W9-BCE-972

The Secret Life of Sparrow Delaney

Suzanne Harper

Greenwillow Books
An Imprint of HarperCollins*Publishers*

I'd like to thank Deb, for talking about all matters related to Sparrow, spirits, and psychics; Aaron, for shedding light on the nature of brotherly affection; Clare, for offering enthusiasm and insight; Mitchell, for representing the book so well; everyone at Greenwillow, for helping in a myriad of ways; and my family, for encouraging me.

The Secret Life of Sparrow Delaney

www.harpercollinschildrens.com

The text of this book is set in 12-point Garamond 3.

Library of Congress Cataloging-in-Publication Data
Harper, Suzanne.
The secret life of Sparrow Delaney / by Suzanne Harper.
p. cm.
"Greenwillow Books."
Summary: In Lily Dale, New York, a community dedicated to the religion of Spiritualism, tenth-grader Sparrow Delaney, the youngest daughter in an eccentric family of psychics, agonizes over whether or not to reveal her special abilities in order to help a friend.
ISBN-13: 978-0-06-113158-5 (trade bdg.) ISBN-10: 0-06-113158-X (trade bdg.)
ISBN-13: 978-0-06-113159-2 (lib. bdg.) ISBN-10: 0-06-113159-8 (lib. bdg.)
[1. Psychics—Fiction. 2. Family life—Fiction. 3. Lily Dale (N.Y.)—Fiction.] I. Title.
PZ7.H23197 2007 [Fic] 22 2006041339

First Edition 10 9 8 7 6 5 4 3 2 1

Greenwillow Books

For Virginia Duncan

Chapter 1

It was three minutes past midnight, and the dead wouldn't leave me alone. I pulled my pillow over my head to shut out the voices floating up from downstairs, but it didn't help. Tonight it was Grandma Bee, my mother, and my sister Oriole who were channeling messages from the Other Side.

First I heard Grandma Bee. "I see an older woman. She's short, a little pudgy, her dentures don't fit well, and she's squinting. Looks like she has a migraine. Hmm. And maybe a touch of indigestion."

Then the voice of my grandmother's visitor: "That's my great-aunt Agatha! That's her to a tee!"

"Hmmph." Grandma Bee loathes being interrupted. I can just imagine the irate glare she's leveling at her visitor. It's been months since we've had enough money to get my grandmother's glasses fixed, so they sit askew on her nose, one side held together with a large safety pin. The thick lenses magnify her eyes and make them look rather wild. The crooked tilt of the frames make her look slightly mad. The combination—plus Grandma Bee's death-ray stare—usually silences . . . well, everybody.

This woman, however, kept gushing. "I can't get over it! It's absolutely uncanny! You've described her perfectly!"

I knew what Grandma Bee would like to say: Of *course* I've described her perfectly. I am after all a *professional medium*. And your great-aunt is standing *right here in front of me*.

But it's not good business to snap at paying customers, so she contented herself with a louder *hmmph* and an irritable clack of her dentures before continuing. "Now I'm getting something else. . . . Oh, she says you're not using enough salt when you make her potato soup." A note of boredom entered Grandma Bee's voice. She hates it when ghosts talk about recipes; she only deigns to turn on the stove when she wants to brew some of her homemade weed killer. "And she says to add some bacon grease, for heaven's sake. A little fat won't kill you."

"Oh, *thank* you!" The visitor sighed happily at this seasoning tip from beyond the grave. "Would it be all right if I asked just one more little question? It's about the number of onions she said to use. . . ."

I threw my pillow on the floor and gave a huge, irritable yawn. Earlier in the evening I had sat at my bedroom window and peered down at tonight's visitors as they walked up our cracked front sidewalk. I counted five people, meaning that the reading should have lasted about two hours, but the spirits were very chatty tonight. We were closing in on three hours with no end in sight.

Unfortunately, I have always found it impossible to fall asleep until every stranger, living or dead, has left our house. This has led to many late nights and cranky mornings because my grandmother and mother have been hosting psychic readings—or, as spiritualists say, serving Spirit—in our front parlor since before I was born.

I closed my eyes and tried to relax, but it wasn't just the ghosts that were keeping me awake. Tomorrow was my fifteenth birthday—undoubtedly the begining of a new and brilliant future!—and right after that was the first day of school. And this year the start of school was even scarier (and more thrilling) than usual.

The reason was simple: I had always assumed that I would go to Jamestown High School, just as my six (yes, count them, *six*) older sisters had. But some sort of redistricting plan was put into place last year. After all the lines had been redrawn, it turned out that I lived in a borderline area, so I could choose to attend either Jamestown High or a huge, recently consolidated high school thirty miles away.

Hmm, let's see . . . I could go to the school where my sisters had spent years making a, shall we say, *vivid* impression, and where I would attend classes with people I had known since kindergarten. Or I could go to a brand-new school and meet brand-new people and make a brand-new start on my life. What to do, what to do?

We had three months to decide. It took me about three seconds.

I was the only person in my town who chose the new school, mainly because nobody else wanted a forty-five-minute bus ride each morning and afternoon. I didn't care. I would have traveled twice as far to end up in a place where I didn't know anyone and, most crucially, no one knew me.

Because when you have a deep, dark secret to hide, a new beginning is a very good thing.

* * *

12:15 A.M.

I stared at the ceiling. Through a quirk in our old house's heating system, the hushed voices on the first floor floated up into my attic bedroom with perfect clarity.

"May I come to you?" Oriole asked another visitor. (There are several ways that mediums can ask if a person would like to hear a message from beyond the grave. Some people say, "May I share your energy, my friend?" while others say, "May I enter your vibration?" The important thing, my mother says, is to ask. "It's only polite, my darlings," she always adds.)

The sound of my sister's voice brought her image in front of me as clearly as if I were sitting opposite her in the dimly lit parlor: She sits on a faded green couch, the perfect backdrop for her long silver blond hair. Candlelight flickers over her pale, luminous skin. She is gazing into the distance, an otherworldly look on her face. (She spent months practicing that expression and then ended up looking like Joan of Arc's less stable sister.)

"You have suffered a disappointment in love recently," Oriole said.

The visitor caught her breath with amazement.

Visitors always do, even though just about everyone has suffered a disappointment in love recently, depending on how you define *disappointment*, *love*, and *recently*. A few months ago a woman cried out, "Yes, that's right! My little dog Sammy ran away just last month!" I have yet to experience any disappointment in love, since I have yet to experience love in any form whatsoever. Still, I hope that when I do, it will be with a dashing, bold, and charismatic hero, not a disgruntled terrier.

"Your grandmother Rose is here. She says that you must keep thinking positive thoughts," my sister said.

"Oh?" The visitor sounded skeptical of this vague suggestion.

"She also says that true love is on its way. Watch for a dark-haired man, perhaps someone who works in computers."

"Oh!" That perked her up.

After a brief pause Oriole added, "Mmm. He *may* like to fish."

"Oh." Clearly this news was not so welcome.

"Rise above it," my sister said on behalf of Grandma Rose. "He's not going to be crazy about your teddy bear collection either, but true love involves *compromise*."

* * *

Earlier in the evening my grandmother and Oriole had asked me to join them, of course, just as I knew they would, and I had said no, of course, just as they knew I would. About every three months my family bands together and tries to persuade me to take part in a reading, using cool logic, sweet reason, or deliberate provocation, depending on personal style.

"Dear Sparrow, what are you afraid of?" my sister Dove will ask, her large gray eyes filled with sympathy. "Even if you don't get any messages, that doesn't mean you've failed. It just means you haven't succeeded . . . yet." Dove has the round, pale face of a medieval saint and a sweet nature to match. That makes it hard to lie to her. But I do.

"I'm not afraid," I always answer.

Lie number one.

"We could treat the readings as experiments," my sister Wren says, her brown eyes sparkling at the thought of a project requiring massive amounts of time and organization. "I could chart all your hits and misses and compare them with various outside factors, like the age of the visitors, the weather, and what you had for dinner. Then we could make some hypotheses about when you're most likely to contact the spirit world."

"No, thanks," I always respond. "I just don't have much natural ability. I've accepted that."

Lie number two.

"But Sparrow, I'm sure you'd find that you're extremely gifted if you would just put forth the slightest effort!" At this point my mother actually manages to focus her eyes on me, rather than the shadows and misty shapes that typically lurk on the edge of her vision. "You have to be! After all, you're the—"

And then the chorus from everyone: "—seventh daughter of a seventh daughter!"

My sisters usually roll their eyes a bit as they chant the phrase that has followed me since birth. When we were much younger, one particular sister (Raven, of course) would even give me a jealous pinch under the table.

I can understand their reaction. After all, I'm even more tired than they are of hearing that folktale about how the seventh daughter of a seventh daughter is supposed to possess enormous psychic talent.

"That's just an old wives' tale," I insist. "It doesn't mean anything except that you come from an extremely fertile family. I don't have any psychic ability at all. Nada. Zero. Zip."

Lie number three.

"You can't escape your destiny, Sparrow Delaney," my sister Linnet intones in a hollow, spooky voice. "It is your fate!"

Her twin, Lark, usually chimes in at this point with a dramatic whisper: "You *will* see dead people!" and then they both chortle wildly. Lark and Linnet are leggy, athletic blondes who are almost identical (Lark's eyes are bluish green; Linnet's are greenish blue). They agree on absolutely everything, including their shared opinion that they're the funniest people in the known universe.

"Let's just drop this, okay?" I always snap at this point. "It's about time we all gave up on the idea that I'm some kind of superspiritualist in training. I have never, ever, not even for a *split second*, seen a ghost!"

And that, of course, is the biggest lie of all.

Chapter 2

The truth? I've been seeing spirits for most of my life.

Since the moment I was born, my grandmother has watched me with the sharp eyes of a carny barker, alert for any sign that I have inherited the family's psychic gene. Little does she know that her fondest hopes and dreams came true when I was only five years old. It was a sunny, cold morning in November. I was sitting on the kitchen floor while Grandma Bee hunted wildly through the refrigerator for a bottle of milk. She emerged holding a spinning top she found tucked behind an ancient jar of pickles. She handed it to me, said, "Here, entertain yourself for ten minutes," and dashed down the street to the store.

I sat on the yellow linoleum in a shaft of sunlight

and spun the top over and over again. Our house was always filled with noise and confusion and, most of all, people, so I remember feeling quite content to be by myself for once. When I finally looked up, I saw a plump older man sitting at the kitchen table.

His white hair stood up in damp little spikes that made him look like a genial hedgehog. (I later learned that this was a holdover from his earthly life as a baker, when he spent long days in a hot kitchen.) His blue eyes were wide with happy surprise, as if he had just seen a dozen firecrackers go off, showering the world with exuberant light. There was a dusting of flour on his white baker's jacket. I smelled cinnamon, nutmeg, and sugar, a scent that later let me know when he was about to manifest (and always gave me an instant, insatiable craving for doughnuts). In other words, if you had to be haunted by somebody, Floyd Barnett was, without a doubt, the person you'd choose.

He looked so happy to see me that I smiled and said hello. I don't remember being afraid or wondering how he had suddenly appeared in the kitchen. He told me his name, and we talked until he heard Grandma Bee come in the front door. Then he put his finger to his lips in a shushing motion and disappeared.

Grandma Bee must have heard our murmuring

conversation because she entered the kitchen with an eager smile.

"Who were you talking to, honey?" she asked, a bright note of hope in her voice. "Did you see someone . . . special?"

But I didn't need my new friend's warning to know that I didn't want to share him with anyone. For once in my five short years of life, I had something that was all mine.

So I looked my grandma right in the eye and said, "Nope." Then I went back to spinning my top.

Thus began my career as a serial liar.

12:37 A.M.

The plastic numbers on my bedside clock flipped over with a loud click.

"Your grandfather wants you to know that he's happy and that he's watching over you." That was my mother's voice, as warm and comforting as an old faded quilt. No wonder she's booked six months in advance. "I'm getting the date November twelfth. Does that mean anything to you? No? Well, keep that day in mind. Your grandfather is telling me that it will be a *most* auspicious day."

I flopped over, trying to get more comfortable. Now

my mother was asking someone else, "Does the name John mean anything to you? No? What about Joanna?"

I sighed and turned over again. Not only was tonight's reading keeping me awake, but the messages were boring, boring, boring.

People who don't deal with ghosts on a daily basis always imagine that the experience will be like the movies: lots of drama, special effects, maybe a cameo appearance by an evil entity or two. The reality is quite different. Like anything else, after a while the supernatural can become a bit . . . well, predictable.

Oh, there are occasional moments of high drama. We've had tearful reunions (the quintuplet who was thrilled to talk with his four siblings who had already Passed On; he confessed he'd been feeling a little left out). We've witnessed the healing of old estrangements (the woman who for twenty-five years hadn't spoken to her best friend—something about a missing ingredient in a cake recipe). On a few memorable occasions we've had profitable revelations, like the time a woman explained that she had hidden her emeralds in the basement deep freeze to keep them safe from burglars. Her husband rushed home, sold the earrings he found in the ice tray, and sent my grandmother 10 percent of the money as a thank-you present.

But most of the time the spirits say exactly what everyone thinks they should say: "Tell her I love her. Tell him I'm watching over him. Tell my family I'm still with them. Let them know that I'm all right." That is all very reassuring and comforting, I know, but it does get tedious after you've heard it a thousand times.

Downstairs my mother was still nattering on. "I see an older man with thick white hair. He's wearing a navy blue suit with white pinstripes—very snappy!" (She likes to describe people's clothes as a way of establishing their identity. After all, there are a lot of older white-haired men on the Other Side.)

"Oh, and I also see—"

"Please," I said imploringly to the ceiling, "not the tie."

"—a wide tie with palm trees!" she said, delighted.

I groaned. When my mother starts talking about accessories, the reading can go on forever.

"I'm also picking up, let's see . . . do silver cuff links make sense to you?"

Cuff links! Pretty soon she'd be discussing the polyester content of his socks! I was about to bury my head under my pillow in utter despair when I smelled smoky incense and heard a voice say, "I would not dismiss your mother's observations so cavalierly if I were you. You can learn much about a person from the cut of his jib."

I sat up and saw the ghost of Prajeet Singh sitting in the lotus position on the rug. As always, he was nattily dressed in black pants, navy sweater, and starched white shirt. He's Indian—not as in Native American, but as in from the teeming subcontinent of India. He passed over in 1903, when he was only twenty-two years old, the unfortunate victim of a vicious monkey bite.

"I'm not dismissing it. I'm just begging that we postpone it to another day." I protested, but I was smiling.

Prajeet's quite a dreamboat, with dark eyes, floppy brown hair, and a kind, flashing white smile. He showed up five years after Floyd came to visit. By that time I was quite good at hiding Floyd from my family, so I just added Prajeet to the list of secrets I had to keep.

He cocked his head to listen as my mother's voice floated up through the vent. She had finally exhausted her fashion commentary and was passing on messages from the spiffy dresser with the palm tree tie.

"He's smiling and happy—"

"And he wants you to know he's all right," I chanted

wearily. "Now if he would just go be all right someplace else and let the rest of us get some sleep—"

"Not a very gracious attitude, I must say, Sparrow," a new voice said tartly. Professor Edna Trimble was shimmering at the end of my bed, accompanied, as always, by the brisk scent of liniment. She had been in her eighties when she Passed On and long retired from her career terrorizing students at an academically rigorous women's college. However, she still dressed in a tweedy, professorial way and wore her gray hair in a severe bun. Her wintry blue eyes eyed me sternly over silver-framed bifocals. "I really expect better of you."

"I'm too tired to be gracious."

She gave a disapproving sniff. "Even when utterly exhausted, one should always demonstrate common courtesy to others."

I fell back on my pillows, knowing better than to argue. Professor Trimble appeared about a year after Prajeet and immediately began nagging me about my homework (sloppy), my posture (bad), my manners (careless), and my general attitude (poor). After her first alarming appearance I asked Prajeet, with some trepidation, if my bedroom would soon be crowded with ghosts, offering unwanted advice and commenting on whether I had made the bed.

"No, no, do not worry," he had said. "You see, we three are your spirit guides. You have heard of such beings, have you not?"

I had, of course. Unlike friends or relatives who Cross Over and then come back with specific messages for their loved ones, spirit guides are assigned to watch over people here on Earth for longer periods of time. I had always found the concept comforting, although I began to revise that opinion after meeting Professor Trimble.

"So you're here to help me, right?" I had asked, just to be sure.

"Yes, indeed," Prajeet had said. "Guidance, support, a helping hand, they are all part of our brief. We each have our little specialties, of course. Floyd, for example, is your gatekeeper, who has watched over you since birth. I have a certain humble talent for explaining metaphysical concepts. And Professor Trimble is here to, er . . ."—he had paused, his eyes sparkling with mischief, then continued diplomatically—"I suppose I should say she is here to make sure you fulfill your potential."

"Oh." I'm sure I sounded rather gloomy at this news. Even then I had sensed that Professor Trimble and I were going to have very different ideas about what fulfilling my potential meant.

"So why are you doing all this?" I had asked. "It sounds like a lot of work. I thought the afterlife was supposed to be kind of, I don't know . . . relaxing."

"An excellent question, my dear Sparrow!" he had said with delight. "The answer is quite simple. Helping others enables us to advance to a higher spiritual level on the Other Side, just as it does here on Earth."

"Really? What's the next level? Do you get promoted to angel or something if you do a good job?"

But apparently even Prajeet couldn't (or wouldn't) reveal all the secrets of the universe at one go. He had just smiled a little and said, "Ah, well, the universe offers many mysteries to unravel—but not tonight, I think." And I could never get him to utter another word on the subject after that.

I rather liked having spirit guides, even if I did have to be careful to talk to them only when no one else was around. But shortly after that conversation I began seeing other ghosts, ghosts that definitely weren't interested in achieving a lofty spiritual goal through unselfish assistance to others. No, they wanted *me* to help *them*. They would come up to me anytime, any place—in my bedroom, on the front porch, at the dinner table, in study hall, at the bus stop. The only place that seemed to be off limits, thank goodness, was the bathroom. I really didn't want to have to deal with spirits in the shower.

"They're everywhere!" I had complained. "Like flies at a picnic!"

"More like moths to a flame, honey," Floyd had answered.

"What does that mean?"

"It means," Professor Trimble said, "that you have an extraordinary amount of psychic talent."

"That's ridiculous," I'd said, uneasy. "If I'm so talented, why didn't I show signs of it before now?"

"That was my doing," Floyd had said, pleased with himself. "You remember when I first came to you? You were already demonstrating all four kinds of psychic ability, but you were such a little thing. I knew we had to take it slow, so I didn't let other spirits approach until you were ready. It's like baking a soufflé. You don't want to overbeat the eggs, or it won't rise. You don't want to keep opening the oven door, or it will fall. You don't want to—"

"I have four kinds of psychic ability?" I had interrupted. Floyd's baking metaphors tend to be long and elaborate. Plus they make me hungry.

Prajeet held up one finger. "Clairvoyance. The ability to see spirits." He held up another finger. "Clairaudience.

The ability to hear spirits." Two more fingers. "Clairsentience, the ability to feel or sense the presence of spirits. And clairgustance, the ability to sense smells or tastes associated with a spirit. Most mediums have only one such gift. It is quite rare indeed to possess all four."

"Oh." That did sound overwhelming.

Professor Trimble had nodded austerely. "It will require discipline and work and many hours of study for you to learn to control your abilities."

That had sounded daunting.

"Fortunately," she had added smoothly, "we are here to help you."

That had sounded terrifying.

Now, as I listened to a reading that was heading into its fourth hour, I didn't feel overwhelmed or daunted or even particularly terrified. I just felt very tired. As an experiment, I closed my eyes to see if I would miraculously fall into a dreamless sleep despite the ghosts in my bedroom and the people downstairs. . . .

"Sparrow! Wake up!" Professor Trimble snapped.

I pretended to snore.

"I know you're awake. I want to talk to you," she said. "I notice that you have once again turned down a perfect opportunity to begin fulfilling your potential."

I opened one eye. "Excuse me?"

"You could be downstairs right now, instead of lollygagging about in bed—"

"Lollygagging? It is *after midnight*! And it's not healthy," I added piously, "for adolescents to get less than eight hours of sleep a night."

Professor Trimble narrowed her eyes. "This is not about losing sleep, Sparrow. It's about offering people hope, comfort, and a connection to the world of Spirit. But most of all, it is about accepting—no, *embracing*—your destiny."

If I had learned only one thing from four years of arguing with Professor Trimble, it was this: how to keep my mouth shut. So I bit my lip to keep from saying something I would seriously regret and settled instead for reciting the words that had become my mantra: "I do not want to be a medium!"

"You keep saying that," she replied tartly. "I'd like to know what kind of life you think you *do* want."

"Anything else," I said. "Anything at all. I mean, I could be an accountant in Santa Fe, or a pastry chef in Paris, or a real estate agent in Sandusky, Ohio, or—"

"Those choices sound very agreeable for some other person," Prajeet chimed in. "But as far as you are concerned, they are mere piffle and poppycock."

"Piffle and poppycock?" I said, betrayed. "Prajeet! I thought you were my friend!"

Then I smelled a sugary fragrance and saw the air in front of the window shiver. Floyd's outline wavered a bit, as if he were uncertain of his welcome.

"Come on in, Floyd," I said with weary resignation. "The party's just getting started."

He firmed up and smiled at me. "Thanks, honey."

"At least I know *you're* on my side," I said, with an accusing glance at Prajeet and Professor Trimble.

"Of course I am!" He turned to the others. "Sparrow is still young. She has a right to be a little confused at this stage in life."

"Thank you," I said with dignity. Finally, someone who understood how I felt, who could see my side of things, who wasn't always telling me what to do—

"Although," he said comfortably, "I do think you should consider going to the last message service of the season."

I gave him my best you-must-be-kidding look. He gave me his best I'm-just-making-an-innocent-suggestion look in return.

Go to a message service? Was he *insane*? It was bad enough to sit in a crowded auditorium for an hour while one medium after another passed on spirit messages to people in the audience. What was even worse was the idea of skulking in a corner, trying to escape the attention of all the ghosts who would also be there. I shuddered.

"Message services," I said. "Ick."

"Ah, well." Floyd looked downcast. "It was just an idea."

I felt a little tug of guilt. I hated disappointing Floyd.

Now Professor Trimble was shaking her head sorrowfully. "You have so much potential. So much untapped talent."

"It is not right that you toss it to the dogs," Prajeet agreed.

"I'm not tossing anything to the dogs, and what does that even mean?" I threw my pillow at him.

He didn't bother to duck. It flew right through him and hit my oak dresser. His image trembled a bit, but his serene expression didn't change.

"It means throwing away something valuable, tossing it aside as if it were garbage—"

"Okay, okay, I know what it means."

"We are just trying to offer you a little guidance, that is all," he added. "Do not be angry."

"I'm not," I muttered. "But do you even remember what it's like to be a teenager? I'm going to be in high school! I don't want people to think I'm a freak!"

Professor Trimble raised one eyebrow. "And why should anyone think that?"

"People think Emily Lawson is a freak just because she plays the oboe," I replied. "If they knew I talked to dead people—"

"Not the same thing at all," Professor Trimble said. "The oboe is a horrid instrument."

"That's not the point—oh, never mind." I sighed. "I just—I don't want any more guidance, all right? I want to make my own decisions about my life."

There was a brief, fraught pause. Then, to my surprise, Professor Trimble actually conceded the point.

"And so you should. An excellent idea." Her tone was brisk. "It really should have nothing to do with us, should it, Prajeet?"

She caught Prajeet's eye, and he quickly shook his head. "No, nothing to do with us," he said. "Nothing at all." Then he paused to listen. "Ah, I think your guests are leaving."

Sure enough, I could hear the murmur of thank yous and good nights as the visitors drifted out of the house. A few moments later I heard my sisters arguing about whose turn it was to clean up the parlor and then mutually agreeing (as always) that it could wait until morning.

"Good," I said. "Now I can finally get some sleep."

Professor Trimble added, "Yes, my dear, you do that." She began to flicker. "And thank you for your honesty, Sparrow. You have given me much to think about."

"Sweet dreams, cupcake." Floyd winked.

They all vanished.

And I was left, of course, staring at the ceiling, wide awake until dawn.

Chapter 3

If you took a wrong turn off the highway and drove through Lily Dale by accident, you'd see what looks like a normal, if slightly dilapidated, small town. Most of the houses are Victorians—not reproductions but houses that were actually built when Queen Victoria sat dumpily on her throne. Very few have been painted or repaired since. Every house leans a little to one side or the other (ours tilts north-northwest), most porches sag in the middle, and a fair number of windows are either cracked or boarded up with plywood.

(Well, as Grandma Bee always says, a spiritual life is not a lucrative life. That's why we buy our clothes in thrift shops, or at least my sisters do. They complain bitterly about this, but I point out that there's something worse than wearing thrift store clothes, and that's wearing thrift store *hand-me-downs*.)

If you actually stopped here after taking that wrong turn, you'd find out that my hometown is not normal at all. That's because Lily Dale was founded in 1879 as a Spiritualist community, a place where mediums could live and work. Here talking to the dead is as normal as pumpkin pie, although we don't actually say that people have died. We say they've Passed On or Crossed Over or Gone to Summerland, which sounds much less scary and morbid and, well, *final*.

My great-great-grandmother moved here in 1912 to hang out her shingle as a medium, and Delaneys have been serving Spirit in Lily Dale ever since. Grandma Bee, my mother, and Oriole all have passed the test to become registered mediums, which means that they are allowed to give public readings. But everyone in the family has some psychic talent. Raven is quite skilled at picking up messages that warn of doom and disaster; coupled with her long black hair, sharp black eyes, and sardonic expression, this has kept her from attracting many customers. Oriole is attuned to communications dealing with love, romance, and hair-styling tips (she's very popular). Dove specializes in weepy messages of reconciliation. Wren usually gets information about unfinished housekeeping details (the will that was hidden a little too carefully, the stock certificates that were lost in the attic). Lark sees auras, and Linnet creates spirit drawings, done with pastels.

And we're pretty run-of-the-mill compared with our neighbors. Mrs. Winkle, who lives next door, believes that fairies live in her garden. Who's to say, she might be right. Her backyard is a wild, overgrown quarter acre of wildflowers and weeds. A troupe of circus clowns could be living there, and no one would ever know.

Three streets over, Mr. Sanderson channels a spiritual sidekick named Ojai Cinnabar. He gets a lot of business, even though he usually just tells people to eat more vegetables and to exercise every day. They often report back that they feel amazingly better and have lost several inches off their waistlines.

Mrs. O'Malley sits on her back porch every evening and watches long-dead Iroquois Indians walk by single file, tomahawks in hand. They never speak to her, but she claims that their "energy vibrations" give her warrior strength. She's sixty-five years old and runs a marathon twice a year. I have to admit that imparts a certain authority to this claim.

Miss Robertson lives with nine cats, five dogs, three

gerbils, and a rabbit. She specializes in contacting the spirits of dead pets. Even in the afterlife, she reports, cats are standoffish, dogs are devoted, and gerbils speak nothing but nonsense. She refuses to channel rabbits because, she says, "they have only one thing on their minds, and I prefer to focus on more *elevated* topics."

Truthfully, I would love to live in a boring suburb where kids play soccer, dads grill hamburgers on the weekend, and moms divide their time between high-powered corporate jobs and PTA meetings. Still, I must admit that there are some good things about growing up in Lily Dale. You learn to be open to the mysterious and the unexplained. You learn not to judge people as nuts until you've known them for years. Then, even if you decide they *are* nuts, you realize that you already like them, so that's okay.

But even if Lily Dale had its good points, I knew that I didn't want the life that my family had planned for me here. Their dream was that I would discover my psychic ability, join the family business, and settle down to many years of buying clothes at thrift stores, worrying about the electric bill, and having everyone in the outside world think that I was seriously weird.

That was most emphatically *not* the future I wanted.

I wanted a world that was bigger than Lily Dale and a life that was absolutely ordinary in every way. And I was determined to have both.

I woke up late on my birthday and wandered down to the kitchen, yawning, at noon. My mother is normally far too distracted to cook (or at least to cook without setting the dish towels on fire). However, for each of our birthdays, she rises early, concentrates fiercely, and produces our favorite breakfasts without incident. As I walked into the kitchen, still blinking the sleep from my eyes, she greeted me with a floury kiss on the cheek and a smile that made her deep brown eyes crinkle warmly.

"Happy birthday, Sparrow," she said happily. "What a wonderful morning! I feel quite certain that today is going to be a *most* auspicious day!"

"Thanks, Mom." I smiled and sat down to a plate of blueberry pancakes. Every year my mother tells each of us, her voice trembling with thrilling conviction, that she can sense that our birthday is a "most auspicious" day. We tease her about it, but we all would be very upset if she ever forgot to say it. It's the only day that I can count on feeling that my life is going to be completely fabulous in every way.

After breakfast I walked to the lake and spent the afternoon swimming and lying in the shade, reading. That evening we gathered to eat my favorite dinner (pot roast and potato pancakes). For the finale, Wren proudly carried my birthday cake into the dining room and set it down on the table with a flourish.

"Ta-da!" she said as triumphantly as if she had traversed the Antarctic to deliver it.

Actually, crossing a polar landscape might have presented less of a challenge; at least there wouldn't be as much to trip over. Tonight, for example, Wren had to dodge Mordred, our one-eyed malevolent tabby cat, who kept weaving between her feet in a deliberate attempt to trip her. She had to step over a pile of laundry that someone (I suspect Lark) had left on the floor. And she had to squeeze by the battered old piano, grandfather clock, and three end tables that had been pushed against the wall to make room for last night's reading.

I saw a faint flicker out of the corner of my eye, caught a whiff of nutmeg, and knew that Floyd had joined us. I glanced casually to my right. He gave me a little wave as my family, oblivious to his presence, chatted on.

Well, I guess there is some truth to that old saying

about the seventh daughter of a seventh daughter. At least, I'm the only person in my family who can see ghosts anywhere, at any time. My mother and Grandma Bee can also see spirits, but it usually requires great concentration and focus. None of my sisters has ever seen a manifestation (a source of much sorrow for Oriole, Dove, and Wren and a matter of true indifference for Lark and Linnet, while Raven claims bitterly and unconvincingly not to care a bit).

This means of course that I constantly have to remember not to react to random ghosts walking down the street or floating up the stairs. For years I've been practicing my poker face, ignoring whispered pleas in my ear, and learning to look past pushy ghosts with a blank and uncomprehending stare.

Sometimes I have slipped up, especially in the beginning, but there are distinct advantages to being the youngest in a large and disorganized family. People often don't notice that you're acting strangely because they simply don't notice you at all. Even if your behavior does attract attention, well, before you've finished explaining just *why* you were talking to the wallpaper, there's bound to be another, much more urgent crisis that conveniently takes the spotlight off you.

Now, I cautiously crinkled my nose at Floyd in

greeting. He examined the cake with professional interest, then heaved a disappointed sigh.

The cake was lopsided and listed to one side, as if its grip on the plate were so precarious that it might slip off at any moment. It had been decorated in a slapdash manner with bright pink icing on the top and white icing on the sides. Candy sprinkles had been scattered randomly, so that they collected in multicolored clumps in some areas and were as sparse as diamonds in others. *Happy Birthday Spa* was spelled out in icing with so many flourishes and curlicues that it was clear that the person writing the greeting (I suspected Oriole, who has a decided preference for style over substance) had run out of room before finishing my name.

"Too much baking powder," he said. "And the cake didn't cool enough before they took it out of the pan. Plus it looks as if someone ran out of frosting there at the end." He shook his head sadly. "Why don't people ever want to hire a professional?"

"It's going to be eaten in fifteen minutes," I said without thinking (this is what happens when I let my guard down for one split second). "Who cares what it looks like?"

Wren looked both hurt and uncertain. "I followed

the recipe exactly," she said. "Down to the last teaspoon. I don't know what happened!"

"No, no, it's lovely!" I said quickly, shooting a venomous look at Floyd. He retreated to the far corner of the room, abashed.

"It was supposed to look like a launchpad, with a little toy rocket ship on top," Wren went on mournfully. "You know, kind of a metaphor for launching yourself into another year of life and going to a new school and everything? But Lark broke the rocket—"

"That thing was ancient; it was about to fall apart anyway," Lark grumbled under her breath.

"—and then the middle of the cake fell in—"

"Yeah, it looks more like a bomb crater than a launching pad," Raven put in, her black eyes glittering with malice. "Hope that's not a bad omen!"

"—and now the entire concept is ruined!" Wren finished with a wail.

"That's okay," I said soothingly. "I'm sure it will be quite tasty. In a metaphor-free kind of way."

"Time to light the candles and make a wish!" my mother trilled. The cake, I now noticed, had only eight mismatched candles.

As if she could read my mind, Raven said, "Sorry we didn't have fifteen candles." As usual, she didn't sound sorry at all. "That's all we could find in the junk drawer."

My mother put a hand in her pocket. A worried look crossed her face. "I could have sworn . . ." she murmured, checking another pocket. "Now, where did I put those matches?"

"You just had them!" Raven said, irritated. "I saw you pick them up off the kitchen counter!"

"You're right!" my mother said happily, seizing on this with relief. "I picked them up with this hand—" she stared at her right hand, her brow furrowed with thought—"and then I did . . . what?" She kept looking at her hand, as if it would offer another clue.

The hand stayed stubbornly empty and clueless.

"I'm sure they'll show up," Oriole said in a faraway voice. She was sitting at the end of the table, wearing an outfit pulled together from the cobwebby recesses of our basement: a tattered antique wedding dress, fake pearls, worn opera gloves, and an ancient pair of button-up boots. She should have looked like a mentally unstable refugee from a music video. Instead she looked like a gorgeous (albeit eccentric) fashion model.

"Dr. Snell probably got at them again," Grandma Bee said as she sneaked a finger in the icing. She popped it in her mouth and added fondly, "He's such a rascal."

Complete silence greeted this remark. Grandma Bee has been nurturing a crush on Dr. Snell for decades. He was apparently a respected member of the medical community when he was alive, but now that he's Crossed Over, he's become a poltergeist, one of those annoying ghosts that get a kick out of playing pranks throughout eternity. He's always dumping flour on the floor or ringing the doorbell at three in the morning or hiding certain items (like matches) just when they're most needed.

I used to think it strange that ghosts could move objects so easily. You'd think that not having a body would pose a problem. But Prajeet explained that it just requires a bit of mental effort, although most ghosts don't care to take the trouble. Unfortunately, Dr. Snell is *very* motivated in this regard.

The last time he dropped by, for example, he found a box in the attic that contained a scattering of dried-up flies, roaches, and silverfish. He proceeded to dump them on the heads of the visitors at that night's reading. Grandma Bee tried to pass this off as his way of telling people that there is Another World That They Know Not Of, but even she had to admit that business dropped off sharply for months afterward. Dr. Snell is beyond annoying, but if any of us complain, Grandma Bee just gets a moony look in her eyes and says something like "If you girls could only see the man! Handsome doesn't begin to describe him!"

Now she called out sweetly, "Oh, Dr. Snell! Are you here, dear?"

"Don't encourage him," Raven muttered.

We all glanced nervously around the room. I've only seen him a few times—he's a natural-born lurker—but I knew I'd recognize him. He looks like a human cockroach, with his shiny brown suit, beady bright eyes, slicked-back hair, and nasty smile. I surreptitiously sniffed the air—he always brings a whiff of stink bomb with him—but smelled only pot roast and, through the open window, the faint scent of fresh-cut grass.

"We'd love a visit if you feel like manifesting," Grandma Bee cooed.

My mother looked worried at this. "Mmm, well, perhaps he doesn't want to intrude," she murmured tactfully. "A family gathering, you know . . ."

"Nonsense!" Grandma Bee got up and began wandering around the room, peering nearsightedly into dark corners, as if hoping to find him hiding in the shadows. "Dr. Snell is always the life of the party!"

The rest of us rolled our eyes at one another behind

her back as we remembered, vividly, other parties with Dr. Snell (curtains catching on fire, salt poured on ice cream sundaes, shoelaces knotted together under the table so that we all fell into a heap when we stood up).

"Could we please stay on task for once?" Wren suggested with barely concealed impatience. "We were looking for the matches, remember?"

Lark and Linnet began conducting an antic and utterly useless search of the dining room, which involved such comic gestures as turning soup tureens upside down, scrabbling around under the table and tickling people's legs, and energetically lifting the carpet, raising clouds of dust and making everyone cough.

Grandma Bee wandered back to the table and plopped down in her chair with a sigh. "Who needs matches?" she said, disgruntled. "Let's just turn on the stove and light the candles there."

"We tried that six months ago for Wren's birthday," Raven snapped.

"At least now we know the average response time of the fire department," Dove said philosophically.

My mother kept murmuring, "They were right here in my hand, and now they're gone! Gone!"

After five minutes of this Wren stalked off to the

kitchen, where the last known sighting of the matches took place, muttering phrases like "madhouse," "disorganized beyond belief," and "pigpen is an understatement" as she went.

She returned almost immediately, saying, "They were still on the counter. You must have put them down when you brought in the pot roast." Then she coolly lit the candles as everyone else collapsed in their chairs in exaggerated relief.

"Make a wish, Sparrow," Dove said.

I squeezed my eyes shut and pretended to think hard. There was really only one wish that I desperately wanted to come true.

I wish I were normal.

I opened my eyes to see Professor Trimble, Prajeet, and Floyd standing in the shadows behind my family. Their outlines were wavery and the light was dim, but I could still make out their expressions. Professor Trimble looked disapproving, Floyd looked thoughtful, and Prajeet just smiled his white, white smile and shook his head, as if to say, "You may make that wish, but it is mere tomfoolery, you shall see."

I scowled at them, took a deep breath, and blew. The flames guttered, flared, and disappeared; thin columns of smoke wafted to the ceiling; my family cheered and applauded and broke into a raucously off-key rendition of "Happy Birthday."

As I looked around at their smiling faces, I felt the strangest sense of warmth and well-being, as if this year my wish really would come true.

Chapter 4

The signs for my first day of high school were, as my mother would say, most auspicious. The sun rose right on time. A few clouds drifted picturesquely across a clear blue sky. Birds chirped merrily, as if they didn't have a care in the world.

Of course they didn't; they were just *birds*. I was the one with a knotted stomach, sweaty palms, a dry mouth, and a clear, sure sense of impending doom.

I had spent most of the previous day obsessing over my clothes and creating dozens of different combinations, hoping to discover that the perfect outfit had been languishing in my closet, unnoticed until now. As I looked in the mirror, however, I realized that no amount of mixing and matching could make my clothes look hip. Or cool. Or trendy. Even bohemian/funky was a stretch.

I sighed and gave myself a smile in the mirror, just to practice. A small smile, not too desperate, not too toothy.

Mmm, not great. I looked smirky and insincere.

I tried a bigger smile. Agghh, I looked like a manic flight attendant.

"Sparrow, honey, why don't you try being yourself?"

I smelled sugar and butter and turned to see Floyd settled in the comfortable old rocking chair I had rescued from a dark corner of the basement. He smiled fondly at me, his white hair standing up around his head like a spiky halo. "You're such a pretty girl. You don't have to work so hard!"

"Who's working hard?" I asked defensively. I hate it when my spirits pop in at embarrassing moments (perfect example: when I'm trying out facial expressions in the mirror).

Floyd just smiled sunnily and continued to rock—nothing put him in a bad mood—so I turned to scowl at the mirror.

My hair looked like a bird's nest. Built by a bird that was very disorganized and quite possibly insane.

I swiped my brush through it and rooted through my top drawer to find a stray hair accessory among the mismatched socks. "Anyway, I am being true to who I am." I glanced into the mirror and saw Floyd looking at me skeptically. "I'm being true to the person I was meant to be," I clarified. "I'm being true to the person I could be, except that everyone in my life already has a picture in mind of who I am, so they can't see the real me. *That's* who I'm being true to."

"Oh, I see." He folded his hands on his round stomach. "Well, that's all right then. We all deserve a chance to transform ourselves into who we really are."

"Exactly." Aha! I pulled my favorite tortoiseshell headband from the bottom of the drawer and put it on. Now I looked more like the person I secretly knew I was. Fun. Friendly. And even better than that: Absolutely Ordinary. "Perfect."

"Mmm." Floyd didn't seem impressed. "Well, good luck, sweetheart. I'm sure you'll have a great first day."

An hour later I stared up at my new school, trying not to feel intimidated. It was six stories high and seemed to stretch for acres. A broad flight of stairs led up, up, up to enormous double doors; it looked like the entrance to Mount Olympus.

I stood absolutely still, frozen with sudden fear, complete with shaking knees and the awful feeling that I might throw up at any moment. I watched the other students stream through the double doors, laughing and talking with their friends, until I was standing by myself, stranded on the sidewalk. But maybe it was all right that I was alone. Maybe it was a sign that I didn't really belong here. Maybe I should go home right now and give up the idea of a fresh start—

"What utter nonsense!" A voice behind me snapped the words with the authority of a marine drill sergeant. "Get a grip on yourself this instant, and walk up those steps!"

I closed my eyes briefly, willing her to go away.

It didn't work. I opened my eyes to find Professor Trimble standing in front of me. Well, perhaps if I played to her softer side . . .

"My knees are shaking," I said, trying to sound pathetic and doing an embarrassingly good job.

"Of course they are," she snapped. "It would be a miracle if they weren't."

"Thanks for the sympathy," I snapped back, now feeling more pissed off than pathetic. "That helps a lot."

"You don't need sympathy; you need bucking up," she declared. "If you want to feel scared, try defending your doctoral dissertation! *All* of my students thought they were going to die." She smiled grimly. "I never lost one."

"There's always a first time," I muttered just as a bell clanged inside the school. I jumped, not sure whether that meant I was already late.

Professor Trimble grandly ignored it as she continued. "First, stand up straight. No, straight, Sparrow! Has your spine turned into a cooked noodle overnight? Now, plant your feet. Feel the ground beneath you, and *own your space.*"

Hmm. This sounded a little New Agey for Professor Trimble, but I didn't have time to argue. I planted my feet, felt the ground, and owned my space.

She nodded in satisfaction. "There. Doesn't that feel better?"

"Yeah," I said, surprised. "It does."

"Good. Remember: *You are not a cream puff.* I expect more from you, the universe expects more from you, and, most important, *you* should expect more from you. Now *move.*"

And without making a conscious decision to do so, I moved. Up the steps, through the doors, and into a wide hallway, jammed with people. It sounded like every single person was yelling hello and "How was your summer?" to someone else. I looked at the sheaf of orientation papers I was clutching. My locker was number 261. I glanced at the nearest locker. Number 1429. That seemed an awfully long way from 261, and I had only four minutes to get to class.

My heart began beating faster. I tried to take a deep breath, but my lungs didn't seem to be working very well. I focused on the paper in my hand, but now the words and numbers were swimming in front of my eyes, there was a faint buzzing in my ears, and my head felt as if it were floating a few inches above my body. I was wondering if this was what happened right before you fell over in a dead faint—

"No need to get in a kerfuffle, Sparrow," said a voice close to my ear. "I shall be glad to lend you my assistance."

I turned to see that Prajeet had materialized next to me.

"Follow me," he said with a reassuring smile. Then he turned and walked rapidly away. I trotted after him, staying as close as I could as we wove through the crowded hallway. We made a left turn, then a right, then another left, and finally stopped in front of a locker. Prajeet pointed to it with a flourish.

Number 261.

I let out my breath. Until that moment I hadn't

realized I was holding it. "Thanks," I whispered.

"No problem whatsoever," he answered airily. He leaned forward and added, "Here's a trick that I used in university when I suffered from nerves. Breathe in slowly, to a count of three. Hold the breath for a count of five. Breathe out to a count of seven. You have that firmly in mind? Three, five, seven. It will calm your mind and body and bring you peace, guaranteed. Try it today, all right?"

I smiled and gave a tiny nod.

"Good." Prajeet's gaze floated over my right shoulder, and his smile broadened. "I bid you farewell then. Until we meet again."

He was gone, and behind me a laughing voice said, "This is *crazy*, isn't it?" I turned to see a girl about my age with bright red hair, freckles, and blue eyes sparkling with excitement. "I'm Fiona Jones. Tenth grade. I'm new here!"

"Me, too." Brilliant. Eloquent. A sterling display of witty repartee. "Um, my name is Sparrow."

"Sparrow?" she asked, puzzled.

"Right. Like the bird."

Her face lit up. "Oh! How totally cool! What's your first class? History with Mr. Grimes—awesome! Me too! Come on, let's see if we can find room twelve-B."

She kept talking, throwing comments over her shoulder to me as people jostled us from every side. "I have no idea where anything is. I'm sure I'll be completely lost for weeks. This is utter madness, isn't it?"

I trailed in her wake, breathing deeply. In for three, hold for five, out for seven . . . A feeling of peace and calm spread through my body. Prajeet was right! I thought. Mindful breathing does work!

So feeling relaxed and confident, I followed Fiona into room 12B.

I grabbed a seat, stowed my backpack under my chair, and scanned the classroom. In the back row a few extremely large guys were crammed into seats that had clearly been designed for wispier people. A cluster of four fashionably dressed girls stood in the far corner, staring raptly into their pocket mirrors. My gaze slipped past other faces—a boy with red hair and a goofy grin, a girl with braces and thick glasses, a shy boy staring down at his desk, a girl who kept twirling her curls through her fingers—until it landed on the boy sitting one row over and one seat back.

He was slumped in his chair, head down, zoned out listening to his iPod. His dark hair just brushed the collar of an old army jacket that was a couple of sizes too large. He wore a worn gray T-shirt, and faded jeans. He looked as if he had woken up late and grabbed the first clothes that he could find. Probably clothes that had been lying on the floor, considering all the wrinkles. As I looked at him, I caught the faint scent of woodsmoke and autumn leaves and felt a little grayness in my soul at the reminder that summer was really and truly over. . . .

At that moment he raised his eyes and looked directly at me. I blushed, embarrassed to be caught looking back.

"Are you finished?" he asked curtly.

I blinked in surprise at the anger in his voice. "What?"

He pulled off his earbuds and leaned forward. "I said, are . . . you . . . finished?" he repeated very slowly, as if talking to a small and rather dim child.

"Um . . . with what?" Even to my own ears, I sounded ridiculous.

"Staring at me. I'm not an exhibit in a zoo."

I heard a girl in the next row giggle. "I wasn't staring," I said hotly.

He smirked. "Right."

"I was glancing casually around the room and you happened to get in the way," I said loftily.

The left side of his mouth slipped upward as his grin widened. "Yeah, sure."

He slipped his earbuds back in and went back to staring at the floor.

I could feel other girls in the class sneaking looks at him, and I could guess why.

He *was* good-looking, I thought, trying to be fair. In a moody, sullen, sarcastic, defensive, slovenly kind of way.

As I pointedly looked past him, I noticed the guy sitting behind Army Jacket Boy. He had shaggy dark blond hair, hazel eyes, and a lively, interested expression. He caught my eye and smiled warmly, as if we shared a secret. Then he flicked his finger at the back of Army Jacket Boy's ear. He didn't get much of a response, so he did it again.

Flick.

Nothing.

Flick.

Nothing.

Flick!

Finally! Army Jacket Boy moved his head with irritation.

Flick again. This time to the left ear.

That got his attention. He turned, scowling, and

looked around the room, as if wondering whether someone had been shooting spitballs at him from the back row. Then he shrugged, turned back around, and slumped down even further in his chair.

I glanced over at Army Jacket Boy's tormentor and found myself staring right into his eyes.

Aagghh! Direct eye contact! Twice in one day! What was *wrong* with me?

I blushed. He winked. I could feel myself blush even more, but I smiled back.

Army Jacket Boy gave me a strange look and turned to look over his shoulder. When he turned back, he was frowning. "Are you all right?" he asked.

"Yes," I said. "Of course. Why wouldn't I be all right? I mean, why do you ask?"

Damn. Note to self: Work on witty, intelligent, scathing comebacks at home tonight. Practice until certain people quake in fear at the mere thought of talking to you.

Just then a breeze blew through the open window, and everyone groaned as papers flew into the air. I saw the boy sitting behind A. J. Boy go all shimmery. . . .

Then he was gone.

I must have looked startled, because A. J. Boy turned around again to see what had happened. Of course he didn't see a thing, so I had seemingly been overcome with shock at the sight of an empty chair.

He turned back and gave me a look.

"Right," he said sarcastically. "That chair is really scary, and you're perfectly fine. My mistake."

"Mind your own business!" I snapped.

He shrugged. "Just thought I'd offer a helping hand of compassion."

"Thanks, but I don't need any help."

"Glad to hear it. I really hate all that helping-hand-of-compassion stuff." He put the earbuds back in, his legs thrust carelessly into the aisle.

I turned back to the front of the class and blinked hard a few times to discourage any stray tears from falling. Before I had a chance to wonder why any spirit in his right mind would choose to spend part of eternity in a high school history class, our teacher walked in the door and instantly commanded everyone's attention.

"Good morning, class. My name is Sergeant Grimes." He wrote his name on the blackboard as everyone in the class gaped at him. Sergeant Grimes was a tall, imposing man with a gray hair, a laser stare, and posture that was so straight I wasn't entirely sure he could sit down.

"Before I was assigned to a tour of duty here at Cassadaga Regional High School, I spent twenty years in the Eighty-second Airborne, the roughest, toughest, most hardcore soldiers in the entire U.S. military." He looked us over with steely eyes. "I expect the same level of discipline, hard work, and devotion to duty from you that I expected from my men. Is that clear?" There were a few intimidated nods as we all sank a little lower in our chairs.

He began to take roll, snapping out each name as if we were on a parade ground.

"Mr. Andrews? Justin Andrews?"

"Here!" The redheaded boy waved his arm as dramatically as if he were guiding a plane onto an aircraft carrier. (Just as I suspected: goofy.)

"Respond by saying 'present,'" Sergeant Grimes said. "Cut out the semaphore. And use my name when you answer."

Justin looked a little puzzled—I had the feeling that "semaphore" threw him for a loop—but he lowered his arm and said, "Present, Mr. Grimes," in a subdued tone.

"Negative." Sergeant Grimes seemed to be getting more annoyed by the minute. "Mr. Grimes is my father. You can call me Sergeant Grimes. Or you can call me Sergeant. Or you can call me sir." He paused, then snapped, "Do we understand each other?"

A murmur of yeses answered him.

I expected him to bark out, "I can't *hear* you!" just like in the movies. But he just nodded, still not smiling, and went on with the roll. I learned that the elegant girl near the windows was named Jeannie Bartlett and that she sounded bored and superior. The girl with glasses and braces also had a most unfortunate adenoid problem and answered almost inaudibly to the name Sarah Carlton. And Army Jacket Boy turned out to be Jack Dawson.

He was called on three times before he heard his name, leading to his iPod being confiscated and the rest of us being subjected to a rather tedious lecture titled "Sergeant Grimes's Rules Regarding the Use of Electronics in Class" (short version: "Don't Even Think About It"). When Jack finally answered, his face was blank, his voice flat. He should have appeared difficult and surly; instead he came off as extremely cool, further evidence (as if it were needed) that the universe is fundamentally unfair.

"Ms. Delaney? Sparrow Delaney?"

I was so lost in thought that it took me a second to realize that Sergeant Grimes was calling my name.

"Yes. Here," I answered. "I mean, present. Sir. Er, Sergeant."

"Very good. Now try to stay present, if you don't mind," Sergeant Grimes said dryly as he checked off my name.

Finally we got to the end of roll call, and Sergeant Grimes took us through what the year had in store. A lot, it seemed. Reading six chapters in the massive textbook every month, writing a short essay on a historical topic every week, and—wait for it—working in teams on a semester-long research project that would teach us "how to effectively find, analyze, and summarize primary and secondary source materials."

No one dared groan, although a certain feeling of anguish reverberated throughout the room.

"Any questions? No? Outstanding." The sergeant picked up his roll book and began assigning us to teams of two. He did this by simply running down his list and pairing us off according to the alphabetical listing of our last names.

All around me people were turning pale with dismay at not being able to choose their own partners, but I would have gladly traded my fate with any one of theirs, because my research partner was none other than Jack Dawson.

I glanced over my shoulder. He was staring at the floor, a slight frown on his face.

"Your research project should focus on some aspect of local history," Sergeant Grimes continued. "All topics must be chosen and approved by me by the end of next week, so that you have sufficient time to complete your project. I strongly suggest that you meet with your partner outside class in the next few days to decide on your chosen area of research."

He would have gone on, but at that moment the bell rang. We all grabbed our books, ready to escape to the next class, but Sergeant Grimes held up his hand.

"Class!" he barked. The single word sounded like a thunderclap. Everyone froze.

"One final rule: Even if the bell rings, you don't leave until *I* say so."

He paused for a long, dramatic moment as we held our breaths.

Finally he snapped, "Dismissed!" and we all bolted into the hall.

The rest of the morning passed in the usual first-day blur of trying frantically to find the next classroom, being issued stacks of textbooks, fumbling with a new locker combination, and signing up for extracurricular activities. All in all, I barely had time to breathe, let alone think about the strange start to my new school year.

By the time I found the cafeteria, I had only fifteen minutes to eat the soggy tuna fish sandwich and bruised apple I had brought for lunch. I spotted Fiona waving to me from across the room, threaded my way through a dozen tables, and plopped down gratefully in the chair next to her.

"What did you think of Sergeant Grimes? History is going to be a complete horror!" Fiona exclaimed with delight. She had spread out a clean napkin—real cloth, I noticed, and snowy white—and arranged her lunch on it like a work of art: PB&J sandwich with the crusts cut off, a red apple so shiny that it must have been polished, and what looked like homemade chocolate chip cookies.

Her eyes sparkled even as she moaned about the rest of her classes. "I'm going to be *completely* in over my head in algebra, I can already tell, and Mr. Crane in English said we have to read twenty novels in thirty-six weeks and if we don't make it, we'll have to keep going in summer school! I think he was joking, but *still*! Are you taking Spanish? Well, then you're just incredibly lucky because you should see the homework assignments we already have, and this is only the *first day*!" Fiona took a neat little bite from her apple and sighed happily. "High school is going to be so much harder than junior high! I just don't know if I'll make it!"

"Mmm," I said. Totally inadequate, I know, but I couldn't talk about what was foremost on my mind—namely, cute ghosts that disappeared into thin air.

"Where's your schedule? I hope we have at least one more class together this afternoon. That would be such fun! Hi, Clare! Hey, Jill!" Fiona managed to keep chattering even as she ate her lunch and waved at various people as they walked by.

"You seem to know a lot of people already," I commented.

"Well, I'm a natural-born extrovert; at least that's what my dad always says," she said cheerfully. "He's a psychologist, so he's always diagnosing people. I think I get it from my mom, being an extrovert, I mean. She's a TV reporter. People always end up telling her things they wouldn't admit to another living soul!"

I nodded throughout this flow of words, making a mental note to avoid being around Fiona's mom whenever possible.

"Of course one of the bad things about being an extrovert is that you tend to talk too much." She frowned suddenly. "Am I talking too much right now? Am I boring you? You have to tell me if I'm boring you. It's vital to my personal development."

"No, not at all." I hastened to reassure her.

"Good. Because I *am* a little hyper today, I admit it!" Fiona rattled on. "I'm just so so *so* excited! What clubs are you going to join? I was secretary of the drama department at my last school. My mom and I just moved here a month ago—did I already say that? Anyway, she got a job at the local station. She's still a reporter, but the station is a network affiliate, so her chances for advancement are much better. My parents are divorced, and my dad lives in Rochester. Once a month I go there, and once a month he visits me, and of course we e-mail all the time, because my dad wants our relationship to remain strong and connected." She paused to take a breath. "What about you?"

"Um, what?" I had relaxed a little bit as Fiona chattered, figuring that I wouldn't have to say much. "What about me?"

"How many sisters and brothers do you have? What do your parents do? What are your hobbies? You know."

"Oh. Well. I have six older sisters . . ." I said cautiously.

"Six! That sounds like so much fun!" She looked wistful. "I'm an only. I always wanted—"

"No, you don't. Believe me." I didn't want to hear her big, happy family fantasy, which I was already pretty sure would feature madcap adventures that ended in a group hug. "They drive me crazy. Anyway, my mom's a, er, counselor." Which was almost true. "And my grandmother lives with us, too."

"That sounds amazing." Fiona was wide-eyed. "And your dad?" The way she asked the question, I knew she guessed the answer. Her voice had a careful quality that she had probably learned from her father.

I replied briefly, "He's not around right now."

Fiona nodded and dropped the subject as I looked around the crowded cafeteria. I was beginning to feel a little nostalgic for the claustrophobic cafeteria of my old school, with a few dozen drearily familiar faces, when I spotted Jack Dawson. He was sitting by himself three tables away from us. Well, almost by himself. The ghost was sitting next to him, looking at me expectantly.

"What are you looking at?" Fiona, curious, turned to follow my gaze. "Ooooh, I see! Your new research partner."

"No, no!"

"He's just so so cute, isn't he?"

I sneaked a quick look. Jack was now sitting quite alone.

"He looks a little bit like a movie star, don't you think?" Fiona whispered. "I mean, the kind who would act in independent films and really *care* about his art."

"Oh, sure." I sniffed. "The kind who plays a heroin addict and ends up dying in the end."

"The kind who then wins an Oscar and goes on to have a fabulous career playing tortured souls and making millions," Fiona finished cheerfully. "Anyway, I don't care what you say. I think you are just so *so* lucky to be his research partner." She caught her breath. "Oh, no, he saw us checking him out!"

"Us?" I asked, stung by the injustice of this. "I was just trying to eat my lunch—"

But Fiona wasn't listening. "I am so *so* embarrassed!" She giggled (sounding anything but) as Jack stared at us, his scowl practically igniting the air.

I grabbed the remains of my lunch and stood up, knocking my chair over in my hurry.

"Come on, let's get out of here."

"But you haven't finished your lunch," Fiona said.

"I'm not hungry," I muttered as I picked up the chair and tossed my lunch bag into the nearest trash can.

"Oh, I understand completely. I've been a nervous wreck all day long—"

Mercifully Fiona kept chattering as we careened down the hall, keeping me from thinking about the fact that I had now made a fool of myself in front of the entire cafeteria.

Or at the very least, in front of Jack Dawson. Which was even worse.

Chapter 5

When the final bell rang, I raced out of the school, ran up the street to the bus stop, and paced impatiently at the curb until the bus finally lumbered into view. I climbed on board, grabbed a seat, and settled back to calculate the day's rating in my head.

Plus two points for finding my locker and making it to every class on time.

Plus seven points for meeting Fiona, possible new best friend.

Minus seven points for seeing yet another ghost.

Plus six points because the ghost was friendly and cute.

Jack Dawson, however, posed a bit of a conundrum: plus five points for being relatively good-looking, minus five points for being sarcastic and surly, resulting in having no effect on the day's rating in any way.

Total score: a solid eight.

Not bad. The best day of my life so far had rated a sixteen (Christmas Day, seven years old, when I found my first bike—used and repainted, but it was *mine*—under the tree). When the bus pulled up to my stop, I grabbed my backpack and started walking home. The afternoon was sunny and warm. By the time I'd gone a few blocks, I was feeling quite happy.

As I passed our mailbox, I knocked on it—three taps, then one, then two—before opening it. I pulled out the mail and rifled through it, hoping, as always, for something other than bills and free circulars. No luck, as usual. In fact there were five bills, and three of them were stamped "Overdue." We also received offers to have our carpets cleaned (we didn't have any), our house painted (could advertising flyers be accused of sarcasm?), and our lives changed through the miracle of energy realignment (only if it was guaranteed to bring a flow of money energy our way).

As I opened the gate, Grandma Bee yelled from the backyard, "Is that Sparrow Delaney I hear?" I could see her head, clad in the white pith helmet and veil of a professional beekeeper, bobbing about behind the towering trees and overgrown bushes at the far end of the lawn. (She tried keeping bees last year, but faced with her irritable monologues about the lack of honey production, they all had decamped months ago for a presumably less stressful environment.)

"Hi, Grandma," I yelled back as I headed purposefully for the house.

"Don't go hide in your room!" she called. "Come over here and talk to me!"

I sighed and cast a wistful look at my bedroom windows, golden with reflected sunlight, high up in the trees.

"Sparrow!"

"All right! I'm coming!"

I headed in her direction, cursing a bit as thorns from vicious raspberry bushes scratched my arms. Finally I stepped out into a small clearing. Grandma Bee was sitting on a boulder, looking mournful and (incidentally) presenting her best profile to her audience (me).

There were four small granite headstones arrayed in front of her. Each one bore the name of a former husband. My sisters and I had given each a name based on the epitaph he had been assigned. The Dearly Departed was Grandma Bee's first husband, whom she married at a very young age ("I was a mere child!" she always said. "A babe in arms, practically!") after a dramatic elopement that involved climbing down a drainpipe from her bedroom window. The Beloved Husband was William Charles Emerson, my grandfather. The Sadly Missed was her third husband, an irascible oil baron whose fortune turned out to exist largely in his own mind. The Late Lamented was her fourth and (so far) last husband, a sickly man who could take Grandma Bee's forceful personality for only eighteen months before turning up his toes and joining his predecessors in the backyard.

My grandmother sighed deeply, wiped a nonexistent tear from her eye, and said, "I do so hate coming out here to tend their graves, my poor dead darlings. It's such a mournful thing to do. But after all"—she leaned down and delicately plucked a strand of crabgrass from the Late Lamented's grave site—"it is my duty."

She turned her magnified gaze on me. "Unless," she added thoughtfully, "I could find a loyal and loving granddaughter who was willing to shoulder this burden for me."

"Oh, for heaven's sake!" I admit this heart-tugging performance used to work on me, but by now I had now spent far too many afternoons on my hands and knees, pulling up weeds and scrubbing headstones with extra-strength kitchen cleaner. "No one wanted them buried in the backyard in the first place! They should be in the cemetery where they belong!"

"But I wanted my darlings close to me," she said mournfully. "It's such a comfort to know that they're nearby."

I sighed and dropped resignedly to my knees. I began pulling up weeds in a desultory fashion as Grandma Bee sat back, content now that she could direct operations from her rocky throne.

"You missed a dandelion, Sparrow," she said. "Over there, by your hand. No, your left hand. That's it, dig those rascals out by their roots! Oh, and as long as you're down there, here are the garden shears. Trim that grass in front of Everett's stone, dear. I can barely make out his name."

I started clipping as quickly as I could, totally focused on getting to the privacy of my bedroom as soon as possible. Unfortunately I was going so fast that my hand slipped, and the shears accidentally scraped the Dearly Departed's headstone.

"Sparrow! Watch what you're doing!"

"Sorry."

"I don't know what's wrong with you these days," Grandma Bee commented. "You've had your head in the clouds for a week now."

I muttered something about having a lot on my mind.

She leaned closer, her eyes fixed intensely on me. "Mmm. And what kinds of things do you have on your mind, I wonder?"

I moved on to the Beloved Husband, conveniently allowing me to edge away from her stare. "Just the usual. Nothing much. You know."

"Mmm." I could tell she wasn't buying this. "How old are you now, Sparrow?" she asked ever so casually.

I sat back on my heels. "You *know* I just turned fifteen!"

"Well, I *am* getting older, you know." She tried adding a pathetic quaver to her voice, but her glance at me was sharp and glinting.

"Don't try to sound like you're about to go to Summerland. We had my birthday party *two days ago*!"

She dropped the act and flapped a hand dismissively. "Well, there are so many of you girls. And when you get to be my age, you've been to so many birthday parties. It's hard to keep track." She took my chin in her hand so that she could peer into my eyes. "Hmm."

I didn't like the sound of that *hmm*. I pulled back and scooted to the next headstone.

"Fifteen," she said. "A tricky age."

I bit my tongue. I would not ask.

"Very, very tricky."

I refused to ask.

"Quite dangerous, in fact. Full of perils big and small."

I Absolutely Positively Would Not—

"Especially for someone like you."

She lifted her veil and fanned herself with it as she gazed over the fence at Mrs. Winkle, who was pouring milk into the saucers she had set out in her backyard. "I see Mary Ann Winkle is still suffering from delusions. Quite sad, really," Grandma Bee said conversationally. Unfortunately her conversational voice is extremely loud. One might even call it booming.

"Shh!" I hissed. "She'll hear you!"

"Oh, who cares? The woman's certifiable. Always has been, from the time we were children."

Grandma Bee and Mrs. Winkle have been archrivals since third grade, when Mrs. Winkle first piped up with tales of fairies in her garden and Grandma Bee countered with stories about ghosts in her living room. They've been waging a pitched battle ever since over who is the most sensitive, the most spiritual, and the most sought-after medium in both this world and the next.

"Only sentimental fools who have never grown up believe in fairies," Grandma Bee went on. Her voice, I noticed, was not just loud; it was penetrating.

"Grandma Bee, please!" I whispered urgently. "Keep your voice down!"

"Why, hello, Sparrow!" I looked up to see Mrs. Winkle standing a few feet away, next to the fence. She glanced at my grandmother and said, rather distantly, "Bee."

Grandma Bee nodded regally but didn't speak.

"How was your first day of school?" Mrs. Winkle asked me.

"Um . . . fine."

"Oh, I wish I were your age again! I loved my school days!" Mrs. Winkle's round face flushed rosy as she stared into the distance, a remembering look in her eye. "My favorite subject was science."

This inspired a disbelieving snort from Grandma Bee.

Hastily I indicated the still-empty saucers near the fence. "The fairies must have been hungry last night."

"Even more so than usual." She beamed. "Do you know, I put out a dozen saucers? And this morning they were all empty!" She lowered her voice. "I think my fairies are starting to bring friends!"

She smiled down at me, her blue eyes round with delight.

"Mary Ann, have you ever noticed the dozens of cats that roam wild through Lily Dale?" Grandma asked tartly. "I'm just curious what conclusion you might draw from that. Given your scientific mind-set and all."

"Um, I'm sure the fairies really appreciate everything you do for them," I interjected quickly. I put an extra ounce of sincerity in my voice to make up for Grandma Bee.

"Oh, yes, they do," she said. Mrs. Winkle turned to go back into her house, then stopped, a little frown creasing her forehead. "Well, that's odd. I just had a little vision. I don't usually have those, you know, dear."

"Oh, really?" I wasn't sure where this was going.

"Oh, please," my grandmother muttered.

"You're not the only one around here with talent, Bee!" she snapped. Then she turned back to me. "I saw you standing at a crossroads. You have to make a choice about which way to go."

"Not a very *specific* vision," Grandma murmured, adding sweetly, "After all, wouldn't that apply to most teenagers?"

Privately I agreed with Grandma Bee, but Mrs.

Winkle had a strange look in her eye that made me uneasy. This was not the cheerful, ditzy Mrs. Winkle I had always known. This was a seer, a prophet, a woman who could see into the future and predict all kinds of strange and wonderful and dire outcomes. The fact that her frizzy gray hair was held back by tarnished bobby pins or that I could see a dab of toothpaste at the corner of her mouth did not lessen her authority as she stared intensely into my eyes.

"I see a young man," she intoned. "He is pointing down a road."

Mrs. Winkle looked past me, narrowing her eyes as if to bring the vision into greater focus.

"He is watching out for you."

I blinked.

"Hmm. You don't want to take the path he is showing you, but he wants you to know that you should not be afraid."

A little thrill of dread ran down my spine.

Then Mrs. Winkle blinked distractedly several times, as if she had just come out of a trance and needed a moment to readjust to the ordinary world. She smiled sunnily at me, as if nothing had happened.

"You see, dear, there's no need to worry. You'll have help with whatever the future holds. Well, we all do, don't we?" she said. "Now, I'd better get back to work! Have a nice day, dear." She nodded coolly to my grandmother. "Bee."

She waved merrily and floated back to her own backyard.

"That was so strange. What do you think it meant?" I asked my grandmother. My mind went back to what she had been saying before Mrs. Winkle came over. "And why is fifteen a tricky age? And what do you mean, for someone like me?"

Grandma Bee cast a disdainful look at Mrs. Winkle's garden and muttered, "Fairies!" in a tone of utter scorn. "That woman is a complete noodle."

"Grandma Bee!"

She turned her attention back to me. "Yes?" she asked, the picture of innocence.

"Why is fifteen such a tricky age?"

"I'm so glad you asked," she said smugly. "Most mediums have realized their talent by the time they're sixteen. So, someone like you, who hasn't shown any signs of psychic talent whatsoever—" She pursed her lips, as if daring me to contradict this statement.

"Right," I said tensely. "Not one iota."

"Mmm. Well, either you are supremely untalented, in which case this year will be one of waiting with less and less hope as the months go by, or you are simply repressing your gifts, in which case this year will be one of upheaval and tumult and disorder and confusion, as all that spiritual energy comes to a boil and then"—she flung her arms wide—"bursts out into the waiting universe!"

This dramatic gesture was ruined only slightly by the fact that one arm had become tangled in the netting that hung over her shoulders, which then pulled the beekeeper's helmet off her head. She picked it up, dusted it off, and settled it back on her head with aplomb, despite the twigs and leaves caught in the veil.

"You make me sound like a volcano," I said, feeling even more uneasy.

"Well, according to you, you have nothing to worry about." Grandma Bee pointed to the Sadly Missed. "Now would you mind brushing those maple leaves away? Poor dear Johnny always had such terrible allergies in the fall."

Chapter 6

I went inside and tossed the bills on the kitchen table. My mother was sitting there, sipping a cup of tea and talking to the ghost of Mr. Tillman, a local farmer who had Crossed Over in April.

"I don't think you have to worry anymore about Eddie," she was saying calmly. "I was at Rita's house just the other day, and he's doing fine. Back to eating table scraps and running all over the lawn."

I carefully didn't look in his direction. "Mr. Tillman?" I mouthed at my mother. She nodded yes, then took another sip of tea as she listened. Mr. Tillman was a burly, red-faced man who wore faded overalls and a constantly doleful expression. The latter was due to the fact that, as my mother said, he just Could Not Let Go. For the last six months they had covered everything from whether the chickens were laying to how the old barn was holding up. His current fixation was a pig named Eddie, who, I gathered, had been much more than a pig. More like a member of the family.

"I don't trust that Rita," Mr. Tillman said. "I don't know why Frank married her. And she never liked Eddie. I wouldn't put it past her to have him butchered!" He added darkly, "That woman craves pork chops, you know."

My mother glanced through the mail as she said, "Oh, no, she knows how much he always meant to you." She shook her head at the bills and then absent-mindedly stuffed them in a cracked sugar bowl.

"Well, if you say so." Mr. Tillman didn't sound too convinced. "Maybe you'd let her know that Eddie loves potato peelings in his dinner—"

I ran up one flight of stairs and heard doors banging and voices yelling, sure signs that at least two of my sisters were already home. I dashed up another flight, darted into the sanctuary of my bedroom, and closed the door with a sigh of relief. As I walked over to open a window, I caught a brief glimpse of myself in the tarnished dresser mirror.

I stopped and looked more closely. In the last year or

so I've found myself doing that more and more often, frowning into mirrors, turning my head this way and that, trying to answer an imponderable question: What do I really look like to other people?

My mother says that I'm pretty, but she has to say that; it's her job as a mother. I'm afraid to ask my sisters. Some of them (Oriole, Wren, Dove) would reassure me, but I would suspect that they were just being kind and then I would sink into a depression at the thought that I was really ugly but no one wanted to tell me. Others (Raven, Lark, Linnet) would laugh and joke or make some sarcastic comment that would make me both angry and insecure, and then I would sink into a depression at the thought, etc. etc.

The weird thing is that sometimes I think I look, well, maybe not *pretty* pretty, but pretty enough. On good days I like my eyes because they're large and fringed with dark lashes and an unusual color (gray), and I like my dark brown hair (even though I wish it were curly, instead of straight as string), and I like my pale complexion. But on bad days I think I look like a troll: pasty-faced from living in some underground cave, with googly alien eyes and lank hair in a particularly boring shade of brown.

Obviously, both propositions can't be true at the

same time. One must be true, and one must be false. But how to know which is which?

Normally I can spend hours contemplating this philosophical problem, but today I had other things to think about. I threw myself on my bed and looked around my room, gloating (for the hundredth time) about the sweet deal I'd made last year when I moved to the attic.

Before that I had a room on the second floor, along with all my sisters. After one too many nights spent listening to the endless family drama—shouting, tears, graphic threats of death and dismemberment—that echoed through the halls on any given night, I'd grabbed my pillow, sheets, and quilt and traipsed up the stairs. Now I was farther away from our one bathroom, and I had another flight of stairs to climb every night, but that was a small price to pay for being able to live in solitary splendor, high under the eaves of our rambling old house.

There was enough room for a huge oak bed and dresser, an old rocker, a wall of bookshelves, and a castoff kitchen table that I use as a desk. True, none of the walls is exactly square, it's drafty in winter, and there's an eccentric alcove to the right of the closet door that serves absolutely no purpose, but I love it.

The very best part, though, are the two large windows that look out over the backyard. Our house has a double-decker porch that runs around two sides of the house. Soon after I had moved into the attic, I discovered that I could crawl out onto the roof of the second-story porch. From this lofty perch I could survey the houses and yards and streets for blocks in each direction.

The sky was darkening already, and I had a lot to think about, so I grabbed my dad's binoculars and slipped out the window. I raised the glasses and focused on the evening star.

If only Mrs. Winkle wasn't always so *vague*. Her sudden backyard vision had raised more questions than it had answered.

Like, for example, who was the young man who was pointing out the right direction for me? The first person I thought of was the ghost that had mysteriously appeared in the midst of an otherwise ordinary history class.

Then I had another thought that wasn't quite so cheerful. What if the young man was my father? That would mean my father had actually—I forced myself to think the unthinkable—died. The fact that Mrs. Winkle said he was young didn't mean anything. First, everyone under the age of fifty looked young to her, and second, many spiritualists swore that in the afterlife you got to return to the age when you were happiest in this life.

And it would make a horrible kind of sense that my father had been happiest when he was young, before he got married and had seven daughters.

I shivered. The air was getting chilly, and my thoughts weren't exactly warming. I scooted back inside and flopped down on my bed. Staring at the ceiling, I tried to turn my mind to more cheerful topics, but it was no use. All the old tapes about my father's disappearance started playing in my head with tedious monotony.

It happened when I was very young, so I can't swear to his motives, but this is how the story was told to me: He was an amateur naturalist (people often wonder why my sisters and I are all named after birds; that's one mystery solved). He was lured out west by a roaming band of graduate students from a nearby university. They had a grant, they told him; they wanted to study a rare ornithological species rumored to be nesting in Colorado or Wyoming; they needed someone to help them take notes, drive the pickup, and cook their dinners by the campfire. Would he join them?

He packed his suitcase in five minutes. As he ran out the door, he called good-bye to us all and promised to write. Eight postcards, with barely legible but cheerful scrawls on the back, came that first year. Three postcards, even less legible and perhaps a touch more desperate, arrived in year two. One more postcard, postmarked Paraguay and stained with what looked like either blood or cherry cough syrup, arrived the next year. And then nothing.

I asked my mother to tell me that story so many times that sometimes I think that I can actually remember it all happening. My own memories of him can be counted on the fingers of one hand.

I remember that he was a lanky man with smiling blue eyes and a bald spot on the back of his head.

I remember that he used to carry me piggyback up to bed, taking the stairs at a run so that I squealed and laughed.

I remember that he loved roaming through the woods, searching for leaves, twigs, and berries to make a foul-smelling tea, which he claimed cured a dozen ailments from the common cold to absentmindedness.

I remember that he was mild-mannered on the surface and incredibly stubborn down deep, where it really matters. When he was asked to do something he didn't want to do (and I have a feeling that he was badgered on an hourly basis, based on personal experience of living in this family), he would at first simply say no.

If the petitioner continued trying to convince him that really, if he only thought about it, he actually *did* want to adopt five homeless cats or fix the sagging front porch step or build an elaborate treehouse in the backyard during a late-summer heat wave, he would then say, "I would Rather Not." Somehow he managed to capitalize those last two words just by making his voice a little frostier, and his listener would be unable to utter another word of protest or persuasion. End of argument. No further discussion needed. Case closed.

Now that I'm older, I think about what the days must have been like for him, living in a huge rickety house with nine females, not to mention all the ghosts, which, even if he couldn't see them, still managed to make their presence felt. All in all, I can understand why he might run.

A few years after he left, well-meaning friends and neighbors began to suggest that we should conduct a special reading to see if he had gone to Summerland. My mother refused all offers with a vague smile.

"Oh, I'm sure he's still among us," she would say. "I

would feel it if he were no longer walking this earth."

Of course, that's what I wanted to believe, too. But sometimes I wonder. If he had died, surely he would contact me? Surely Sparrow Delaney, who sees everybody else's loved ones on a far too regular basis, would get a visit from her own father? The fact that I haven't seen his spirit makes me feel both hopeful and depressed.

Hopeful, because that meant he was probably still alive.

Depressed, because if he's still alive, why hasn't he come back?

Hopeful, because maybe he just hasn't come back *yet*. Maybe he wants to return, dreams of it even, but he's been imprisoned in a South American jail or icebound in the Antarctic or shipwrecked on an atoll in the Pacific.

Depressed, because the worst thing would be to know that he has died and still chooses not to come back for one last message.

As always when I think about my father, I turn my head to stare at my bedroom walls. Soon after moving in, I papered the walls with old maps from the local junk store. They're interestingly faded and discolored and look particularly nice in the golden glow of my bedside lamp. When I stare at the tapestry of small towns and hidden back roads, I try to sense my father's presence somewhere in the wide, wide world.

On good nights I imagine him traipsing through the southwestern desert or sitting in the piney woods up north, peering through his new binoculars. After a moment he lowers the binoculars, a faraway look on his face as he suddenly realizes that he misses us. He grabs his gear and heads for his battered pickup, determined to drive night and day until he gets back home.

On bad nights I imagine him sitting in front of a small campfire in a tropical jungle clearing, sipping a cup of herbal tea, and thinking about the family he left behind. Weighing the pros and cons, perhaps, of returning. And somehow, every night, deciding that when it comes to a joyous homecoming, he would Rather Not.

Chapter 7

By noon the next day I was already down five points for getting lost on the way to French, up two for a fast sprint that got me to class just as the late bell rang, then down three for discovering that I had forgotten everything about how French people use the past imperfect tense in conversation (or, indeed, why they would want to).

After struggling through an hour of *le français*, I walked to my locker. Jack was leaning against the wall. He was wearing his army jacket again, despite the heat, and surveying the passing crowd like a scornful prince deciding which commoner should be thrown into the dungeon. He spotted me and raised one eyebrow in recognition; other than that he didn't move a muscle.

"Hey," he finally said.

"Oh, hi!" That was terrible. Too bright, too enthusiastic, too head cheerleader for words. Dial it down a bit, I told myself, even as I felt myself hold out my hand like a glad-handing businessman and heard myself say, "I'm Sparrow."

Jack looked down at my hand, then glanced up at me with an ironic smile. He took my hand and shook it solemnly.

"Yeah, I know. You sit one row over in history, remember? But it's nice to meet you *formally*."

I blushed and pulled my hand away. "Yeah, me you too," I muttered idiotically.

Jack's smile widened. "It's okay. I don't bite."

"What's that mean?" I snapped defensively.

"Nothing. You just seem nervous, that's all."

"I'm not nervous!" Even more defensive, even more snappish, and now I sounded shrill too. This was going *so well*.

"My mistake. You're cool as a cucumber." He seemed ready to change the subject. "Look, I thought we'd better get together and talk about our history project."

"Yes, good idea," I said, my entire being focused on nodding intelligently and looking bright and interested.

I smelled autumn leaves and woodsmoke. Behind

Jack's left shoulder a shape flickered, then solidified into the ghost of room 12B. He winked. I frowned and pointedly turned my attention back to Jack . . .

. . . Who had moved on to complaining about our history project. "We only have a few more days to get the topic approved, and then there's all the research Grimes wants us to do," he was saying. "Ten sources, footnotes, a bibliography! He must think his class is the only one we're taking!"

Behind his back the ghost was watching me intently. At least he wasn't trying to talk to me. But somehow I found his steady, silent gaze even more unnerving. In fact he looked as if he were taking my measure in some way.

"Mmm," I murmured, trying to sound suitably outraged while keeping my eyes firmly fixed on Jack's face. "Well, I was thinking maybe we could research the Seneca. You know, the Indian tribe that used to live in this area . . ."

My voice trailed off in the face of his disbelieving stare.

"Don't you think that's a little, I don't know, fourth grade?" he asked. "What are we going to do, make a diorama out of modeling clay and Popsicle sticks?"

I clenched my hands, willing myself to remain

unflustered. (This was especially hard because my mind had immediately flashed back to my own wobbly model of a Native American longhouse that I had, indeed, made in fourth grade.)

He seemed to read my mind. "Don't tell me." He grinned.

"It was papier-mâché, not Popsicle sticks, and I got an A, for your information," I said. He laughed. I bit my lip to keep from smiling, but it didn't work.

"Okay, scratch that idea. Maybe something with politics? I think there was a congressional debate held around here back in the 1800s, I'm not sure of the exact date, we could look it up—"

"Too obscure."

Jack was still smiling. He seemed to be taking an evil delight in shooting down my ideas one by one. I should have just shut up. But one of my great personality flaws—according to Professor Trimble, who keeps a long and detailed list—is stubbornness.

So instead I suggested, a bit wildly, "Well, in the nineteenth century, one of the main industries around here was textiles. That could be kind of interesting—"

Even the ghost was shaking his head sadly at this.

Jack looked at me for a long moment, his expression blank. Then he said just one word. "Textiles?"

The delivery was so deadpan that I almost smiled again, but I caught myself in time. "Fine! You think of something then!"

"I already have. I heard about this place—"

The first bell rang. I glanced nervously at my watch. "We'd better get going."

"Oh, yeah," he said. "We wouldn't want to be *tardy*." Jack gave the last word a sarcastic twist, as if he thought the only people who cared about being late were grade-grubbing, authority-obeying morons. He started moving in the direction of our classroom, but I think his pace could fairly be described as leisurely.

"So you heard about this place?" I prompted as I walked next to him, but just a little bit faster.

I could feel a deep chill as the ghost strolled companionably at my side. I tried to ignore it, but there's really nothing worse than the bone-numbing cold that spirits give off. It makes you feel as if all the air has been sucked out of your lungs and you'll never be able to breathe again.

"I think we should do a report on Spookyville."

"Spooky—" I almost choked. Spookyville, of course, was what some people called Lily Dale. It was not an affectionate nickname.

"Yeah, everyone there says they can talk to ghosts,"

Jack went on. "I think it sounds cool, in a freaky kind of way. And it's been around for more than a hundred years, so it's historical."

My mind raced as I tried to think of an argument, any argument, to counter this reasoning.

"I'm not sure how *interesting* that would be," I said weakly.

He gave me a look of utter disbelief. "Are you kidding? Everyone's interested in ghosts. Even my parents were talking about it last night. Within ten minutes a perfectly normal conversation became this huge argument—" He stopped in mid-sentence. I glanced over at him, but his gaze skittered off mine, and he seemed to develop an unnatural interest in a nearby poster that implored someone, anyone, to run for student council.

"Why?"

"Why what?" Now he was suddenly moving faster. Now, it seemed, he couldn't *wait* to get to class.

I sped up until I was practically double-timing it through the hall. "Why did they start arguing?"

He wouldn't meet my eyes. "Ah, my mother's more of a believer, I guess. My dad thinks that psychics are all con artists."

"Why does he say that?" I tried not to sound indignant.

"He's read about all kinds of tricks they use to fool

people," Jack said. "Like, some psychics have friends who hang out with the audience before the show starts and listen to what they're saying about their dead relatives, then they give the psychic notes. The psychic goes onstage and miraculously has all the details, right down to what brand of dentures Grandpa used to wear."

We stopped in front of the classroom door. His voice had been getting louder, and his face was a little flushed. "They make money off of people's grief," he said, finishing up. "It's disgusting."

He paused for a second, as if recalibrating his tone, dialing it back from unreasonably irate to offhandedly casual. "But even if it is all a con, it would be kinda cool, to figure out how they do it," he said. "You know, like in that old movie *The Sting*, when Paul Newman and Robert Redford outcon the con men?"

"I never saw it."

"My brother loves that movie—" Jack looked down at the floor and shook his head slightly. Then he looked back at me, his eyes shuttered. "You should watch it some time. It's on DVD."

I didn't want to admit that we didn't even have a working TV, let alone a DVD player. I matched his voice. Cool for cool. "Oh, yeah, I'll check it out," I said airily.

We went into class and sat down, with the ghost taking his usual seat behind Jack.

"All right, people, settle down," Sergeant Grimes's voice boomed out.

Jack leaned forward and whispered, "I think we should start by visiting the Spookyville museum. I've got stuff to do this weekend, but maybe next Saturday?"

I stared at him. My mind was blank.

Then the ghost helpfully snapped his fingers in the air. I jumped and blurted out, "Yeah, sure. That sounds fine."

The ghost nodded encouragingly just as Sergeant Grimes exclaimed, "Delaney! Dawson! Class is now in session!"

Jack slumped back in his chair and closed his eyes.

I blushed and turned to face the front of the room, but not before one last glance at the ghost. He gave me a wink and disappeared.

Chapter 8

"You know, Sparrow, tonight is the last message service of the season," my mother said to me a few days later. It was Saturday; I was having lunch with my mother, Wren, Lark, and Linnet and considering what I wanted to do with the day. Usually I lounged around, maybe went on a bike ride, and thought vaguely about getting an early start on my homework without, of course, actually doing anything of the sort. Today, however, all I could think about was *next* Saturday, when I would be meeting Jack at the museum.

And now my mother, who was not a wheedler by nature, had decided to start wheedling about going to a message service. I quickly took a big bite of my grilled cheese sandwich to avoid answering. "Mmm," I said instead.

"It would be so lovely if you would come with us." My mother's vague gaze drifted off to the far corner of the kitchen. "Dear, please don't sniff the red wine. You know it gives you headaches."

I glanced over and saw the prune-colored image of a woman wearing a hoop skirt, a sunbonnet, and a sour expression lurking between the sink and the stove.

"Is Mrs. Witherspoon manifesting again?" Lark asked. She used her spoon to slingshot a cherry tomato in the direction of my mother's gaze.

"Lark!" my mother said. "Manners!"

"Sorry," Lark said blandly as Linnet giggled. "It just got away from me."

Mrs. Witherspoon, who Crossed Over right after the Civil War, is not a family favorite, to put it mildly. Even my mother has come close to losing patience with her. Perhaps because of the many, many travails she suffered on Earth, Mrs. Witherspoon used to take a nip now and then when she was alive. Now she just inhales the fumes from any wine bottles that happen to be around and then comments disapprovingly to my mother about the behavior of "young ladies these days," meaning, of course, my sisters and me.

My mother cocked her head to one side and listened for a moment. Then she turned to us and said, "Mrs.

Witherspoon says that you should use your napkins a little more and try to smack your lips a little less—"

A chorus of boos greeted this etiquette tip from Beyond.

"It's just food for thought, darlings, all just food for thought." Then she turned back to me. "About tonight's message service—"

"No," I said. "Of course not. No."

The first time I went to a message service, I was horrified to discover that ghosts had no qualms about standing right next to my seat, leaning forward so that their faces were only inches from mine, and yelling over one another to get my attention. I finally told my mother that I'd developed a migraine (which turned out unfortunately to be true) and ran from the auditorium.

Gradually I got better at ignoring the spirits, but I never became truly comfortable. For one thing, it's exhausting to maintain the illusion that I don't see anything out of the ordinary. And then there are the physical symptoms I get from spending too much time around too many ghosts. My chest starts to feel tight, I begin to shiver uncontrollably, my nerves feel as jangled as if I'd drunk a pot of coffee. And I always end up with a killer headache.

So I quit going. My mother thought that I was disheartened by my lack of psychic success, so she kept coaxing me to "just try one more time, darling, I'm sure you'll get a message tonight!"

I had been steadfastly refusing for so long that we could now conduct our discussion almost entirely in shorthand.

"I'm sure you'll find it—"

"No, I've told you—"

"If you'd just try—"

"But I have, and anyway, it's so—"

"No, darling, it's not boring, not really—"

"Yes, it is! In fact, it's—"

Just as we reached round three and I was opening my mouth to take an irritated bite of sandwich, I felt a little nudge, right between my shoulder blades. A freezing cold little nudge.

I turned around. Oh, no. The ghost from school was perched on the kitchen counter. The nudge I had felt was from his foot, which was swinging lazily as he watched our family discussion.

He nodded a cheery hello.

I deliberately turned my back to him and tried to remember where I had left off with my mother.

Ah, yes.

"It is *beyond* boring," I said truculently.

There it was again. Another nudge, harder this time. It made my elbow slip off the table. (All right, that means it was *on* the table while I was eating. Mrs. Witherspoon isn't totally wrong about our manners.) My soup slopped onto the tablecloth. Wren looked martyred.

I almost said a very bad word. I stiffened my back, trying to send a clear message to the ghost—Go away, you're not welcome here, don't you have something important to do in the afterworld?—through sheer force of mind.

"Sparrow? Is something wrong?" My mother was watching me closely.

"What's wrong is that I just washed and ironed that tablecloth yesterday!" Wren said. "It took half an hour!"

I followed family tradition and ignored Wren; after all, she was the one who insisted we use tablecloths at every meal, including lunch, and everyone knew she secretly loved to iron. "I was just saying that I don't think I can make it tonight because—"

Another . . . okay, that wasn't a nudge. That was a *shove*. I heard a whisper from behind me: "Sparrow. Go."

Somehow, without meaning to say those words *at all*, I heard myself snap, "Oh, all right! I'll go!"

Everyone stopped eating. Everyone looked at me. Then everyone looked at one another, as if to check that she hadn't been the only person who had heard what I just said.

"Oh, Sparrow!" My mother's eyes were shining. "Really?"

I shrugged. "It's no big deal," I said, even though I could already feel my breathing getting shallow. I sneaked a peek behind me. The ghost was gone.

As the day wore on and the time for the message service approached, I could feel my stomach starting to jump.

It's only one hour out of your life, I kept telling myself. You can do this. After all, you know how to handle spirits.

Indeed, I had learned a lot about ghosts over the years, thanks to a few pointers from my spirit guides and my own observations. For example, I discovered that people's personalities don't change a lot when they Cross Over. There are calm ghosts, jittery ghosts, angry ghosts, and (most annoying) ghosts that sigh and roll their eyes to the ceiling and say things like "I don't want to be any trouble. Really. If it's too much to ask for you to let my grief-stricken family know that I'm all right, well, I understand." Just think of every kind of person you've ever met in your life, and I can guarantee there's a ghostly counterpart.

I also found out that no matter how different their personalities are, they all have one thing in common: It takes an awful lot to discourage them. However, I did finally develop, through trial and error, three simple rules to keep all but the most persistent ghosts away from me.

Rule 1: Refuse to acknowledge the ghost's presence.

When ghosts approached me, I stared steadfastly into the distance and pretended that I didn't see them. Even if they waved their arms. Even if they jumped up and down. Even if they got so close that they were seriously invading my personal space.

Rule 2: Think boring thoughts.

Ignoring someone who is trying desperately to get your attention requires a lot of concentration. I found that it was easier if I focused on something tedious enough to make my mind go blank but complicated enough to demand a certain amount of focus—mentally reciting the twelve-times multiplication table, for example, or conjugating French verbs. I also memorized several endless poems by Longfellow and entire sections of the judicial code for just this purpose.

Rule 3: Finally, never, ever talk to them.

This is the most important rule of all. Saying something to a ghost means you've made a connection. And once you've made a connection, you're hooked, like a fish that has fallen for a particularly entrancing lure.

After I followed these three rules for a while, the ghostly grapevine gradually began working in my favor. I was branded a poor sport in the spirit world. Fewer and fewer ghosts dropped by for a chat.

They left me alone. I left them alone. And everyone—and by everyone, I mean, of course, *me*—was quite happy with that state of affairs.

So as I walked with my family to the auditorium, a barnlike wooden building in the middle of town, I was wondering how, how, *how* that pushy ghost from school was getting me to do things that I had sworn I would never do again.

We joined the crowd of people flowing into the building, talking in low but excited voices about what was about to transpire. My mother said coaxingly, "Sparrow, why don't you sit next to me? I'm sure you'll serve Spirit tonight! I've been seeing the most auspicious signs all day—"

"In a minute," I said. "I need to run to the rest room first—"

"Time for Sparrow's world-famous disappearing act." Raven's voice was acid.

"I'll be right back," I said untruthfully.

"Yeah, we'll save you a seat," Lark said with weary disbelief.

As Grandma Bee led the Delaney contingent boldly down to the front row, I edged my way toward the side wall. There were huge windows on two sides of the building, kept open to catch any hint of a breeze. Lattice screens were set up a few feet in front of the windows to hide all the miscellaneous items, such as extra chairs, hymnals, and office supplies, that the people working the entrance might need. The screens also offered a convenient place to hide, if that was the kind of mood you happened to be in. I ducked behind one, took a seat, and watched as the audience got settled in for the service.

The rows of folding chairs were already packed with the last group of summer tourists, and when it came to spirits, it was standing room only. Already at least two dozen misty figures were scattered through the hall. I shivered, and scooted back a little farther behind the screen.

At seven o'clock on the dot Miss Canterville, a tall, thin woman with curly white hair and piercing blue eyes, took the stage.

"Good evening!" she called out.

"Good evening!" the audience chorused in response.

After saying a brief prayer and leading the room in a ragged but heartfelt hymn, Miss Canterville looked around the room. "I can see that a lot of you brought spirits in with you," she said. "We have quite a crowd today!"

There was an excited buzz. Some people glanced over their shoulders, and at least half the audience shifted to the edge of their seats.

"Please look down and notice what you're wearing." Miss Canterville went on. Heads bowed as everyone checked—let's see, did I put on the white T-shirt or the fuchsia blouse today?—then looked up, memories refreshed. "I ask you to do that because our mediums will often point to someone in the audience and say, 'I have a message for the man wearing the blue and white striped shirt.' "

She gestured toward a man wearing just such a shirt. He sat up a little straighter, eyes wide, as if he suddenly realized that he might actually be selected to hear a message from the spirit world. The people sitting around him stirred in anticipation.

"It helps keep things moving if you can remember what you put on this morning," she said in a light-hearted tone that was calculated to make the crowd chuckle. They did chuckle, right on cue. You'd never know that Miss Canterville had repeated the same patter at least once a day for the entire summer.

"First, I'd like to ask Sylvia Robertson, a registered medium here in Lily Dale, to come forward and serve Spirit."

Miss Robertson walked eagerly to the front of the room and scanned the faces in front of her. After a moment she pointed to someone in the fourth row and said, "The woman wearing the green blouse. May I come to you?"

The woman nodded eagerly.

"Please say something, dear, I need to hear your voice for Spirit to come through. May I come to you?"

The woman cleared her throat and said, very loudly, "Yes, you may."

"I see a dog sitting right by your feet, it looks like a pug, do you understand that?" Miss Robertson said rapidly.

"Yes!" the woman cried as a friend gave her a significant nudge. Clearly Miss Robertson had scored a direct hit right off the bat.

"I'm getting the name Barry or Bob, do you understand that?"

"His name was Bart!" the woman squeaked.

"Yes, Bart, he was quite a pistol when he was on this plane, wasn't he, dear? Quite the ladies' man."

The woman was nodding so much she looked like a bobble-head doll.

"Yes, I see that he already has a special friend on the Other Side." A ripple of laughter ran through the audience. "He wants you to know that he feels like a young pup again." She paused to listen, smiled, then added, "And he's so happy that you took in that little stray from down the street, but he wants you to buy a new dog dish. He doesn't like seeing someone eat out of his bowl. That's why he keeps pushing it behind the refrigerator."

The woman looked a little stunned.

"And I'll leave you that with blessings, my dear," Miss Robertson finished up.

She strolled to the other side of the room, her eyes searching the audience. She drew out the moment a bit (Miss Robertson loves her moment in the spotlight) but finally pointed to someone else. "May I come to you?"

She passed on an entertainingly sarcastic message

from a Siamese cat ("I *told* you I was sick, but would you listen?") and a golden retriever's slobbery declaration of adoration for his former owners ("I really really really love you, yes, I do, I really really do!"). Then the gerbils started coming through, and Miss Canterville sensed that people's patience was wearing thin. She said crisply, "Lovely, dear. Such comforting messages, as always. But I believe there are other spirits anxious to communicate with their loved ones."

Miss Robertson walked back to her seat, and Mrs. Winthrop stepped forward to take her place. She usually wears a long purple caftan in the hope of looking more spiritual, a hope that is dashed by the inevitable egg stain on the front and the torn hem dragging on the ground. She breathed deeply to prepare herself, then looked expectantly around the room.

A ghost standing in the middle of the aisle waved her hand to get Mrs. Winthrop's attention. The spirit was a small woman carrying a thick book, her finger holding her place. She had the distracted, impatient look of someone who had been interrupted just as she got to the good part of a new novel. Her impatience only grew over the next ten minutes, as the medium laboriously figured out that the spirit was a librarian who wanted to contact her sister Jane.

At one point the librarian glanced desperately in my direction. "This is so irritating," she said to me. "I left five books under my bed, and now they're more than three months overdue."

I stepped back a little farther behind the screen.

The librarian drifted back into my eyesight and waved a hand in the air, as if maybe I was such a completely oblivious idiot that I hadn't noticed her before.

"Hello?" she called. "A little help here? I know you can hear me."

I pointedly looked away.

As I watched the ceiling fans whir gently under the high ceiling, I heard her plead. "I want to get back to my book. If you could just pass on one little message for me—" I began to run through a list of U.S. presidents in my mind, concentrating fiercely on getting the chronology exactly right.

"Oh, all right, *fine.*" She sounded exasperated, but she turned back to Mrs. Winthrop, whose forehead was now beaded with sweat as she tried to tune in to the spirit's voice.

"I'm getting an anxious energy?" the medium said uncertainly.

Grandma Bee shifted in her seat and gave a fierce clack of her dentures. Mrs. Winthrop glanced nervously at my grandmother and added, "I think there's something worrying her?" It was definitely a less than commanding performance. I think I actually heard Grandma Bee growl.

Many, many agonizing minutes later the mission was finally accomplished. Sister Jane, weeping, agreed to return the library books and pay all overdue fines. Mutual expressions of love and caring were exchanged.

However, the damage had been done. The librarian had picked up on my presence, and other spirits had taken note. A small, nervous man with thinning brown hair and buckteeth glided around the screen and looked beseechingly at me. "Please, I don't mean to bother you," he said in a high, nasal voice. "My message is very short. I wouldn't want to take up much of your time."

I stared fixedly at the windows as an extremely large woman wearing an extremely bright flowered dress elbowed him aside. "He only Crossed Over last week!" she bellowed. "I've been waiting for almost a decade! And my message is of the utmost importance! It's a matter of life and death!"

Even the other spirits, who were now edging closer to me, rolled their eyes at this. "There's always one drama queen in every crowd," a small elderly woman murmured. She looked like the Hollywood version of a sweet grandmother, complete with fluffy white hair and rosy cheeks, but her tone was acid.

I pressed my lips together to keep from smiling, and her gaze sharpened. She took two tiny, tottering steps forward and gazed up at me with a winning, hopeful expression.

"You seem like such a nice girl," she said sweetly. "Surely you'll help a poor old woman contact her great-grandchildren, especially little Joey? He misses me so much, poor dear."

I moved farther back in the shadows and started to do algebra equations in my head. She scowled and stamped her little foot. "You're just like all the other young people these days!" she scolded me before moving on. "No consideration for others! No consideration at all!"

For the next ten minutes I meditated on double-entry bookkeeping, cinder-block motels, highway exit ramps, Latin grammar, shag carpeting, and mall parking lots. If thinking boring thoughts were an Olympic event, I would have won the gold. Finally all the ghosts drifted away, muttering darkly to themselves.

The service went on for another half hour, but I stopped paying attention. I sat behind the lattice screen and watched the light fade from the sky and listened to the faint chirp of crickets. Once in a while I glanced at my family, who also seemed ready for the service, and the season, to end. I could see Raven yawning and Lark and Linnet drawing elaborate designs on each other's arms with ballpoint pens. Even Oriole was now absorbed in a minute examination of her fingernails, and my mother's usual warm smile was beginning to slip.

Then a draft of cold air swept across the back of my neck, bringing with it the faint smell of autumn. I turned to see the ghost from history class standing right behind me.

I whipped my head back around and stared steadfastly at the maroon velvet curtains that framed the stage.

Rule 1: Refuse to acknowledge the ghost's presence.

Within the blink of an eye, the ghost had manifested in front of the curtains, gazing at me as if I were his last hope of heaven.

My eyes locked with his, and I forgot to breathe.

Luckily my body remembered. After a few airless seconds my lungs drew in a deep, shuddering breath. My eyes darted to the clock on the back wall.

Before I could blink twice, the ghost was standing under that clock. He was farther away than before, yet somehow his presence was even more . . . present. He grinned at me.

I frowned back. Rule 2: Think boring thoughts.

"Our legal system is based on the principle that an independent, fair, and competent judiciary will interpret and apply the laws that govern us," I mentally recited. The State Bar Association's code of judicial conduct usually puts me into a semiconscious trance within one or two sentences. I relaxed into the familiar cadences, much as I would have relaxed into a hot bath, feeling happy and victorious.

Then I heard a deep, warm voice say, "Nice try, Sparrow."

Startled, I opened my mouth for an indignant reply—and just in time remembered Rule 3.

Never, ever talk to a ghost.

I snapped my mouth shut and ran out the back door, congratulating myself on my escape and wondering why it had been such a close one.

Chapter 9

I didn't wait for my family. I knew they would linger after the service to gossip with neighbors and enjoy the relaxed, relieved feeling that comes with the end of yet another season. I ran home, avoiding the worst potholes and enjoying the feel of cool air on my face and the sweet, sad scent of the last summer flowers, still bravely blooming around every house.

I was used to vanquishing unwanted ghosts in minutes. But this one . . . he was proving to be troublesome. And I couldn't figure out why.

I walked into a bizarrely silent house and trudged up the stairs. At least I don't have to worry about going to another message service for a while, I muttered to myself as I pushed open my bedroom door. The only thing on my mind was my comfortable bed and warm quilts and soft pillows. So when I stepped inside and found the ghost of room 12B lounging comfortably in my rocker, my reaction was not a happy one.

In fact I actually closed my eyes for a moment, hoping against hope that I was seeing things.

I opened my eyes. He was still there.

"Hello, Sparrow."

I turned my back on him and began organizing my desk.

"I enjoyed the service tonight."

I neatly stacked my textbooks into a serious, scholarly tower. I straightened the No. 2 pencils, freshly sharpened, that already stood at perfect attention in a chipped mug.

I sat down, flipped to a fresh page in my notebook, and stared down at it, my thoughts racing as I tried to figure out how to get rid of him. After a few seconds I couldn't resist sneaking a quick peek over my shoulder.

"Perhaps you couldn't see much from your hiding place," he commented, "but people are always so happy when they receive a message from one of their loved ones." He looked wistfully into the distance. "I wish—"

Wish what? I almost said it out loud. I caught myself just in time and quickly opened my trigonometry textbook, searching for the dullest section I could find.

The Pythagorean theorem. Excellent. Boring enough to keep any ghost at bay. I started reading: "Label the right angle C and the hypotenuse c. Let A and B denote the other two angles, and a and b the sides opposite them. . . ."

Instantly a gray fog of boredom began creeping into my brain. La, la, la, I hummed to myself, feeling pleased as punch. You, Sparrow Delaney, are a force to be reckoned with. You can hold off the spirit world with one hand tied behind your back. You can take on all comers and dismiss them in the first round. You are a champion!

Well, as Professor Trimble always says, pride goeth before a fall.

Two minutes later, in the midst of an enormous yawn, I looked up to see that the ghost was standing beside my desk, looking down at me inquiringly.

"Must be tedious work, keeping ghosts away," he said. He would have sounded sympathetic if it hadn't been for the hint of laughter in his voice.

Scowling, I slammed the book shut and started to stomp out of the room. Halfway to the door I stopped. What was I doing? This was *my* room! If anyone was going to leave, it was going to be the dead guy.

I whirled around, only to find that he had moved

again to stand right behind me. Now we were facing each other, only inches apart, close enough so that I caught my breath at the sudden freezing cold.

I took a quick step to the right. He moved just as fast to block my way.

I moved left, he moved with me.

Well, I wasn't a third-grade dodgeball survivor for nothing. I'd mastered a few tricky moves in my day.

I feinted right, then moved left, *fast*, and—

"*Get out of my way!*" I yelled at the ghost, who was standing mockingly in front of me.

There was an awful silence as I realized what I'd done.

"I was wondering how long it would take to get you to talk to me," he said. "Five days might be some kind of record, if anyone bothered to track that kind of thing." He sat down in the rocker and leaned back comfortably. "So, now that you have, why don't we get to know each other?"

I looked at him for a long moment.

"Damn," I said.

"Mmm," the ghost murmured sympathetically. "You were doing such a good job blocking me out, too. Just goes to show what having a bad temper will do." He shook his head sadly.

"I don't have a bad temper!" I snapped, sounding (I realized too late) extremely bad-tempered.

"Of course you don't," he said solemnly. "My mistake."

I bit back a sharp—well, all right, bad-tempered—remark and took a deep, calming breath instead. "Look," I said evenly, "I know you're only here because you want something from me."

"You make me sound so selfish."

I raised an eyebrow in polite disbelief. "If you didn't want something, you'd be drifting around in the afterlife somewhere, thinking ghostly thoughts," I pointed out with devastating logic. "You wouldn't be hanging out in my history class. Or the cafeteria. Or my *bedroom*."

"Point taken. But—"

"Ghosts never come back to answer questions," I continued, warming to my theme. "It's always a one-way conversation with them. Tell my wife I love her, I buried the silver in the backyard, don't let the fire insurance lapse, blah, blah, blah. It's always about what *they* want."

"Yes, but I think that if you heard about my particular case—"

"And I might as well tell you right now. Whatever you want, I can't help you."

He raised his eyebrows slightly at that. "Can't?" He stood up and wandered over to my dresser. He bent down to look in the mirror, which reflected nothing but the room. He shook his head. "I never know how my hair looks anymore," he remarked absently.

Then he turned back to me. "Can't, as in it's physically impossible for you to help me because you don't have the skills or the talent or the intelligence?"

He paused, as if he were really waiting for an answer.

When I didn't respond, he went on, "Or can't as in I could if I wanted to, but I won't?"

"Well, since you ask. Won't. It's a matter of policy," I explained.

"That sounds very official. But aren't you being a little unreasonable? Considering that we just met?" He smiled in a way that I think was supposed to be winning. I scowled back. "You don't even know my name."

I sat up a little straighter, folded my hands in my lap, and gave him a demure look.

"You're absolutely right," I said. "So. What's your name?"

"Luke."

"Luke. Very nice to meet you," I said formally.

He matched my tone. "Likewise, I'm sure."

"And how long have you been dead?" I continued, still using that ultrapolite voice that adults bring out when they talk to people they barely know.

"Almost a year now. See, we're getting to know each other better all the time."

"Not to be rude or anything," I said, "but I don't want to know anything more about you. And I don't want you to know anything at all about me."

He leaned back and squinted at me. "Oh, I already know a great deal about you."

"You do?" That made me feel uneasy. "Like what?"

"Well, your name, for one thing. And that you're a sophomore in high school. It's a new school, so you're nervous. You want to make friends without revealing too much of yourself, a terrible plan, by the way. Doomed to failure. You worry too much about all the wrong things. Your best subject is English, your French is *très misérable*, you need to pay more attention in biology, and—let's see, what else? Oh, yes, you've got a tremendous psychic gift, which you're determined not to use. How am I doing so far?"

After a long moment I said, "I'm doing just fine in biology."

"Mmm. Well, you're going to have a pop quiz next Friday," he said. "So we'll see."

My pulse jumped a little at this news.

"But enough about you. Let's talk about me."

"Oh, yes. Let's," I muttered sarcastically.

"You see," he announced, "I have a mission." He hummed a few bars of the *Mission: Impossible* theme song.

"Of course you do," I said, rather pleased with the way I had colored my voice with a bitter, knowing edge.

Then I had a sudden, brilliant thought. "Why don't you contact my mother? Or my sister Oriole? They would *love* to help you!"

He tilted his head, considering this. "I *could* do that," he said thoughtfully.

I relaxed a tiny bit.

"I'm sure they'd understand why you had to give me a referral, instead of using your gifts to help a poor lost wandering soul." He smiled innocently at me. "Is that really what you want me to do?"

I glared back. Somehow he knew that this was the last thing I wanted and that he had just got the upper hand. "Oh, forget it," I snarled.

"Then I guess we're back to Plan A." He added woodenly, "Help me, Obi-Wan Kenobi. You're my only hope."

I gave him a cool look. "That's a terrible Princess Leia impression."

"The worst in the tristate area, if not the entire eastern seaboard," he said cheerfully. "Unfortunately doing bad impressions of pop culture icons is pretty much my only party trick. Although," he added, "people did seem to like it when I flipped my eyelids inside out." He demonstrated.

I winced. "Yuck."

He shrugged and flipped his eyelids back to the position that most people consider both normal and desirable. Then he gave me a melting look (one that I'm sure worked on all the girls when he was alive, one that I'm sure he used to practice in the mirror every night). "I'm serious, Sparrow. I need your help."

I propped my book on my lap and put my hands over my years. "Doing homework," I said in a singsong voice. "Ignoring you."

"Hanging around," he said, mimicking my singsong exactly. "Still haunting you."

I stared furiously down at the page, trying not to smile. "I'm only going to say this one more time," I said as clearly and distinctly as I could. "I . . . will . . . not . . . help . . . you. Now, *go away*."

"Oh, right." He snapped his fingers, as if suddenly

remembering something. "That reminds me of another thing I know about you. You're incredibly stubborn."

"Yes, I am," I said proudly.

He nodded, as if pleased. "Good. So am I."

As he shimmered out of sight, I heard him say, "This should be fun."

Chapter 10

The next morning I found myself looking over my shoulder, wondering when and where Luke would pop up next. I felt jumpy and paranoid, like a spy who knows her cover has been blown and is just waiting to be taken in for questioning. But when several days went by and nothing happened, I decided that he had found some other psychic. Someone more agreeable. Someone more helpful. Someone altogether more charming and friendly and fun.

Which was a good thing, I kept telling myself. Because that, after all, was exactly what I wanted.

Then one morning I woke up to find every chair and table in my bedroom upside down. The battered cigar box that held my makeup, the chipped vase that occasionally held flowers, the plaster pig that was a souvenir of a long-ago trip to the county fair—all the little knickknacks that I kept on my dresser were also upended. The few pictures I had hung in my room now faced the wall. All my books had been turned around so that their spines were toward the back of the bookshelf.

I jumped out of bed and glared at the mess. "Very funny. But if you think this is going to make me change my mind," I informed the air, "you are completely wrong."

I pulled a sweater and some sweatpants from my dresser, then stomped over to the closet, muttering, to grab my sneakers. I shoved my right foot into the shoe. My toes encountered a thick, gooey substance. I pulled my foot out and saw what looked like blood dripping to the floor. For a single shocked moment, I thought it *was* blood. Then I smelled a sweet fragrance that brought to mind crisp toast and melting butter and my brain finally figured out what my toes already knew: The sneaker was filled with raspberry jam.

"Ahhhh!"

Ten seconds later Dove was at my door. She opened it a crack and peered in at me with a worried expression on her round face.

"Sparrow? Are you all right?"

"Fine," I growled as I wiped the goo off my foot.

She started to inch her way inside. I hopped to the door, holding my sticky right foot in the air.

"Halt," I commanded.

She blinked, her gray eyes brimming with owlish sympathy behind her glasses. "I thought you might need some help," she said. "I just wanted to give you a hand."

She sounded hurt, but I held firm. This room was my sanctuary. No one was allowed inside.

I put one hand on the doorknob to balance myself. "I don't need any help, but thanks anyway."

She leaned on the door a little more. "Are you sure? You look a little . . . *frazzled*."

"I just, um, have a big test today. And I don't have anything to wear. And doesn't everyone scream when they're feeling totally frustrated?"

She paused to consider this. "Well," she said slowly, "*I* usually have a good cry."

"No kidding," I said, deadpan. Dove has a good cry about three times a week, because someone spoke sharply to her, or she read a really, really sad book, or she found an earthworm drowned in a puddle. Almost any reason will do. We've learned just to hand her a tissue and go on with our lives.

"I don't cry," I said, barring the door more firmly with my body, "and I'm fine."

"Well, all right," she said reluctantly. "But if I can help in any way, please, please, *please* let me know. Do you promise, Sparrow?"

"Yes, yes, all right, I promise," I said. The door closed, finally, and I leaned against it, heaving a huge sigh of relief.

My relief was short-lived. Seconds later I heard hooting laughter from the front lawn. I leaned out my window and saw five of my bras festooned on tree branches in the front yard. And not just any bras. Back in the spring I had snagged an unusually lucrative babysitting job (holding the Thompson twins at bay for five hours, a task so onerous that their mother had guiltily doubled my fee when she returned home). I could have used the money for many dull and worthy items. Instead I had splurged at a Victoria's Secret sale.

Now my flaming red bra waved from the treetops like the flag of a defiant army, and the leopard-pattern bra fluttered saucily from a lower branch.

Lark and Linnet were dancing beneath the trees, their long blond hair flying as they jumped up, trying to grab the bras. They were laughing insanely, as if they had never seen underwear before. (To be fair, they had probably never seen it dangling from tree branches, but I wasn't in the mood to be terribly fair at that moment.)

I raced down the stairs two steps at a time and burst out the front door.

"Sparrow, are these yours?" Lark yelled, jumping in the air and trying to grab the super low-cut version in bright purple. "Ooh, you are a sexy lady!"

"Give me that!" I snatched a sunny yellow bra from Linnet's hands. "Stop laughing! Stop yelling! Just . . . stop!"

Fortunately Wren and Dove, alerted by the noise, came out of the front door, instantly figured out what was happening, and sprang into action. Wren ran for a broom and used it to dislodge the bras that still dangled from a high branch; I grabbed each one as it fluttered gracefully to the ground. Dove gently but firmly made the twins hand over the bras they were waving in the air. Ten minutes later I had an armful of underwear and a bright red face.

"Thanks," I muttered to my two good sisters.

"Thanks a *lot*," I snarled at my two bad sisters.

Wren looked from me to the trees, then back to me. Even after all that running and jumping and waving of the broom handle, she looked neat and composed.

Every glossy hair of her short brown bob had fallen back into place, her crisp white shirt was still tucked into her skirt, and there wasn't a grass mark or smudge of dirt to be seen on her gleaming white sneakers. "How in the world," she said, "did your bras end up in the *trees?*"

Ah. Good question. I opened my mouth, then closed it again when I realized that I had no good answer. And now all my other sisters were staring at me with bewilderment gradually dawning on their faces as well.

I was saved by, of all people, Raven. She stomped out onto the porch, her black hair flying around her head like a thunderstorm. She had worked the late shift at the convenience store again and was clearly not happy about being awakened by all the commotion. In fact she looked like an ancient goddess, the kind that strikes people dead with lightning bolts just for fun.

"*Dr. Snell,*" she hissed.

Everybody's face cleared.

"Of course," Lark said.

"This is just the kind of thing that stupid ghost would think was funny!" Linnet said.

"I keep telling Mother we should hold an exorcism," Wren said, automatically leaning down to pluck a weed.

"I could get the whole thing organized in a few days."

"That seems a bit harsh," Dove said. "Grandma Bee does like him so much—"

"Talk about a match made in heaven!" Raven snapped. "I'm going back to bed, and nobody'd better *wake me up again*!" She stormed back inside, slamming the door behind her.

"Well, at least he makes life more interesting," Lark said. She spotted a garden gnome that had tipped onto his face in all the excitement and cried out, "Oh, no! Dudley!" As she knelt to place him upright, the rest of us rolled our eyes at one another. A few years ago Lark began collecting tacky garden ornaments at garage sales. There are now fifteen gnomes scattered across the front yard. We *think* they're supposed to be ironic.

Linnet was gazing thoughtfully at me. "Spar-row," she said, a delighted sparkle beginning to shine in her eyes, "when did you get a *Wonderbra*?"

I looked down at my armful of underwear and blushed. I looked up to see Luke leaning against the tree, laughing, and blushed even more.

"Never mind!" I snapped.

Then I ran inside, mentally cursing all ghosts, those in my past, those in my present, and those, I was sure, lurking somewhere in my future.

* * *

The Upside-Down Bedroom Incident, closely followed by the Raspberry Jam Affair and the Underwear in the Trees Scandal, made me late getting ready, late catching my bus, and late for the first bell.

I race-walked to my locker. I feverishly twirled the combination, missed the number nineteen on the last spin, and, cursing under my breath, started over. I flung the locker door open, reached inside for my history textbook, and gasped as my hand encountered a solid, gummy mass. At first I couldn't even understand what I was seeing. Then, gradually, the details seemed to fill in, like a photograph developing in a darkroom.

Somehow, my entire locker had been filled with a shimmering block of blue Jell-O. Even as I was registering the fact that my books, papers, and gym bag were, thankfully, not entombed in gelatin but stacked neatly on the floor; even as I distractedly wiped my sticky hand on my skirt; even as I wondered how the Jell-O had solidified, given that my locker was not refrigerated; even as all those thoughts were running through my mind, I was dimly aware that this was the not kind of event that would go unnoticed. I grabbed the locker door, preparing to swing it shut, but I was too late.

"Hey, what's that stuff in your locker?" A boy was peering over my shoulder and grinning with delight. I knew him vaguely. He played football, he was a junior, his name was . . . Clay? Ben? Jayson with a *y*? "Cool! I've seen lockers filled with Ping-Pong balls or whipped cream or Silly String, but Jell-O! Man!" He nodded appreciatively, a connoisseur of pranks acknowledging the work of a master. "Now *that's* original."

"Well, I've always wanted to go down in history for something," I said tersely.

I grabbed the door again, but the football player held it open with his mighty football-playing arm and bellowed across the hall, "Hey, Reggie! Come over here, and take a look at what someone did to this chick's locker! It's awesome!"

Reggie sauntered over. "Dude, how did they get the Jell-O to, you know, gel?" he asked. Well, at least he was bringing scientific inquiry to bear upon what was turning out to be one of the top ten most embarrassing moments of my life.

The football player looked puzzled. "It's Jell-O, man," he explained.

Reggie slapped him on the side of the head. "You gotta mix it up and stick it in the refrigerator for hours, you idiot! Haven't you ever made Jell-O?" He prodded the blue mass experimentally. It quivered but held its shape. "Hmm. Pretty solid consistency . . ."

"Hey, Deemsy, come over here! Take a look at this!" Clay or Ben or Jayson yelled. "It's awesome, dude!"

Within moments I was surrounded by a dozen of my fellow students, most of them members of the football team, a jolly bunch that apparently considered a lockerful of Jell-O the height of sophisticated humor. They all were laughing loudly and jostling for a better view and speculating about who could have pulled off this amazing prank and how they did it and why they had picked on me.

"You sure you don't have a clue about who did this?" Deemsy said to me. "You gotta have *some* idea. When Mark Rabucci put itching powder in my jock, I knew it was him right away. Within seconds." He stopped grinning long enough to add grimly, "And then I pounded him."

"Yeah!" a couple of his buddies said together, their eyes lighting up at the memory.

"'Course, turns out that Mark didn't do it; it was Danny Ramos." He shrugged. "Oh, well."

He turned back to the mystery at hand. "You must have made somebody really mad."

"No, I haven't!" I was flustered at being the center of so much attention, worried about how I would clean up the mess, and—the bell rang—now late to class as well.

I was saved by Assistant Principal Donovan, a small man with beady, suspicious eyes. "What's going on here?" he asked.

The crowd melted away as everybody suddenly remembered that they really had to get to class, there was a quiz scheduled in geometry, Mr. Hines hated it when people were late. . . .

I was left alone with Mr. Donovan, who stared at my locker as if it held evidence of some sort of massive conspiracy. He said, "I'll call the janitor to clean this up."

"I think someone already did," I said, nodding toward an older man who was walking stiffly up the hall, carrying a mop and bucket and shaking his head wearily.

"Oh?" Mr. Donovan looked over his shoulder, then turned back to me, frowning.

Too late I felt a wintry chill, tasted chalky antacid tablets, and noticed that the man's work shirt had a certain vintage look. "Twenty years of cleaning up messes at this school," the ghost was muttering sourly. "Twenty years."

I met Mr. Donovan's puzzled gaze. "I thought I saw someone down by the office," I said weakly.

"And here I am," the janitor said, scowling at the melting Jell-O. He set the bucket down with a clang and plunged the mop into the water. "*Still* cleaning up messes."

I closed my eyes briefly. Could this day possibly get any worse?

"Sparrow?"

I opened my eyes. The janitor had vanished, but Mr. Donovan was looking at me as if he thought I should either book a session with the school counselor or get a prescription for some excellent drugs. Or, preferably, both. "Are you all right?"

"Yes, of course!" I said quickly.

He squinted at me, clearly running through a mental checklist ("Ten Warning Signs of Imminent Mental Breakdown in High School Sophomores"). Finally he said, "I don't suppose you know who did this." It was a statement, not a question, but I answered anyway.

"I have absolutely no idea." My voice rang with conviction.

"Hmm." He looked at the locker again, and his pale eyes suddenly sharpened with interest. He reached past me to pull something from the sticky mess.

It was a plastic sandwich bag. Inside was a piece of paper, folded as precisely as origami into a tiny hexagon.

Mr. Donovan gingerly pulled the bag open, trying not to get his hands sticky. "Perhaps we have found our first clue," he said. "Why don't you read that note out loud?"

Reluctantly I unfolded the paper and read the message, which had been written in a beautiful, almost calligraphic script.

"Surrender, Sparrow," the note said. "Resistance is futile."

Mr. Donovan eyed me suspiciously. "You're sure you don't know what that means?"

"No," I said, all wide-eyed innocence. "I don't have a clue."

And I thought, Luke, if you weren't already dead, I would kill you.

Chapter 11

I was running behind all day and totally exhausted by the time I got to my last class. Because it was Wednesday, that class was gym, the most loathsome hour on my schedule. As I rushed breathlessly into the empty locker room (so late, so late!), I saw that no matter how bad your day has gone, there's always the potential for it to get worse.

Luke was lounging on a bench, absently twirling a combination lock and humming a little tune.

"Well, Sparrow, what do you think?" he asked without looking up. "I'd make a pretty good poltergeist, don't you agree?"

"Dandy," I said. "Although it's a low and shabby ambition."

"I know." He tried to look shamefaced and failed

miserably. "But you made it quite clear that you won't help me—"

"And you think that what you put me through today is going to change my mind?"

"—even though I most urgently need your help," he went on, ignoring me. "What we have here is a classic problem." He pointed to me. "Immovable object."

"You got that right," I muttered.

He pointed to himself. "Irresistible force." He smiled smugly and added, "Emphasis, of course, on *irresistible*."

I eyed him coldly. "You flatter yourself."

"Constantly," he agreed. "Helps keep my spirits up."

Before I could respond, I heard the dulcet voice of Coach Drogoszewski, the football coach who had most unwillingly been forced to take over the girls' PE classes when the regular teacher quit after the first day.

He marched into the locker room, scowling. "Delaney!" he barked. "Get dressed and get on the court in five minutes, or this will be the most miserable hour of your life!" He started to storm out, then turned and fixed me with a basilisk stare. "For your information, this is the sixth class I've taught today, and you are now the thirteenth girl to be tardy. I'm warning you! I'm near the end of my rope!"

He slammed out the door. I opened my gym bag and began pulling out the hated uniform as quickly as possible.

"Will you get out of here?" I snarled at Luke just as I realized that I had forgotten my socks.

Luke leaned over to pull a stray volleyball from under the bench and began pushing it back and forth with his foot. "Oh, I don't know," he said. "I kind of like it in the girls' locker room. There are distinct advantages to being invisible to most people."

I was on my way to change inside a stall, but I stopped to look at him with an awful suspicion. "How long have you been lurking here?" I demanded.

He grinned. "Long enough."

"That is disgusting," I said through gritted teeth. "Despicable!"

I jumped into the stall, slammed the door closed, and began tearing my clothes off. "Chauvinistic! Shameful! Inexcusable! Degrading to women!" I continued to yell through the door.

"You are so right," Luke said complacently. "Not to mention horrifying, appalling, dreadful, and wicked."

I burst out of the stall, red-faced and breathless. I tried to put on my right sneaker while standing on left foot—never a good idea—and promptly fell over. "If you think

I'm going to give in, just because of a few pranks—"

I pulled myself up onto the bench, jammed my left foot into the other sneaker, and began to fumble with the laces.

"Two minutes, Delaney!" Coach Drogoszewski yelled from the hallway. "I can see the end of the rope from here!"

I shoved my bag in my locker. "I don't have time to *talk* about this, he's going to *kill* me, you have no idea what a *fiend* he is—"

"Sparrow." He put his hand on my shoulder. The sudden cold shocked me, and I jerked away.

He held up a hand in apology. "Sorry. But . . . *do* you know what happens when an irresistible force meets an immovable object?"

I threw my hands up in despair. "I don't know! Nothing, I guess."

"Exactly! Because they can't both exist. If the force is irresistible, the object will move. If the object is immovable, the force is not irresistible." He paused a second to let that sink in, then added, "One of us will win, and that means one of us will lose. Unless—"

"Unless what!" I didn't have time for this.

"Unless we call a truce and figure out a way for both of us to win."

I began frantically searching for my lock, then realized it was still inside my gym bag, which I had stuffed in my locker. As I pulled the bag back out again, I said testily, "What kind of truce?"

"I won't play any more pranks if you'll let me argue my case with you. All I want is the chance to convince you to help me."

"Convince me how?" I asked cautiously.

"Through reasoned and intelligent debate."

I shook my head. "No, thanks. I have enough ghosts arguing with me already."

He nodded, conceding the point. "All right. How about if I agree to visit you once a day? And furthermore"—he held out his hands, palms up, as if to demonstrate how completely sensible and fair and conciliatory he was being—"furthermore, I will stipulate that at each visit I get to make one, and only one, argument on my behalf. Now, that is a more than reasonable offer, right?"

"I don't want you droning on and on," I countered. "Each argument will last no longer than five minutes."

"Fifteen."

"Ten."

"Done."

I stopped. I looked at him. I considered. "Wait. This is a negotiation, right?"

"Ye-es . . ."

"So what do I get in return?"

He tilted his head to one side. "What do you want?"

"Delaney!" I jumped as Coach Drogoszewski's voice echoed through the room. "This is your *last warning*!"

"You have to answer one question a day," I blurted out. "In exchange for making me listen to you."

"Questions about what?"

"About being, you know . . ." My voice trailed off.

"Dead?" he suggested helpfully.

"Well"—I cleared my throat—"yes."

He paused, as if considering, then nodded with decision. "Agreed."

"Okay," I said. "It's a deal."

"Excellent." It wasn't until I saw his shoulders relax that I realized that our negotiation had actually meant something, maybe even a lot, to him.

But before I could consider that at length, I heard Coach Drogoszewski yell, "All right, Delaney! You had your chance! I am now officially *at the end of my rope*!"

"Bye," I said hastily, then ran up the stairs to the gym to a grim hour of wind sprints, frog jumps, and push-ups.

* * *

When I got home and limped upstairs to my bedroom, Luke was sitting at my desk. I was happy to see that he had finally used his ghostly powers for good, righting my room so that everything was back in order. He was gazing with interest at my dad's postcards (lifted from my mother's bedside table one dark and nervous night), which I had pinned to the wall. I had typed out all the messages and then pinned that sheet of paper next to the cards themselves so that I could see the pictures on the front and remember what he had written on the back.

When I read them all at once like that, the words, which were a model of economy and noninformation, almost started to seem like a poem. I preferred thinking of them that way, actually. A poem from my father. With a title like "Thinking of You, More Later."

Dear family,
The adventure continues to go well, but
the food is bad.
Since I am the cook,
I can't complain.
Thinking of you.
More later.

Dear family,
Funds are low, but
spirits are high.
Moving to new camp
tomorrow.
Thinking of you.
More later.

Dear family,
Had to leave Peru
suddenly.
Don't believe
Anything you hear.
Thinking of you.
More later.

"'Dear family, Heading to India in search of mountain quail,'" Luke read out loud. "'Sorry couldn't afford trip home at Christmas, thinking of you—'"

"More later," I said as I reached over his shoulder and pulled the paper off the wall. This close, the cold that came off his body nearly stopped my breath. "That's private."

He stepped back. He put one hand over his heart. "My apologies."

I gave him a long look, then nodded. "Accepted."

He glanced at the wall. "You like maps."

"Yes." I waited, wondering where this was going.

But all he said was, "That will be helpful." He sat down in the window seat, pulling his feet up to rest on the cushion. "Now, I'd like to make a brief opening statement before launching into my first argument—"

"Let me guess," I interrupted, flinging myself into the rocker. "Your spirit cannot rest."

There was a long pause.

He glared at me. Finally he said, "Well, it *can't*."

"Uh-huh." I nodded, unimpressed. "And that's because—let's see, what could it be?" I snapped my fingers. "You have unfinished business!"

"Well, I do," he said coldly.

"So you need to pass on a message from beyond the veil? And I'm sure there's some kind of unfortunate miscommunication that needs to be cleared up?" I sighed condescendingly. "All *very* standard."

He swung his feet to the floor and stood up. He paced back and forth a few times, running his hands through his hair and muttering to himself. Then he turned to face me. "The stakes are much higher than that. I need you"—he paused here for dramatic effect—"to right a terrible wrong!"

"Oh, well, then, that's different," I said in mock surprise. "But you know what? It sounds like it might be a bit beyond me." I gave him a wide-eyed look. "Maybe you should try a more experienced medium."

"You can't just dismiss my points out of hand—"

"Oh, but I can. I do."

He shook his head sadly. "How did such a young, innocent girl develop such a cold, cold heart?" he asked the air.

"Practice," I told him.

For the next few minutes the room was quiet. I opened my civics textbook and began reading chapter three. Luke stared out the window, frowning.

Finally I said, "So, now it's my turn, right?"

"What?"

"I get to ask you a question," I reminded him. "That was our deal."

"Oh, right." He steepled his fingers in a parody of an ancient Eastern philosopher. "It is good to see a thirst for knowledge in one just starting on the path to enlightenment. What do you wish to know, young Sparrow?"

My mind flashed on how many times I had tried to wheedle information about the afterlife from Professor Trimble, Floyd, and Prajeet. Even when I tried asking questions in the most offhand manner possible. I was always met by bland smiles and a change of subject. Once Professor Trimble did snap, "Well, if you really want to know, the best thing about the afterlife is that I no longer have to carry a purse," which was not helpful *at all*. So now I asked the first question that came to mind.

"What was it like? Dying, I mean."

"Not as bad as you'd think. Although it wasn't my first choice of things to do that day."

"I guess not." I'd heard other mediums say that sometimes when people die suddenly, they don't figure out what's happened right away. The medium actually has to break the bad news (Hey! You, with the sudden ability to walk through walls! You're *dead*, you idiot!) and then nudge them toward the Other Side. "Did you know you were dead?"

"Oh, yes," he said wryly. "There's no mistaking that feeling."

"Good?" I asked. "Or bad?"

"Oh, good, good," he said quickly. "Peaceful, calm, all my cares gone away, just like the songs say. I felt like myself, only a whole magnitude better. Luke, version two-point-oh."

I was struggling to imagine this. "Better how?"

"Well . . ." He paused. I saw the mischief in his eyes, but I couldn't help leaning forward in anticipation.

"Yes?"

"I could never get a tan while I was alive. Now look." He pushed his sleeve up his arm to reveal the golden glow of a perfect—all right, I'll say it, heavenly—tan. "Almost makes it worth dying."

"I'm *serious*," I began, with some indignation.

But he held up his hand to stop me, his head cocked as if he had heard something. He grinned suddenly at whatever it was, then said, "Next time," gave me a wink, and was gone.

A second later I heard footsteps pounding up the stairs and Lark yelling, "Sparrow! It's your turn to set the table!"

"Okay, okay," I yelled back.

She hammered on my door. "Hurry up! We're all starving!"

But I stood very still for another long minute, staring at the window seat where Luke had been sitting.

Chapter 12

The next day at lunch Fiona couldn't wait to discuss every detail of the now infamous Jell-O incident.

"Do you have any idea who did it?" she asked, then went on without waiting for an answer. "Maybe Sean Miller, but why would he do that to *you*, and anyway, he doesn't seem the type to be able to figure out how to do something that complicated, but maybe Chad Hanson helped him, they're friends, you know, and I heard that last year Chad was *suspended* after he let out all the mice from the biology lab, which he *said* was a protest against animal testing, but honestly, can you imagine Chad Hanson getting all political about *anything*, let alone *mice*—"

"So," I finally interrupted in desperation. "Jack and I

are going to do some research at the Lily Dale Museum this Saturday."

Well, that silenced her. For about two seconds. Then she squealed, "That is *awesome*! You're going on a date with Jack Dawson!"

"Shh!" I hissed, glancing nervously around the cafeteria. "It is *not* a date! It's *homework*!"

Her expression changed to one of solemn concern. "Oh, I totally understand. I'd be a wreck, honestly I would! I mean, Jack Dawson! Every girl in the school has a crush on him!"

I suddenly developed an intense interest in the contents of my lunch bag. "I wouldn't give him many points for his personality."

Fiona unwrapped her sandwich. "He does seem a little quiet—"

Quiet? "Try withdrawn, moody, surly . . ." I ran out of adjectives. "And when he does talk, he's kind of—"

"What?"

"I don't know." I tried to pinpoint what about our conversations made me feel so off-balance. "Sarcastic, kind of. Like he's pushing you away."

"Mmm." Fiona ate a potato chip as she considered this. "Well, maybe he's shy."

"Yeah," I muttered. "Of course, there's the alternative

explanation." She looked at me questioningly. "He's just an antisocial jerk."

At that moment Jack himself walked into the cafeteria, his hair hanging in his eyes, which were focused on the ground. He slouched past five tables of laughing, chatting people to the table that no one wanted because it was closest to the garbage cans. He sat down with his back to the room, pulled a paperback out of his backpack, and started reading as he ate.

Fiona gave me a significant look.

"Deliberately isolated," she diagnosed. "Unhappy, alone, lost. Probably defended against feelings of sadness." She took a dainty bite of her sandwich and added, "You could help him *so much*!"

I sighed. I really did not want to have this conversation.

She gave me a shrewd look. "What's wrong, Sparrow?"

Well, I could hardly say that I was worried because a bunch of ghosts were driving me crazy, and because Jack might soon find out that I lived in Spookyville, and because she was altogether too curious and interested in me for comfort.

So instead I said, "Nothing, really. I'm just a little nervous, I guess, about going anywhere with Jack." I made a big show of frowning and added, in a very worried voice, "And I don't have any idea what to wear!"

As I thought, this distracted her beautifully.

Later that night I was sighing over my trig textbook as Luke looked through the books on my desk. "You're reading *Pride and Prejudice*?"

"For class." I chewed on the end of my pencil and frowned at the first problem in my homework assignment.

"What do you think of it?" He seemed genuinely interested.

"I haven't read that many pages yet," I said. "Actually, I've just read the first two paragraphs. But so far it's okay."

"Just okay?" He put the book down and remarked absently, "Well, you haven't gotten to Mr. Darcy yet."

"Who?"

"Oh, I don't want to spoil the surprise." He gave me a bland smile and stretched out on the floor, his hands behind his head and his legs crossed at the ankles. "So, what's the metaphysical question of the evening?"

"Aren't you going to try to convince me to help you?" I asked suspiciously.

"Eventually. I just thought you might like to go first this time."

"Oh, okay." I pushed my textbook away and slid down to join him on the floor, sitting with my back propped against the bed and my knees drawn up. "Well, this is an obvious question, it's what everyone wants to know, but—"

"What's it like on the Other Side?" He finished for me.

"Well, yes."

"Actually that's hard to say—"

"Oh, no, don't do that," I said.

"What?"

"That whole it's-impossibly-beautiful-but-I-can't-describe-it business that ghosts always pull out of their pockets when someone asks this."

"I was just going to say that I can't describe the Other Side because I'm not actually there yet," he said with dignity.

"You're not?" I hadn't expected this. "So where are you?"

"Well, I'm in a kind of . . . holding area."

I had a sudden vision of the airport's baggage claim area. I imagined Luke and a few other forlorn spirits sitting around like suitcases that people had forgotten to pick up. "That doesn't seem fair," I said.

"It's not too bad. It looks kind of like a huge park—

you know, trees, flowers, ponds." He paused thoughtfully, then added, "And, um, chipmunks."

"Oh, nice," I said.

"Yes, *but*. The Weather Channel seems to be set on mid-November. It's always chilly. That wouldn't be too bad," he said judiciously, then added, "Except for the fog. And the damp."

I shivered.

"So there I am. Stranded in a damp, foggy park all by myself—"

"Aren't there any other people there?"

"I see them come and go, of course, but they all seem to pass through pretty quickly. I'm the only one still hanging around." He sighed. "It does get rather lonely."

"Oh." That sounded even worse than the cold and the damp. "How long do you have to stay there?"

"I'm not sure." He rubbed his hand back and forth on the rug. "I did ask my spirit guide that question—"

"Your what?"

"Oh, didn't I mention her? She was assigned to me when I first Crossed Over."

"You're kidding," I said, appalled at the idea of someone like Professor Trimble haunting me through eternity. "I thought spirit guides just nagged and harassed and annoyed people here on Earth."

"Oh, no. The nagging never ends," he said, laughing. "But on the Other Side spirit guides are more like individual guidance counselors. Someone to help you, you know"—he waved one hand vaguely in the air—"make the transition."

"Oh." I thought of Mr. Campbell, the school's guidance counselor, who had just visited our homeroom to talk about Making Good Choices and Preparing for the Future. I certainly hoped that Luke's spirit guide didn't look as sad and disillusioned about his prospects as Mr. Campbell did about ours.

"Anyway, she has assured me that once I've cleared up that unfinished business—I believe I mentioned it on my last visit?—well, then I will move on to a place that is apparently much nicer, and warmer, and filled with people rather than chipmunks." He paused, then added wistfully, "I'm really looking forward to that."

"Oh."

Then I saw the hint of a smile on his face.

I crossed my eyes to express my disgust.

"Damn, that almost worked!" he said, laughing.

"You are a vile person," I said. "Manipulative and vile."

"It's all true, Sparrow, really," he said, still laughing. "Well, except for the part about the cold. And the damp. And the chipmunks." He tried to look serious. "It *is* kind of foggy."

I eyed him narrowly. "Do you really have a spirit guide?"

"Indeed I do," he said in a wry tone that I didn't quite understand.

"Oh." I bit my lip to keep from asking what this female spirit guide looked like.

He grinned. "Don't ever become a spy, Sparrow. Every thought you have shows on your face." I blushed, and he added kindly, "She's eighty years old and an absolute terror."

He wrinkled his nose. "I think it's time for dinner. Enjoy the brussels sprouts."

I made a face, but no one was there to see it.

Chapter 13

On the Saturday that I was supposed to meet Jack, I got up. I got dressed. I looked at myself in the mirror. And I sighed. A deep, heartfelt, despairing sigh. I looked awful.

"You do not look as bad as you think, Sparrow." I turned around. Prajeet was sitting cross-legged on the bed, looking at me appraisingly. "In fact your appearance is delightful."

"I look like a troll," I moaned. I jerked open a dresser drawer and began rummaging through my clothes. "And I have absolutely nothing to wear!"

He leaned over the drawer and looked inquiringly inside. "Really? And what are those fabric things that used to be folded so neatly in that drawer?"

I pulled out some shirts. "Horrible, horrible," I muttered. I held up a tank top and looked appraisingly at myself in the mirror. No, it was too cold outside. I kept going.

"You just threw a perfectly clean shirt into the laundry hamper, you know," Prajeet said mildly.

I snatched it back and asked, "Why do all my sweaters look like something that only middle-aged women in England would wear?"

"Mmm." Prajeet surveyed most of my meager wardrobe, now spread across my bed and the floor. "You make a good point."

I strode across the room and flung open the closet door. "Look!" I cried. "It's a tragedy!"

He wafted over to the closet and hovered there, about six inches off the floor. "I see why you are a bit flummoxed," he murmured. His eyes slid over to meet mine. "But perhaps you do not have to be?"

"What do you mean by that?" I asked as I went back to staring hopelessly into the depths of my closet.

"I mean," he said, in a crisp voice that sounded remarkably like Professor Trimble's, "that the universe is a friendly place, Sparrow. Learn to ask for help."

I rolled my eyes—did spirit guides have to use *every* moment as an opportunity for a life lesson?—then tilted my head toward my disaster of a closet. "Okay. There's my problem. Can you help with that?"

A quick, gleaming white smile; then he pretended to look serious. "Of course," he said, bowing his head. "May I suggest that perhaps your sisters' closets could offer some attractive options?"

I gave him a long, considering look. "Pra-jeet. Have you been snooping?"

He opened his eyes wide, as if shocked, *shocked, I tell you!* at the very idea. "Sparrow, what can you think of me?" he protested. Then he grinned and said, "Well, maybe a little. I was something of a fashion plate in my day, you know. I do like to see what young people are wearing these days." He looked rather prim. "The standards are a bit lower now, I must say."

And so as Prajeet and I spent a happy and fruitful half hour raiding my sisters' closets, I asked him to help me a little more.

Our plan was simple: Arrive at the museum early. Get Miss Robertson, who was on museum duty, out of the way for an hour. Meet Jack, whisk him through the one room of exhibits, and usher him out without—fingers crossed—seeing anyone who knew me.

I had told Jack that I could meet him at one o'clock, which I calculated would be the safest time of day. Most of my family went to Fredonia to run errands on

Saturday afternoon. The coast was clear—or at least as clear as I could hope for.

I started walking toward the museum, frowning down at the cracked and uneven sidewalk and thinking about how I could steer Jack away from certain displays, such as the chalk and slate that my great-grandmother had used to transmit spirit messages or the trumpet that my great-aunt June had used to amplify spirit voices.

"*Please* watch where you're going," a cultured voice said. My head snapped up just in time to see two women, wearing the flowered hats and long dresses fashionable in the 1890s, walking majestically toward me.

"Oops, sorry," I said, quickly stepping off the sidewalk to let them past. They strolled on, heads held high, the scent of lilac perfume trailing after them.

"Did you see the way that girl was dressed?" I heard one whisper to the other.

"She looks like an urchin," the other said. "Poor dear."

So much for Prajeet's fabulous fashion sense. Well, they weren't the ones I cared about impressing anyway.

When I got to the museum, I was relieved to see that there only two people there, a middle-aged tourist couple wearing matching purple sweatshirts and blue baseball caps. So far so good. Then Miss Robertson caught sight of me and scurried over.

"Why, Sparrow Delaney, I haven't seen you in ages!" she trilled. "How is that darling Mordred doing?"

"He's fine," I said, blinking a bit at the use of the words *darling* and *Mordred* is such close proximity. Miss Robertson was the only person in Lily Dale—and possibly in the entire world—who harbored an affection for our cat.

"I must tell you about the amazing reading I had last night with a parakeet who Crossed Over a month ago," she went on merrily. "The communication was quite clear, which, as I'm sure you know, is rather unusual for parakeets. . . ."

"Uh-huh." I glanced at the clock. Five minutes to one.

The pungent smell of incense wafted through the room, and my shoulders relaxed.

Prajeet drifted over until he was only inches away from Miss Robertson. "You should perambulate home," he murmured in her ear. "There is a distressing situation in the making."

She stopped talking abruptly. "Why, that's strange."

"What?" I asked. The tourists were interested too; I saw the woman nudge her husband, her attention caught by the strange note in Miss Robertson's voice.

"I'm getting an impression from the Other Side right now," she said, rubbing her forehead. "It's just a feeling, but a very strong one, that I need to go home for some reason."

The tourists edged a little closer and tried to look as if they weren't eavesdropping.

"Never ignore a message from Spirit!" I said.

"One of your pets is in trouble," Prajeet said. She frowned and tilted her head as if she couldn't quite hear. He sighed and tried again. "Pet." He enunciated as clearly as possible. "*Trouble.*" He watched for a response and, seeing none, yelled, "Snowball! In a tree!"

She jumped. "Oh, no. I think Snowball is up in that elm tree again!"

Prajeet grinned at me and pretended to wipe sweat from his forehead.

Miss Robertson was rattling on. "I don't know *why* she keeps climbing up there. She *knows* she can never get down; you would think she would *learn*—"

"You'd better go!" I said quickly. "She's probably hysterical by now." Three minutes to one.

The tourists' mouths were hanging open. They exchanged delighted glances. Clearly they were getting their money's worth from their visit to Lily Dale.

"Oh, dear, but I'm on duty!" She glanced wildly around the room. "If something was stolen—"

The tourists sniffed, offended. Two minutes until one.

"I'll keep watch until you come back," I said hastily. "Take your time."

"*Would* you? That is so *thoughtful*. I'll be *right* back, thank you *so* much." She dashed out the door.

Now that the show was over, the tourists left as well. "I hope our astral travel workshop is half as good as that," I heard the husband say as they walked out the door.

"Nice job," I said to Prajeet.

"All part of the service," he said with a courtly bow. "Fortunately it was not difficult to urge Snowball to a very high branch indeed. I think you have forty-five minutes at least. Perhaps an hour." He looked out the door. "Ah, I see your friend approaching, so I shall leave you now."

He disappeared just as Jack slouched up the sidewalk, his hands thrust into the pockets of his army jacket. I opened the door.

"Hey," he said.

I gave him a relieved smile. "Hey, yourself."

* * *

At first Jack just wandered around the room, looking at the various photos and displays. He lifted one eyebrow at the spirit trumpet. Both eyebrows went up as he peered at the slate with a chalked message from Abraham Lincoln. He gave a small snort of laughter at the pastel portraits of Native American spirit guides, most of them wearing full-feathered headdresses. Then he spotted one of the spirit photos on the wall and leaned in to look at it more closely. I braced myself for what he would say.

The spirit photos always made visitors, even the true believers, laugh a little, in a smug twenty-first-century can-you-believe-people-ever-fell-for-*that* kind of way. And they are pretty lame, if you know even the slightest thing about photography.

One photo, an obvious double exposure, shows a woman with her eyes half closed in a trance, a ghostly face floating over her left shoulder. In another photo a man with a handlebar mustache is frowning intensely, his arms outstretched, as he makes a chair float in the air. A third photo shows a flare of light in a bedroom window. Most people would assume this is a reflection of car headlights or the setting sun, but the attached caption claims that, no, it's an actual photograph of an actual ghost. No wonder people giggled and joked when they came to this exhibit.

But, well . . . I mean, I *did* see ghosts, and I knew—only too well—that they were real. So when people laughed, part of me wanted to say, Okay, these photos may be fake, but that doesn't mean that everything here is a hoax. Some of it is really true.

"Gross." Jack had stopped in front of another photo that showed milky fluid pouring out of a medium's mouth. "It looks like she's throwing up."

"That's ectoplasm." He gave me a questioning look. "Some sort of gooey glop. Supposedly it used to come out of the mediums' mouths when they were in a trance. Sometimes it would form into pictures—you know, people's faces or bodies." Too late, I realized that I sounded a tad too knowledgeable about this subject. "I've, um, read about that before," I added lamely.

But Jack was staring critically at the photo. "How did people ever fall for this stuff? I mean, it's obviously trick photography! And look at this one!"

He pointed to a photo that showed a man sitting at a small table. A woman cloaked in a white cloth stood behind him, her arms raised in a classic spooky ghost-like gesture. The man looked blankly at the camera, clearly unaware of the spirit lurking just behind his right shoulder. "That's so fake it's not even funny."

I shrugged. "Those photos are a hundred years old."

"So?"

"So, photography was brand-new back then. Even a regular photo probably seemed like magic. Why wouldn't people believe that ghosts could appear on film?"

He pointed to the photo in question. "She's wearing," he said, "a *tablecloth*."

I leaned in for a closer look. He had a point.

"Still," I said.

He tilted his head toward another photo. This one showed a spirit trumpet floating in midair in front of an amazed audience. Unfortunately the camera also recorded the string that was holding up the trumpet. " 'Spirit trumpets were used to amplify the voices of the dead,' " he read from the sign. He gave a small snort. "I guess ventriloquists could make a pretty good living back then."

"A lot of those mediums were fakes." I conceded the point.

"A lot of them?" A small smile lifted one corner of his mouth.

"Most of them," I admitted.

"But?" he began, teasingly.

"I think some of them were probably"—I hesitated over the word; I didn't want to say *real* for fear of Jack's scorn—"sincere."

He seized on even that mild term with absolute delight. "You don't actually *believe* in this stuff, do you?"

"I don't believe these are really pictures of ghosts," I said carefully.

He grinned. "Uh-huh. But do you believe that ghosts exist?"

"Well, I—" I stopped, flustered. "Do you?"

He gave a short, incredulous laugh. "Of course not."

"Because you've never seen one?"

"Because it's a ridiculous concept. Dead is dead."

"So you don't believe in an afterlife either?"

"Well, I—" Now it was his turn to look flustered. "I don't know," he admitted. "I don't *think* there's anything else, but even if there is, I don't believe that people can come back for a cozy little chat with their friends and family. I mean, if they could, they'd do it all the time. And they don't. So there you go."

"Okay," I said, "but if you *did* see a ghost—"

"I wouldn't."

"I'm just saying *if*—"

"And *I'm* just saying it would never happen." He clipped off each word with finality.

I could feel my face flush with anger. I had opened my mouth to argue some more when I smelled incense and Prajeet's voice whispered in my ear, "Breathe, Sparrow. Count. Relax."

I did, then tried again. "So, *nothing* could convince you?"

He threw his hands in the air at the utter ridiculousness of this question, but he did answer. "I'd have to see the ghost with my own eyes, not just take the word of some crackpot medium," he said. "And the ghost would have to look *exactly* like the person it was supposed to be. Not just some misty shape. Someone I can recognize."

I caught a whiff of a sharp, medicinal odor. "Oh, for heaven's sake! Take the boy over to look at that spirit painting on the far wall," Professor Trimble snapped. "No, the big one in the middle! That's it." She let out a huff of impatience. "*Then* let's see what he has to say," she said, and disappeared.

I steered Jack over to the painting. "This looks interesting!" I said in a chipper voice. I pretended to read the information card fastened to the wall. " 'The mediums used to set a blank canvas next to a bowl filled with powdered pigment. They covered the canvas with a black cloth, and when they took the cloth away, there was a finished picture painted on the canvas.' " I took a few steps back and acted as if this were the first time I had seen the portraits of the young blond woman, the stern army general, and the man wearing a frock coat.

"Another trick," Jack said dismissively, but he came over for a closer look.

After a moment my gaze slid sideways to see what Jack's reaction was. I was ready for mockery and sarcasm, so I was taken aback to see him standing stock-still—rigid, in fact—in front of the painting of the girl. His face had turned pale, and he didn't seem to be breathing.

"Jack?" My voice seemed to vanish in the room like a wisp of smoke. He didn't say anything. I cleared my throat and tried again. "Are you all right?"

He didn't look at me, but he nodded slightly at the portrait and said, in a hushed voice, "Do you see that?"

I looked again. "See what?"

"That face next to her shoulder . . ." He didn't point, exactly, but cautiously flicked one finger at the painting, as if afraid to make any large or sudden movements.

I leaned past him to squint at it more closely. My shadow moved across the glass. "I don't see anything—"

"Damn it!" he snapped, sounding much more like

the Jack Dawson who endeared himself to everyone he met. "What did you do?"

"What did I do?" I snapped back. "I just looked at the stupid painting! And there's nothing there next to her shoulder!"

"Well, *now* there's not," he said, eyeing me accusingly. "You must have breathed on it or touched it or something."

"That's crazy," I said, my voice rising. "All I did was look. Because you wanted me to, I might add."

"Fine. Forget it," he said sharply, but he sounded disappointed.

"If you did see a face—"

He crossed his arms and stared at me.

"Okay, okay, you saw a face." I had a sudden thought. "Wait, could it have been your own reflection in the glass?"

Jack rolled his eyes. "I think I can probably recognize my own face. I see it in the mirror every day."

"I was just asking," I said. "So if the face didn't look like you, then who did it look like?"

There was a long silence as Jack stared at his feet. He stared at them for so long, in fact, that I finally sneaked a peek myself, wondering wildly if the face had now appeared on the toe of one of his scruffy sneakers.

One toe moved slightly. Forward, then back. Finally he muttered, "Never mind. You're right. I probably imagined it."

"Oh. Sure. Only—"

"What?"

"When you asked me to look at the painting, you seemed—" I hesitated over the word, then decided to tell the truth. "You seemed scared."

His eyes shot back in my direction. "I was not scared!"

"Okay." I offered another adjective. "Upset."

"No."

"Concerned? Taken aback? Startled?"

"No, no, and no. I was not scared, I didn't see anything, and I don't want to talk about this anymore!" Jack stomped over to the spirit cabinet and stood staring at it, his hands in his pockets and his shoulders hunched. Even his back looked angry.

"Fine!"

That was the last word either of us said for the next fifteen minutes. Finally Jack glanced at his watch and muttered something about his mother's picking him up. We walked down a back street to the gate at the main road, where visitors pay their entrance fee to drive into Lily Dale. I kept my head down, my baseball cap pulled low over my face, and my pace brisk, like a celebrity trying to avoid the paparazzi. We made it to the gate without being greeted by a single person.

Just as we got to the road, a blue car pulled up. The horn beeped a cheerful little hello—beep beepity beep beep (wait for it) beep beep—that made Jack glance at me and blush slightly.

Jack's mother had the same dark hair and brown eyes that he had. She was smiling as she rolled down the passenger window and leaned across the front seat. "Hi, there," she called brightly. "You're Sparrow, aren't you? Nice to meet you. How did you two do with the big project?"

My eyes met Jack's, then we both looked away quickly.

"Fine," he said with finality.

His mother looked at me, one eyebrow raised.

"Yes, fine." I agreed, then added helpfully, "The museum was very, um, educational."

"Always a good thing for a museum to be," she said solemnly. She held the car keys out to Jack. "Hey, do you want to practice? The traffic's pretty light."

"Sure." He shrugged, trying to look nonchalant, but I could see the gleam in his eyes as she got out of the car and he took the driver's seat.

As Jack started fiddling with the rearview and side

mirrors, Mrs. Dawson walked over to where I was standing. She looked past me at the gated entrance, frowning slightly, clearly lost in her own thoughts. I shifted from one foot to another, not sure how long I should let this silence stretch out. Then a gust of wind blew her hair into her face. She blinked, brushed it away, and turned to me, the spell broken.

"You know, I've lived in this area for almost twenty years, and I've never had the slightest desire to visit Lily Dale until recently." She was smiling, but it was the kind of smile somebody used when she felt like doing anything but. "Isn't that strange?"

"Well," I said cautiously, "a lot of people think it's kind of weird."

"Oh, I know. I have a couple of skeptics in my own family. It makes for . . . well, *interesting* dinner table conversations." She meant to sound rueful, I think, but there was a brittle note to her voice. Considering the scorn that Jack and, apparently, his father had for psychics, "interesting" was probably just another way of saying "tense and argumentative enough to ruin everyone's digestion."

"Lately, though," she said softly, "I feel—well, I hope this doesn't sound too odd, but I really feel *drawn* here for some reason."

Oh, no. I managed not to roll my eyes, but only just. So many of the tourists who come to Lily Dale say they were drawn here in that same exact hushed voice, as if they alone had tapped into a mysterious force beyond anyone else's understanding. I couldn't believe that Jack's mom would be one of *them.*

"What about you, Sparrow?" She gave me such a searching look that I glanced away, uncomfortable. "Do you believe in life after death? Do you think"—her voice quavered a little—"do you think people can actually contact the spirits of the dead?"

"Um." I stared at the sidewalk, wondering just how I had managed to get trapped in this metaphysical and apparently emotionally fraught discussion only two minutes after meeting Jack's mother. "Well, it's hard to imagine that we just disappear when we die," I said finally. "And if people do live on in some way, I guess it makes sense that they would try to come back somehow. Maybe."

It had to be the most lame, halfhearted, weaselly defense of Spiritualism ever uttered, but Mrs. Dawson looked as relieved as if I'd just offered demonstrable proof of the soul's existence.

"Exactly!" she said. "That's exactly what I think! And whether you're a believer or a nonbeliever, you're still choosing your position without proof. So why not have hope that something exists beyond the world that we know?" She leaned forward, intent on making her argument. It sounded like one she had made many times before. "Why not believe in something instead of nothing?"

Her eyes, dark and desperate, locked with mine. I shrank back. I recognized this look. I'd seen it many times before, when people carrying an overpowering weight of guilt or grief entered our parlor. Even observing such anguish from a distance always made me feel totally inadequate, and sad, and a little sick. For a long moment neither of us said anything.

Then there was a blast from the car horn, and we both jumped. Mrs. Dawson laughed a little in reaction, and the strange mood dissipated. Jack was frowning with embarrassment at the dashboard, adjusting various knobs with the focused concentration of a fighter pilot.

"Well," she said, "I think we'd better get going. Can we drive you home?"

My heart skipped a beat at the thought. Had Grandma Bee ever taken down those baboon skulls she had strung across the front porch last month? I couldn't remember.

"No, thanks," I said hastily. "I have a few errands to do in Jamestown. I'll catch the bus."

"Are you sure? I don't like leaving you alone." She sounded really worried, as if we were standing in a dark alley in a bad neighborhood at 3:00 AM.

I thought about the effigy of a hated math teacher that Lark and Linnet had created in the front yard last week. And the attic windows, which Raven had painted with mysterious runic signs for Halloween and then never scraped clean. And the fifteen garden gnomes that stood guard on the front lawn, a few of them even wearing little crocheted hats that Lark had made.

"I'll be fine," I reassured her even as I wondered what kind of menace Mrs. Dawson imagined could be lurking in Lily Dale on a bright Saturday afternoon.

"Well . . . all right. If you're sure . . ."

"Absolutely. Thanks anyway." I gave her a big, bright, all-will-be-well smile. She finally got into the car, and Jack pulled away from the curb without a backward glance.

As I walked home, I kept replaying the scene in the museum, which seemed odder and odder the more I thought about it. Jack didn't seem like the type of person who liked to play practical jokes. And he had seemed pretty spooked when he was looking at that painting, no matter what he said.

So then why had he tried to act as if it were nothing? His furtive manner reminded me of someone, but I couldn't think who. And that strange conversation with his mother—I could sense all kinds of strong emotions under the surface, but I couldn't figure out what they were. It felt strange and mysterious and murky, just when I wanted life to be plain, simple, and straightforward.

It wasn't until later, after I had flopped down on my bed with a plate of graham crackers and a glass of milk, that I was suddenly jolted with the realization of whom Jack reminded me of.

Me.

Me, trying to hide my ghosts from my family.

Me, trying to avoid telling anyone at school where I lived.

Me, doing my best to pass as just another ordinary sophomore.

All of which made me wonder, What was *Jack* trying to hide?

Chapter 14

We had only eaten three or four bites of dinner that night when my mother cleared her throat and said, "My darlings, there's an important matter we have to discuss." Her voice was uncharacteristically firm and focused. "I'd like to call a family conference, please."

As attention getters go, this may not sound particularly momentous. But my mother's normal state was one of dreamy abstraction, so to hear her speak so crisply, like a CEO calling a board meeting to order, had the effect of totally silencing the table.

"Thank you." She paused to collect her thoughts, then went on. "As you all know, this was a rather disappointing summer from a financial point of view."

A sigh rippled around the table. We all knew, only too well, what my mother was referring to. Lily Dale is a summer community, so the mediums make almost all of their yearly income from the tourists who flock to town for those three short months. Like squirrels, we hoard any money made during the brief season of sun and try to live off it during the bleak midwinter.

Also like squirrels, we (that is, my mother) have a tendency to stuff dollar bills in various receptacles around the house and then forget where they're hidden. For years a simple trip to the grocery store meant tossing couch cushions to the ground, flipping through books, and upending vases in search of cash.

Once Wren got old enough to understand the concept of banks, she insisted that Mother open a checking account. This worked better than the previous system, although now we often have to conduct wild searches under couch cushions, behind books, and inside vases for the missing checkbook. But the checking account did give us all a much clearer picture of our family finances.

This year the picture was exceedingly gloomy. For whatever reason—a rainy June, the high price of gas, a subtle misalignment of the planets—Lily Dale had experienced the slowest summer in a decade, even though the season had been extended for a week after Labor Day. We stared glumly at our plates.

"I'm afraid we have to cut some expenses, my darlings," my mother said.

"We've already cut everything we can!" Linnet cried.

"Guess we won't be getting the TV back from the shop after all," Raven said with a certain malicious satisfaction. She fancies herself an intellectual and greatly enjoys despising all aspects of pop culture.

"But the TV has been in the shop for weeks!" wailed Lark, who worships at the altar of pop culture.

"Months," Linnet corrected her. She confronted my mother. "It's ruining our social lives! How do you expect us to fit in with our peers if we don't even have a *television*?"

Mother held up a hand and said, "There's no need to get upset. First, let's make a list of possible—possible, Lark!—places where where we can cut back. Then we will vote, as a family, on where to cut. If everyone wants the TV back—"

"Not if it means cutting the gas budget," Raven said. She used our family car the most, to get back and forth to her job at the local convenience store. "I can't take the bus to work."

"The rest of us take the bus. Why can't you?" Lark said in a snippy tone. "In fact, why do you get to drive the car all the time, while the rest of us are forced to live in the Dark Ages?"

"Hardly the Dark Ages," Dove murmured peaceably. "Wouldn't that be horses and carts?"

Raven glowered at Lark. "I get to drive the car because I actually *have a job*, where I actually *make money* for this family to live on. Furthermore—"

"There's no question of not buying gas for the car," Mother interjected firmly. "I thought we might look at some of our more . . . optional expenses?"

"I suppose you mean my candles," Oriole said, a bit huffily.

"No one else in town burns two dozen candles every time she holds a reading," Wren said.

"Exactly. It gives us a competitive advantage. Not to mention creating a romantic atmosphere—"

"And dripping wax on all the furniture, which I then have to clean up."

"And there was that time Grandma Bee set the couch on fire—" Linnet chimed in.

"*Not* my fault, not my fault *at all*—"

"Of course not, just because you always wave your hands around like some mystical priestess—"

"We're lucky that poor man didn't sue—"

"He wouldn't *dare*." Grandma Bee's eyes narrowed dangerously at the thought.

"So." Wren held up her hand, as if we were taking a congressional vote. "I nominate eliminating all expenditures on candles forthwith." She settled back in her chair, smiling smugly. I could see that she was pleased with that *forthwith*.

"Incense too," she added.

"You have no soul," Oriole said, casting her a look of betrayal.

"We're just brainstorming right now, dear," my mother said. "We'll add candles and incense to the list of possible cuts. Any other ideas?"

"Have you looked in the pantry lately?" Grandma Bee said. "We can't possibly need that many cleaning products."

"Good point," Raven said. "It looks like we've cornered the market on Windex."

Wren bridled at this. "Well, if you actually cleaned a window once in a while, you would know how fast it gets used up around here—"

"I work at a *full-time job*, the only person in this family who does, thank you very much. I shouldn't have to do housework on top of that—"

"Of course not, why should anyone else lift a finger to keep this house in order? I'm surprised it hasn't been condemned by the sanitation department by now—"

"And has anyone else noticed how much we spend on cat food?" Grandma Bee interrupted. She spotted Mordred, who was sitting in the corner and staring fixedly at the baseboard. "When times are tough, the least among us must be sacrificed. Let him find his own dinner."

"We can't abandon a poor, defenseless cat!" Dove cried.

The rest of us glanced shiftily at one another. Mordred might be poor—he was a Delaney, after all—but as for being defenseless…

Dove knelt down to pick up Mordred, crooning, "Poor baby, don't listen to them—ow!" True to his nature, he hissed, swiped at her arm with his claws, then whipped his head back to his floorboard surveillance. In the instant that he had been distracted, a trapped mouse had made a bold but foolhardy decision. It had decided to race for the front door, and freedom.

Shrieks, groans, and general cries of disgust echoed through the room as Mordred vividly demonstrated the law of the wild.

"That's what I'm talking about!" Grandma Bee said, vindicated. "He can hunt for food the way his ancestors did! Eating meals from a can is an insult to his noble lineage."

"That is so gross," Linnet said.

"How lucky that we have enough cleaning supplies to take care of the mess," Wren said, with a cool look at Raven.

My mother rubbed her temples and sighed. "I feel that we're straying from the main topic. Perhaps we should pause for just a moment and eat some of this delicious dinner."

Wren looked gratified at the compliment. Raven had a wild look in her eye that meant that, now that battle had been joined, she wanted to fight on. She opened her mouth, but my mother gave her a quelling look, and she took a bite of mashed potatoes instead. Grandma Bee muttered, "Enjoy it while you can, girls. It sounds like we're headed for bread and water." And for a few moments peace and quiet reigned once more.

It didn't last, of course. Such moments never do in my family.

I had been very quiet during the family conference. I couldn't help thinking that arguments about cat food and candles paled in comparison to worrying about Luke and wondering about Jack.

"Are you feeling all right, Sparrow?" Dove handed me the bowl of green beans, a concerned expression on her face. "You seem so . . . downcast."

"I'm fine," I said as nonchalantly as possible. "I'm just a little tired lately. New school, lots of homework, you know."

Grandma Bee pursed her lips suspiciously, but she just muttered, "Hmmph!" and didn't say another word.

She didn't have to. My mother had been gazing distractedly at a dark corner by the fireplace where Mrs. Witherspoon sat, rocking back and forth and muttering to herself. "Are you sure, dear?" she asked me. "You look a little pale. Mrs. Witherspoon thinks perhaps a dose of cod-liver oil—"

My sisters joined me in a chorus of groans.

"Sparrow's always pale," Linnet said. "As pale as potatoes! Year-round!"

"It's disgusting," Lark said. "If you would just lie out in the backyard during the summer—"

"I'd rather not have skin cancer when I'm forty!" I replied, stung. My fish-belly pale skin was a sore point with me, and the twins knew it.

"How about getting a *date* before you're forty?" Linnet asked, chortling as she exchanged a raucous high five with Lark.

"My mind is on higher things," I said, bringing a

round of jeers from the rest of the table. I ignored them. "Please pass the gravy."

Lark grabbed the gravy boat and handed it across three people, slopping some as she did so. Wren sighed and gazed mournfully at the linen tablecloth (a wedding present for my parents, it was now frayed and dingy and haunted by the ghosts of old spills).

"Oh, come on!" Raven cried. Her black eyes gleamed with evil delight as she purred, "Are you trying to tell us that there's not one boy you're interested in at that new school of yours?"

Grandma Bee stood up. She did it slowly, with a commanding air and a faraway look in her eye that was meant to draw everyone's eyes to her.

It would have been quite impressive if she hadn't pulled that stunt every month or so when she found that she couldn't get a word in edgewise during a particularly lively family discussion. Clearly the magic was gone. No one stopped chattering, and she stood there, a lonely prophet, ignored by her own people—

Until she uttered a mighty "harumph!" and slammed her hand down, rattling the mismatched water glasses.

She turned her head to look around the now-silent

table, her magnified eyes staring through each of us. "I have heard enough," she announced grandly. "My spirits are telling me that mighty and mysterious forces are at work here, and we should not make light of them."

I felt a little shiver go down my spine.

A quiet giggle to my right (Lark?) indicated that not all my sisters felt the same way.

But then, *they* were not attuned to the supernatural the way I was. *They* were not visited by ghosts on a daily basis. *They* were not—

"Falling in love," Grandma Bee was saying.

What was that? I snapped to attention.

"The spirits are telling me that there is a person, waiting in the wings perhaps, not yet known to any of us perhaps, who will have tender feelings for our dear Sparrow," she continued.

A vision of dark blond hair and hazel eyes and a crooked smile flashed through my mind . . .

"Really, Sparrow!" an acerbic voice said. "Try to keep your mind focused on *important* matters, if you please."

Professor Trimble shimmered into view, her mouth drawn tightly in disapproval. She hated hearing girlish chitchat on the subject of boys. She claimed that it distracted young ladies from more vital aspects of life, like Latin declensions and geometric proofs.

"Sparrow? In *love*?" Raven asked in a shocked tone that was, frankly, quite insulting.

The others took up the cry.

"Who is it, Sparrow?" Dove asked.

"What does he look like?" Lark asked.

"Is he cuuuuute?" Linnet added, not even bothering to stifle her giggles.

Professor Trimble rolled her eyes. "Oh, *honestly*."

Oriole murmured conspiratorially, "Is it that boy you're doing the project with? What's his name? Jack?"

I made a face before I could stop myself. "Ugh, no."

"Methinks she doth protest too much," Raven sang out merrily.

I glared at her, my heart filled with murder.

"Yes, yes, confess all!" Lark cried, laughing.

"I have nothing to confess!" I exclaimed. "Or to confide! I'm just trying to eat my dinner in peace."

"Now, dear, you don't have to tell your secrets if you don't want to," my mother interrupted hastily. "Although"—she turned a wistful eye in my direction—"if you'd like to confide in your mother, I hope you know that I'm always here, sweetheart."

My mother's gaze swept around the table as she added sternly, "But the rest of you, leave poor Sparrow alone."

For the second time in one evening she managed to

silence the room, and we ate our desserts without saying another word.

Later, though, my mother came upstairs. She glanced around my bedroom before sitting in the rocker. "I haven't seen your little nest for a while," she said. "It's very cozy."

I sat on my bed and pulled a pillow in front of my chest. "Thanks."

Her eyes flickered over my father's postcards on the wall, and her eyebrows went up a fraction, but she didn't comment.

"I don't mean to pry, Sparrow, but I feel that I would be remiss in my motherly duties if I didn't, well"—she gave a wry shrug—"pry. At least a little."

I grinned. "Sounds like you've been talking to Mrs. Witherspoon. Motherly duties?"

"I know, I know." My mother sighed. "But you know how persistent she can be. And I do like to know how my girls are doing. In general terms at least."

"In general," I said cautiously, "I'm doing fine."

"I'm so glad to hear it!" Mother beamed at me. She lowered her gaze to the rocker's cushion, where her fingers had found a loose bit of thread. As she tried to snap it off, she said, "And school is going well?"

"Yes. I mean, as well as can be expected." I paused, then added, "Gym is horrible."

"Isn't it always?" She finally lifted her eyes from the coverlet. "As for falling in love?"

"Oh, no, absolutely not," I said quickly. "You know how Grandma Bee likes to exaggerate."

"Of course. You have been making friends, though?"

"Oh, yes." I didn't want to seem like a total loser. "Just friends, though. Nothing more."

"Of course." She stood up and, after one last, searching look, gave a satisfied nod. "I admit I'm somewhat relieved to hear that." Her gaze flickered again past the postcards on my wall. As she drifted toward the door, she added, "But you know, Sparrow, if there's anything you ever want to talk about, anything at all . . ."

But now my attention was focused on the postcards as well. Before I could stop myself, I blurted, "Why doesn't he ever write 'love'?"

"I'm sorry?" She sat down again and folded her hands in her lap, leaning forward with a careful, listening expression on her face.

I bit my lip. "On all the postcards he sends us . . . he always writes 'more later.' He never writes 'love.' I was just wondering—" My voice quivered, embarrassingly high. I stopped, cleared my throat, started again.

"I mean, why is that, do you think?"

"Ah. I don't have to think. I know." She looked past me and smiled to herself as if reviewing a bittersweet memory. "When we were dating, he would write me letters, even though we only lived a few miles away from each other." She smiled again, more happily, now totally lost in the past. "*Wonderful* letters. But he would never sign them 'Love, Patrick.' He would always write 'more later.' Frankly, I wondered why, too. I thought perhaps he was trying to tell me that he didn't love me, or he didn't love me enough to say that he loved me, or he had doubts about any love he might have been feeling, or . . . I don't remember all the theories I concocted, but there were quite a few, believe me. Finally I realized that I was doing nothing but upsetting myself and that the only sensible thing to do was just to ask him."

"And what did he say?" I asked in a hushed tone. My mother never talked much about my father.

"He said he thought that *love* was the most overused—and misused—word in the English language. That people said, 'I love you,' when they really meant 'I like going to the movies with you.' Or they said, 'Remember, I'll always love you,' as they walked out the door to be with someone else. So he refused to sign his letters with 'love.' " She shook her head fondly. "That's your father. Very . . . scientific, I guess you'd say. Very logical and precise. He always wrote 'more later' because he considered that . . . well, he would say that it was a promise to the future. That there would always be more, later."

"Oh."

She patted my hand. "Your father may be in South America, or Madagascar, or Tibet, but he's still connected to you. And your sisters." She looked serenely and utterly certain of what she was saying. "And to me. So don't worry, all right?"

I couldn't speak. I nodded.

She stood up. "Good," she said briskly. "Now, do you have a lot of homework?"

"Well, I probably should start reading this history chapter," I said. "I have a test on Friday."

"Good idea." Her gaze flickered past the postcards again. "We should always prepare for the tests that we know about. After all, there are so many that surprise us."

Chapter 15

"May I remind you that this is exactly what you wanted?" Professor Trimble said, with some asperity, just behind my right ear. "A best friend, someone to study with after school and share secrets with and—what is the current phrase? Oh, yes—to *hang out with*?"

I was standing on the school's front steps, waiting for Fiona. We had made plans to go to her house after school. Professor Trimble was standing to my right, grandly ignoring the students who were pouring out of the doors and milling about on the sidewalk, talking, flirting, yelling, and pushing one another.

"I know, I know," I said, trying not to move my lips. "But—"

"Yes?" Professor Trimble sounded as if she were doing her best to sound patient and understanding.

Her best, I reflected—and not for the first time—was not very good.

"Fiona asks a lot of questions."

The professor nodded approvingly. "And then really listens to the answers. Very rare in this day and age."

"Or any time, really." I smelled nutmeg, and Floyd popped into view on my left, dusting off his floury hands. "No wonder everyone likes her. She's a real sweetheart."

This was true. Just today I had watched Fiona walk up to Seth Roberts, one of those shy, genius boys who rarely speak and who, when spoken to, always look both startled and irritated, as if they were just about to solve the mystery of the universe until you so cruelly interrupted them.

"Hi!" she had said. "I've heard you're really good with computers, and I'm having this problem with my laptop. Would you mind taking a look?"

He had glanced at her warily but nodded agreeably enough. As he frowned at the screen and began pushing various keys, she chatted merrily about topics ranging from this week's football game to a recent horror movie marathon on TV. Within two minutes she had persuaded him to say something back. Within ten minutes he was cautiously debating the relative fright factor of zombies versus vampires. By the time the bell rang, they sounded like old friends. He handed her laptop back and wandered down the hall in a daze, a little smile on his lips.

Watching, I just shook my head. "I think your hobby is conversation," I had said, not accusing at all. In fact I was beginning to admire Fiona's warm and openhearted interest in others (as long as it wasn't directed at me). "Endless, unlimited, infinite, never-ending conversation."

"I know! My mom says I even talk in my sleep!" She looked a little smug. "My dad says I have 'an uncanny ability to establish dialogue with a wide range of personality types.' He says it's a gift."

"You must promise to use it only for good," I had said, mock solemn, and she had laughed.

"I mean, she asks *a lot* of questions," I said again.

"I would not worry if I were you." Now Prajeet manifested, lounging on the stone steps. He smiled up at me. "It is not such a terrible thing to have your friends know who you really are."

"Mmm," I murmured skeptically. I would have liked to say more, but I didn't want everyone to see me talking to empty space. As it was, listening to three ghosts was proving to be quite distracting.

"Sparrow!" Fiona was hurrying across the courtyard.

"We shall leave you now," Professor Trimble said.

"Have a good time, honey." Floyd winked.

"Do not worry." Prajeet raised a hand in benediction. "All will be well."

They vanished just as Fiona ran up, breathless. "I'm so so sorry I'm late! I had to talk to Mr. Renfrow about my civics paper, and then I ran into Rachel, who wanted to ask about the biology assignment and tell me about the fight she had with Paul, and then I couldn't get my locker open, and anyway, you know how it goes, blah blah blah, here I am at last!" She grinned and brushed her bangs out of her eyes. "Hey, listen, I'd better warn you about my mother—"

Just at that moment a shiny silver Mercedes pulled up to the curb.

"Oh. That's her." Fiona's face darkened a little—it wasn't a look that worked for her; she looked like a peevish elf—and she said quickly, "Listen, be sure to fasten your seat belt. And whatever you do, don't let her start asking questions!"

A carbon copy of Fiona—at least a Fiona thirty years in the future—sat behind the wheel. She waved a perky Fiona wave, smiled a bright Fiona smile, and called out, "Hi, girls! Sorry I'm a little late, my meeting ran over and then I had to stop and pick up some milk and lines at the grocery store were horrendous and the traffic is just *beyond belief*, but here I am at last! Are you Sparrow? So nice to meet you!"

Fiona rolled her eyes at me, whispered, "My mother is *such* a flake!" and trotted down the steps to the car.

We climbed into the backseat. Fiona's mother pulled out in front of a black SUV with a slapdash style that resulted in a series of angry honks. She waved her hand in carefree acknowledgment and called out, "Sorry! Nice job of braking!"

"Brace yourself," Fiona muttered. "My mother learned to drive the summer she worked at a carnival. On the bumper car ride."

Her mother just laughed as she merged onto the highway, inches in front of an eighteen-wheeler. "Don't listen to a word she says. I've never had an accident. Not once in my whole, entire life." She slipped in between two cars in order to change lanes. Fiona made a small strangled noise in her throat. I gripped the armrest and tried to smile.

After a moment or two, however, I realized that Mrs. Jones was actually an excellent driver, and I started breathing again.

"So, tell me all about your day, girls," she called back

to us. "Every tidbit and detail! I want to hear all!"

And now Fiona, who could normally talk without pausing for hours at a time, stared out the window, as tight-lipped as a CIA operative.

Her mother glanced at her in the rearview mirror and sighed in frustration. "Okay. Let's see . . ." She paused to think. "What was the most startling thing you learned in school today?"

"Nothing, really." Fiona seemed to be fascinated by the passing scenery.

An awkward silence filled the car. "I learned that the giant squid has the largest eyes in the animal world," I volunteered finally. "They're the size of volleyballs. I thought that was interesting."

Her mother spun the wheel, and the car slid over three lanes and onto an exit ramp. My knuckles turned white, and I reminded myself to inhale. "Always good to know," she said. "At the very least it will come in handy at cocktail parties when everyone has run out of things to say."

I tried to imagine myself at some point in the distant future, wearing a silk dress and holding a cocktail and telling a circle of glamorous people about giant squid and their eyeballs. "I guess so," I replied doubtfully.

The car whipped around a corner with a squeal of

tires. Fiona's mother tossed more questions over her shoulder. "Any juicy gossip from the girls' room? What was the most horrific thing you had to do in gym? Are you girls going to the game on Friday? Who are you going with? When's the first school dance? Is there a theme this year?"

The worst part was that after firing each question at us, she waited for an answer and then actually listened to it. Now I knew where Fiona had learned her unnerving technique. Finally even Fiona succumbed enough to utter a few sentences, although she still sounded like a prisoner talking under threat of torture.

At last we pulled into their driveway with one last jaunty swerve and came to an abrupt, screeching stop. As we went inside the house, Fiona's mother murmured something about calling the office and melted away.

"Thank God the third degree is over!" Fiona opened the refrigerator and grabbed a couple of sodas. "You see what I mean? My mom asks billions of questions! She always wants to know everything about my life! I mean, *everything*! Down to the smallest, most insignificant details!"

"Irritating," I said, hiding my smile as I followed her, looking around me with interest.

Fiona's house was so . . . perfect. The kitchen counter gleamed. I could tell, because the only things actually on top of the counter were a polished toaster and a coffeemaker that looked as if it could run the space shuttle. No copies of *Life* magazine from 1982, pots of dried-up cold cream, ancient cat toys, pencil stubs, stray buttons, bird feathers, snakeskins, rusty nails, half-empty boxes of Christmas cards, bent clothes hangers, or mysterious jars filled with murky liquids. We walked through the living room, where the couch and chairs didn't look as if anyone had ever sat on them, let alone spilled a drink or dropped cookie crumbs or dripped candle wax on the cushions. The rug still showed faint track marks from the vacuum cleaner.

Fiona's bedroom was pink and white, with a canopy bed, ruffled bedspread, plush flowered rug, and collection of family photos on one wall. She took her snow white Mac laptop out of her backpack, put it on her immaculate desk, and turned it on. Its blue screen lit up, glowing with an unearthly light.

"Wow." I just stood in the center of her room, trying to take it all in.

Fiona looked at me, a little puzzled. "What?" she asked.

"Your house, your room." I gestured feebly, trying to find the words. "They're so . . . great."

"Really?" She shrugged. "Just a regular house in the burbs. In fact, sometimes I think it's kind of, well, boring, really."

I laughed in disbelief. "Everything's so clean and shiny and *new*."

She glanced around, as if seeing her room for the first time. "I guess so. But it's just so . . . normal. And so *decorated*. I mean, look at this." She picked up a mother-of-pearl tissue box holder from her desk and frowned at it. "Shouldn't life be more odd or mysterious or strange or . . . or something?"

I thought about crooked porches, peeling paint, and cracked windows. I thought about poltergeist pranks, a possibly demonic cat, and a house filled with nine females and one bathroom. I thought about gravestones in the backyard, spirit readings in the parlor, and ghosts wandering the halls.

I shook my head decidedly. "No," I said. "Normal is good."

Fiona shrugged again and flashed me her usual sunny smile. "Well, I guess I can always live in a garret and have an interesting life after I graduate from college, right?" She sat down at her desk and clicked on a few keys. "So, I had a fabulous idea today! We should Google Jack and see what we can find out about him!"

I looked at her with a new appreciation. Clearly she had learned a thing or two from her mother about investigative reporting. "*Awesome* idea," I said, as I grabbed the extra chair and sat down next to her.

"This is so much fun! I'm so glad you could come over," she said as she typed the words *Jack Dawson*. "Maybe I can come over to your house next time."

"Yeah, maybe," I said vaguely, praying that we would move off that topic, fast.

At that moment some higher power—and it seemed its name was Google—answered my prayer. A new screen appeared. The words *Jack Dawson* were listed a dozen times.

Fiona beamed. "Oh, look! There are ten thousand seven hundred fifty-one Web pages about Jack."

I leaned forward to read over her shoulder. There was a Jack Dawson who had published a scientific paper and a Jack Dawson who ran a balloon company and a Jack Dawson who was an actor in summer stock theater—

"Let's narrow it down." She looked over her shoulder at me. "Do you know where the Dawsons lived before they moved here?"

I tried to remember what Mrs. Dawson had said. "I think it was—Collins? Yes, that's it. Collins."

"Great." She added *Collins New York* to the search. She waved her hands over the computer and proclaimed in a spooky fortune-teller voice, "Now the great god Google, which knows all and sees all, must reveal all to us! Oh, great Google, we must know all there is to know about the mysterious Jack Dawson! Hear us and give us our answer! We command thee!"

Usually I wouldn't appreciate such a stereotypical portrayal of a psychic, but I was too interested in what Google might turn up to feel miffed. Fiona lifted her hand high above the keyboard and, with a flamboyant swooping motion, hit the return key.

A mere 0.71 seconds later a list of articles appeared on the screen. Fiona clicked on the first link. Just like that, we were staring at our answer.

The headline said, LOCAL TEEN MISSING.

The subheadline said, HIGH SCHOOL SPORTS STAR VANISHES, COUNTY-WIDE SEARCH IN PROGRESS.

The photo caption said, "The Dawson family (l. to r., Jack, 15; Sarah, 42; Robert, 43; and Luke, 17)."

The photo showed a happy family, beaming at the camera.

"Wow," Fiona said. "Jack looks *completely* different!

It's hard to believe this picture was just taken"—she paused to read the caption—"a little over a year ago. He looks so young! And so . . . I don't know . . . *innocent*."

"Yeah," I said slowly.

But my gaze wasn't focused on Jack. It was riveted on his brother, the lost Luke Dawson. Dark blond hair, hazel eyes, and a lopsided smile.

Luke Dawson was none other than the ghost of room 12B.

And he wasn't haunting me. He was haunting Jack.

Chapter 16

Fiona and I printed out every page we could find on the Internet about Jack Dawson and his brother's mysterious disappearance. There were quite a few pages—104, to be exact. Apparently Luke had been something of a celebrity in his hometown—star quarterback, top student, and (a bit of a surprise here, although it explained how he learned to argue so well) captain of the debate team. His vanishing was much more than a one-day wonder.

In fact for six months the local newspaper had run constant updates on the investigation. After a while actual news seemed a bit scarce on the ground, so the paper had resorted to asking people for their pet theories about the disappearance and then running that speculation under headlines like THE

LUKE DAWSON MYSTERY: WHAT MIGHT HAVE HAPPENED.

"Listen to this." Fiona read part of one article out loud. "'Jack Dawson seems to be a sensitive young boy, clearly distraught over the event that has caused a seismic upheaval in his life.'" She scanned down a few paragraphs and read more. "'He stands at the living room window, gazing wistfully into the night, as if hoping that his brother, Luke, would soon come home again.'"

"Really? That's what it says?" I read over her shoulder in disbelief. The writer seemed to be indulging in a little wishful thinking. Her description of Jack—sensitive, distraught, wistful, hopeful—sounded like some weird, parallel universe version of the person I knew.

"Where do reporters come up with this stuff?" I demanded, remembering, too late, that her mother was a reporter.

But she didn't take offense. She just said, "I know what you mean. Although Jack could have been in shock or something."

"Maybe," I said, although it was still hard to imagine a sensitive or wistful Jack.

We didn't have time to read much more before

Fiona's mother knocked on the door and asked if we wanted an afternoon snack. We said yes, of course, and took the printouts with us into the kitchen.

"Carrot sticks?" she asked, holding out a plate. "Or if you're not interested in the healthy alternative, chocolate chip cookies?"

Fiona defiantly grabbed a cookie. "Mom has to watch her figure. The camera adds ten pounds, you know. But since *I'm* not on TV—"

"I'm a mother," Mrs. Jones said mildly. "It's my duty to push vegetables."

Fiona rolled her eyes at me. I took two cookies as a sign of solidarity and gave her a wink. She grinned back, and we settled ourselves at the kitchen table with the articles spread out before us.

Her mother began unloading the dishwasher as I picked up a paper at random. This article had been written by a different (and clearly more observant) reporter, who introduced Jack by saying: "Jack Dawson, 15, sat huddled on one end of the couch, staring at the toes of his sneakers in grim silence." Now, *that* was the Jack I knew.

"Imagine waking up one day to find out that someone you loved had vanished from the face of the earth!" Fiona exclaimed, her eyes wide.

As she gave a delighted shudder, my mind flashed to a photo of my father, waving good-bye as he bounced down the road in the back of the ornithologists' pickup truck. My mother had snapped the picture as he left, capturing his exuberant wave and his half-guilty, half-gleeful smile as he escaped into another life.

Glad to be going. And, maybe, still glad to be gone.

Mrs. Jones glanced over at us. "What do you have there that's so fascinating?" she asked.

"Oh, nothing," said Fiona.

Her mother gave us a knowing glance, then leaned over Fiona's shoulder to read one of the headlines.

"'Search for missing boy ends after two weeks,'" she read out loud. "'Family increases reward for information to twenty-five thousand dollars.'" She shook her head. "How tragic."

She picked up the first story we had printed out. "Why are you girls so fascinated by this story?" she asked absently as she began reading.

"Jack is in our class," I said. I pointed to his picture. "The missing boy's brother."

Mrs. Jones glanced over at me, her eyes sharp and interested. "Really." Her gaze moved on to rest thoughtfully on her daughter. "I certainly hope you aren't planning to bring up bad memories for this poor boy—"

"We're not going to say anything to him, Mom!" Fiona said indignantly. "Honestly. Give us credit for *some* tact!"

"All right, honey. Just making sure . . ." Her mother flipped through the papers spread out on the table, frowning in concentration. "It looks like this story got a lot of attention."

"It was a small town," I pointed out as a tiny alarm bell went off in my head.

"Mmm." Fiona's mother wasn't listening. She grabbed a pen and memo pad from the kitchen drawer and began jotting notes. "Unsolved mysteries always get great ratings."

"Mom!" Fiona protested. "How is doing a story on this any different from talking to Jack about it? Won't you be 'bringing up bad memories' for him?"

Her mother waved one hand dismissively as the alarm bell in my head rang even louder. "I would approach his parents first, of course."

"I don't know if the Dawsons will want to do another interview," I said hastily. "It looks like they had their share of news coverage last year."

"Yes, *but*," her mother countered, listing her arguments with the ease of long practice. "There's always the chance that someone who knows something will come forward. Newspaper articles are fine, but a television audience is huge. Thousands of people will see the story and be on the lookout for this boy. Someone might remember seeing him."

Fiona nodded slowly as she saw the logic of this argument. "If anyone in our viewing audience has seen Luke Dawson or has any information about his disappearance, please contact Channel Seven News," she intoned in a deadly serious anchorperson voice.

"Or your local police," her mother added, but without much conviction.

That alarm bell was clanging so loudly that I was surprised no one else could hear it.

"They might be too upset to talk," I said, giving it one last try.

"Oh, Mom has a special talent for getting people to open up," Fiona assured me. "Her news director is always sending her on stories where people have suffered some sort of tragedy, because they always start out by saying that they won't talk to *anyone*, they're just too distraught, and then they always end up giving her an exclusive interview. Always."

Mrs. Jones double-checked the date on one of the articles. "The one-year anniversary of Luke's disappearance is in a few weeks," she said to herself. "Good hook."

She asked, "Do you mind if I hold on to a couple of these articles?" even as she was picking them up and heading out of the room. "I think I'll make a quick phone call to Cutler—"

"That's her news director," Fiona explained. "He'll *love* this story! And who knows? Maybe Luke will see the story and decide to contact his family! Maybe someone who saw him will call in with a tip! Maybe Mom will solve the mystery! Wouldn't that be *awesome*!"

She kept talking, but I wasn't listening anymore. I pushed my plate of cookies away. I had that hollow, fluttery feeling you get in your stomach right before a roller coaster plunges straight down at breakneck speed.

Chapter 17

"Sparrow! Come help me, sweetheart!"

I cautiously followed the sound of Grandma Bee's voice, well aware that her use of the word "sweetheart" meant that nothing good was in the offing. Sure enough, as I rounded the corner of the house, I spotted her in the side yard. She was standing in a martial pose, her legs planted in a wide stance and her arms raised as if she were about to deliver a killing blow to an unsuspecting passerby.

She lowered her arms and peered happily at me through trifocals smeared with mud. "*Just* the person I was hoping to see!" she cried. "Sparrow, you are the answer to a weak old lady's prayers!"

"No. My elbow still hurts."

She blinked innocently. "I have no idea what you're talking about, dear."

"Last month?" I reminded her. "Helping you practice judo throws?"

For the past two years Grandma Bee has been creating a new martial art designed for older people. Her belief, based on a completely immodest assessment of her own talent, was that the elderly could be organized into our country's most effective crime-fighting force. "It's so unexpected, you see," she always says. "Who would ever suspect that a man wearing a 'World's Best Grandpa' T-shirt could kill with his bare hands?"

"I promise I won't hurt you," she said, inching closer. She stared into my eyes and spoke slowly and evenly. "Everything . . . will . . . be . . . all . . . right." I had a feeling she was trying to work hypnotic mind control into her technique.

"Forget it," I said, backing away.

"Stand still. You won't feel a thing."

"No, no, no, no, no." I sprinted for the porch.

As I took the steps three at a time, I heard her yell after me, "You know, it doesn't hurt to be rendered briefly unconscious! It's actually rather restful!"

Once safely inside my room, with the door shut and firmly bolted, I pulled the printouts from my backpack and flung myself on the bed to read. An hour later I put the papers down and stared unseeingly at the ceiling.

The most illuminating article was a long feature story written six months after Luke's disappearance. The investigation had stalled. There was no news, good or bad. The newspaper had clearly wanted to run something, however, so the reporter had recapped the facts and then filled in by interviewing almost everyone, it seemed, who had ever crossed paths with Luke.

LOCAL TEEN'S DISAPPEARANCE STILL A MYSTERY

Investigators Stymied, Family Reaches Out to Public, Psychics

BY LITTON HOUSTON BERES

Collins, New York—It happens every day. Someone vanishes without a trace. A toddler is snatched from a supermarket, a teenager runs away, a husband or wife decides to jettison daily responsibilities in favor of a new life somewhere else, somewhere far away. It happens every day, and according to law enforcement statistics, the missing person is usually found. Eventually.

Waiting for "eventually" is the hard part. That is what is facing Robert, 47, and Sarah, 45, Dawson, of Collins, and their son Jack, 15. The Dawsons' son Luke, who had just turned 17, disappeared six months ago. Despite a continuing intensive search, the police have not found any clues to how or why Luke vanished. The mystery has unsettled this small town, where almost everyone, it seems, knew Luke Dawson, and absolutely everyone has a theory about what happened to him.

Neighbors share their speculations at the grocery store or dry cleaners. Classmates talk about Luke in hushed tones between classes or at lunch. But the Dawson family no longer cares to listen to hypotheses or conjecture or suppositions.

They just want their boy home.

The morning of September 30 dawned cloudy and cool. Although the temperature got warmer during the day—Sarah Dawson remembers being grateful for the last bit of Indian summer—it was clear that fall weather was on its way.

For Luke Dawson, an athletic boy who played quarterback for his high school football team, this meant turning his mind to school and sports. An avid hiker, biker, and fisherman, he tended to spend the warm summer months outdoors.

"That kid really liked to get out in nature," says Will Grissom, 65, owner of Grissom's Outdoor Gear. "He was in here all the time, getting information about new hikes he wanted to try. Didn't buy much, though. He was real practical. Had one pair of hiking boots, one old fishing rod, one beat-up hat, you know, one of everything, and he never traded up."

Friends and family say that both Dawson boys loved to hike and camp, but that Luke particularly enjoyed solitary time in nature. He often went on hikes by himself. However, his parents say that he was very safety conscious and always let them know the route he planned to take. They also point out that he did not leave any note or message the day of his disappearance.

The park service conducted searches along Luke's favorite trails in case he had decided to go for a spur-of-the-moment hike and been injured or lost. After two weeks, they found no trace of him and had to call a halt to the search.

"The problem with most wilderness searches is that there's just too much ground to cover," said Park Ranger Georgia Keener, 32. "We were out there from sunup to sundown. He may have had an accident, but we didn't find a trace of him after days of searching."

Others strongly disagree with the theory that Luke could have had a hiking accident.

"That boy knew this area like the back of his hand," Mr.

Grissom says. "No way he had an accident. No way, no how."

Some have suggested that family tensions may have made Luke run away from home. A neighbor says that he often heard Luke and his father fighting, "My wife and I would hear them going at it sometimes," said the neighbor, who asked that his identity be kept confidential.

The Dawsons say that any arguments were typical family disagreements. However, the number and intensity of arguments had increased noticeably in the months preceding Luke's disappearance, according to the neighbor.

Henry Winston, Mrs. Dawson's second cousin, has also said that he watched the arguments between father and son escalate over the years. He adds that any normal adolescent angst could have been magnified by the fact that Luke was actually Robert and Sarah Dawson's nephew.

Sarah's sister, Merrilee, and her husband, Ben Kelly, were killed in a car accident when Luke was five years old. The Dawsons became his legal guardians and, within a year, adopted him. By all accounts, Luke's bond with Jack was particularly strong from the very beginning and remained so until his disappearance. "Closer than brothers, if that's possible," said Johnny P. Jones, head football coach and civics teacher at Collins High School. "It's a tragedy. I feel for the family."

Mr. Winston says that Luke became more interested in learning about his birth parents as he got older, increasing tension in the family. Mr. Dawson had not gotten along with his brother-in-law Ben Kelly, who had enlisted to serve in Vietnam when he was only 17 years old. In contrast, Mr. Dawson had spent several years protesting the war.

Their political differences were only one source of disagreement between the two men. Mr. Dawson blamed his brother-in-law for the accident that claimed his life and his wife's, insisting that Mr. Kelly's habit of reckless driving had led to the tragedy.

"Every time Luke stepped out of line, even one little inch, Robert was all over him," Mr. Winston says. "It was like he was afraid that Luke would turn out like his dad. You know, wild. Then Luke started wearing his dad's old army jacket from Vietnam. I thought it was kind of nice, sort of a tribute. But it drove Robert crazy."

Luke's friends insist that he was not a reckless person or the kind of person who would run away from his problems.

"He always volunteered to be the designated driver when we went out," said one friend, 16, who asked not to be identified because he and his friends have not yet reached legal drinking age. "He said he really didn't like alcohol, but I think he just liked to be in control."

But if Luke did not have an accident and did not run away, the question remains: What did happen to him?

Speculation is rife in this small town, from the plausible to the frankly unbelievable. Some people insist that Luke was kidnapped, even though no ransom note has ever been received. Rumors persist that drug smugglers sometimes travel through the backwoods of Zoar Valley to avoid detection by the local police. If Luke encountered them while on a hike, some people theorize, he could have been murdered as a result.

Silas "Skeeter" McGee, 73, owner of the town's only gas station, insists that Luke was abducted by a Bigfoot-like creature that he says has been spotted dozens of times by hikers and campers over the last fifty years.

Detective Seymour Calhoun, who is leading the investigation into Luke Dawson's disappearance, has not yet ruled out foul play. Contacted for comment, he would only say, "We are keeping an open mind at this point about the case."

Although friends and neighbors are already talking about Luke Dawson in the past tense, his family refuses to give up hope. In fact they took the unusual, but by no means unheard-of, step of hiring a psychic. Joanne Waters, a close family friend, describes the séance held in the Dawson living room approximately three months after Luke's disappearance.

"A woman named Mrs. Rosario called Sarah out of the blue and said that she was getting messages about where Luke was," Mrs. Waters says. "I guess Sarah felt pretty desperate by that point. So she set up a reading, and they asked a few friends to be there for moral support."

Apparently the friends were suspicious of the psychic from the beginning, as were Mr. Dawson and the Dawsons' son Jack, who was also present. Mrs. Rosario did not offer a first name and refused to talk about any previous successes she had had as a psychic, citing privacy and confidentiality concerns. (Several attempts to reach Mrs. Rosario for comment were unsuccessful.)

Her appearance also raised eyebrows, according to Mrs. Waters. "She wore tons of makeup—I mean, tons! It wasn't very warm in the living room, but she was sweating so much that her eyeliner started to run down her face halfway through the reading. And her hair was a mess, just wild, with so much hair spray you could smell it across the room. And she wore a caftan covered with bright red and purple flowers." Mrs. Waters paused, then added, "She just didn't seem trustworthy somehow. We all felt it."

Mrs. Rosario insisted that all curtains must be closed and only one candle lit, plunging the living room into darkness even on a sunny winter afternoon. She then settled into a trance. For an hour, she told the group about images that were coming to her, including a fast-flowing river, a late-model red Ford truck, and the number 638.

Unfortunately, none of these clues meant anything to the family. The information was later passed on to Detective Calhoun, who refused to comment on how, or if, it was used.

Shortly after the séance was held, Mr. Dawson increased the reward he was offering for information about his son's disappearance to $25,000. So far, no one has come forward to claim the reward.

For now, that is where the case of Luke Dawson's disappearance stands. Still a mystery, still a source of bewilderment for this small, tight-knit community, still a matter of deepest grief for his family—

"Now do you have a better idea of why I contacted you?" asked a voice somewhere behind my left ear.

I sat up abruptly, spilling the pages onto the floor and somehow banging my elbow on the bedside table.

"Ow!" I rubbed my arm and glared resentfully at Luke. "Do you always have to sneak up behind me like that?"

"Sorry. Occupational hazard of being a ghost."

I glanced at the papers. "I hope you don't mind. . . ."

"No, it helps, actually." He settled himself in the window seat. "A useful summary and relatively accurate. Although just for the record," he added, "Henry Winston may be my mother's second cousin, but she can't stand him. We saw him maybe once a year."

"So all that stuff he told the reporter about you and your dad—that wasn't true?"

He sighed deeply. "Oh, it was true, I *guess*," he admitted. "I mean, yes, *technically* we were arguing a lot. But he made it sound so sinister. We didn't hate each other. We just got on each other's nerves."

"Your father must feel horrible—" I began, without really thinking through where that sentence was going.

"*Exactly* the point I've been trying to make," Luke said with an air of triumph. "If you had been willing to listen earlier—"

"Okay, okay, *okay*." I started grabbing the papers from the floor. "I got it."

I stacked them in a neat pile, thinking hard.

"And I guess I could help you," I said grudgingly. He opened his mouth to reply, and I hurried on. "*Not* by passing on a message! *Not* by saying that I've talked to you! But maybe there's something else I could do, something a little more anonymous."

"Like passing a note in gym class?"

I refused to dignify that with a response.

He shrugged, smiling. "Well, that's a start. Let's see."

He stood up and walked over to the maps I had pinned on the wall. "Tibet, Patagonia, the Azores," he said, running one finger across the countries. "Don't you have any local maps?"

"Sure. Right there." I moved behind him to point to the map and jerked back when I felt the freezing cold. I shivered and saw him give me a sidelong glance that was both understanding and a little sad.

He knew. He knew that if he were still alive, I'd feel a subtle warmth from his body, not that otherworldly chill. It must be heartbreaking, I suddenly thought, when you truly realize that you can never again interact with people the way you used to, that you've moved across an invisible border and can't cross back.

He very politely took two steps to the left so that I could reach out and show him the county map pasted just over my bedside lamp. "Here's Lily Dale," I said.

He traced a route with his finger, then stopped at a wilderness area about thirty miles south. "And here's Zoar Valley. That's where I died."

Neither one of us moved. We both stared at the map. I tried to focus on the details—elevation, nearby towns, highway numbers—but my vision was too blurry. I had to blink several times in order to see again.

I glanced sideways at Luke. His jaw was clenched, but his voice was calm as he said, "I need you to pick up a more detailed trail map."

"Okay. Why?"

"Later." He ran a hand through his hair, looking uncharacteristically edgy. "Can we get out of here? I need to see some sky."

We sat in the far end of the backyard under the branches of an enormous maple tree, safely screened from the house by overgrown bushes and knee-high grass that no one had bothered to cut for weeks. I sat cross-legged, my back against the tree trunk. Luke was stretched out at my feet, his legs crossed at the ankles, his hands behind his head, his eyes closed. By unspoken mutual agreement, we had moved on to lighter topics, carefully avoiding the subject of Luke's death. I knew we would get back to it eventually, but not now. Not yet . . .

"I love it when the warm weather lasts until September," I said, watching as the shadows of leaves shifted on my legs. "This summer was way too short."

"Summer always is," he said. "And winter is always endless."

The mere thought of dark days and slushy streets made me scoot out of the shade and lay down on the grass a little distance from Luke. "Aah." I sighed in satisfaction. "That feels good."

Luke watched me wistfully and said, "I wish I could feel the sun again."

"You can't?" I asked, surprised.

"Faintly. More like the memory of sun." He shrugged. "Of course, on the upside I don't feel the cold." He held up his right hand and started ticking off other points. "I don't have to worry about losing my keys. I am always appropriately dressed for any occasion. And I don't have to watch my weight."

"Must be nice being a ghost. No worries."

"Well, different ones anyway."

I closed my eyes, enjoying the sun on my face and trying to imagine never feeling it again. I shivered and sat up. "So what kinds of worries do you have now?"

"Oh, I don't know. How to get reluctant psychics to help me pass on a message of vital importance—ow!" He grinned as the pinecone that I threw at him went through his head.

"Don't try to act like that hurt you. I know it didn't." I flopped back down on the ground.

"You're the one who worries too much," he commented.

"I worry exactly the right amount," I protested.

"Given all the many troubles in your life," he said dryly.

I felt vaguely resentful of his tone but too lazy to react with any force. "Is this what ghosts do?" I asked idly. "Make fun of the living and their problems?"

"What problems do you have exactly?"

"My family is nuts, your brother is driving me crazy, and I see dead people." I reeled the list off promptly.

"Your life is a little more complicated than most," he conceded.

"No kidding," I said gloomily. Now that I had laid out all my worries end to end, I felt the weight of them pressing down on me.

"Sparrow." His voice sounded serious. Surprised, I turned my head a few inches to look at him. "A complicated life is an interesting life."

"That sounds very enlightened. Do you have all the answers to life now that you're dead?" I tried to sound sarcastic but didn't quite make it.

"Hardly." He laughed. "But you do see things in a different way. And you realize that all the stuff you thought you had figured out when you were alive was completely wrong."

"In what way?"

He thought a bit. "Like . . . the things you think are

your weaknesses are often really your strengths. The things you think are your strengths are what trip you up. Everything you take seriously doesn't really matter in the end. Everything important in your life is the stuff you're not even noticing right now. And"—he paused until I opened my eyes again and looked at him—"you *really* don't have to worry so much. Everything's going to be fine."

I watched a cloud drift by. Easy for you to say, I thought. *You* don't have to figure out what to wear to school tomorrow.

But as the minutes ticked by and I listened to the faint hum of bees, and smelled the sun-warmed grass, and watched the leaves move lazily in the breeze, I felt myself relax and found myself thinking that it would be wonderful if what he said was true. . . .

The cloud moved over the sun. I sat up, rubbing my hands on my arms in the sudden chill.

"Why did you go hiking by yourself all the time anyway?" I asked, remembering the newspaper article. "That seems like asking for trouble, even if you did let people know where you were going."

He gave a slight laugh that ended with a sigh. "You're right about that," he said ruefully. "At least that's the way it turned out in the end. But I loved to be by myself in the middle of nowhere. It's great just to be quiet, you know, and think about things without other people telling you what *they* think or what you *should* think or what *most* people think."

"So," I asked, "what did you think about?"

He balanced his right heel on top of his left toe and waggled his foot back and forth. "Oh, you know. School. Girls. Football. The meaning of life." He hesitated. "And my parents. I thought about them a lot." He glanced at me and added, "I mean, my real parents."

His words were so casual and uninflected that it took me a few seconds to remember that Mr. and Mrs. Dawson were actually his aunt and uncle.

"So you'd think about your—" I hesitated. "Other" parents sounded too weird. "Real" parents sounded too disrespectful to Mr. and Mrs. Dawson. "Biological" parents sounded too clinical. . . .

"My parents," Luke rescued me. "That's the way I always thought of them. I don't remember them very well, but I had a photo of them holding me right after I was born. The way they looked in that picture, that's the way I imagined them looking forever."

"Oh." I couldn't think of anything else to say.

So for a while we stayed like that, quiet, Luke humming

a little tune, me watching the clouds drift, both of us thinking our own private thoughts.

Then a second-floor window flew open, and Raven leaned out to scan the backyard as if she were a prison guard on the trail of an escaping inmate. "Sparrow!" she yelled. "You were supposed to clean the bathroom!" I could see her squinting against the sun, trying to spot me. "I'm not doing it for you this time! It's your turn!"

Luke grinned up at her. "But soft!" he said. "What light through yonder window breaks? It is Juliet, and she sounds pissed."

"What else is new?" I muttered, trying to edge deeper into the shade of the tree.

"I can see you, Sparrow! And if you're not inside in two minutes, I'm coming down to get you!" The window slammed shut.

"I think I'd better go before your sister gets here," Luke said.

"Coward."

He laughed. "Always."

"Wait." I took a deep breath and said in a rush, "Have you seen your parents now that all three of you are, um"—I hesitated, then finished tactfully—"on the Other Side?"

"Not yet. But my spirit guide assures me that once I take care of that unfinished business we've been discussing"—he flicked a crooked smile my way, then turned serious again—"and I move on to wherever it is that I'm going . . . well, that's when I'll see my parents again." He lifted one eyebrow and said, "And that's argument number three for why you should help me. In case you weren't keeping track."

I stared back at him for a few seconds. Then I said, "That's not fair."

"Oh, come on," he said. "What's a little emotional blackmail between friends?"

"Not fair *at all.*"

"Well, you already knew that life isn't fair, right?" he said. "I guess death isn't either."

Chapter 18

"Did you know that Arthur Conan Doyle believed in ghosts and fairies?" Jack shook his head in amazement. "The guy who created Sherlock Holmes, the most logical and rational detective of all time! You'd think that he would have more sense."

"Yes, I did know that," I said shortly. It was a study period, and we were sitting opposite each other at a library table. Fiona sat at the next table, her nose buried in her history textbook, trying to pretend she wasn't listening to every word we were saying. "Doyle's son died in World War One," I pointed out. "He was desperate to make contact with his spirit—"

"Okay, but *fairies?*" He looked so outraged that I grinned and shrugged in agreement.

"Fairies are a little out there," I admitted, with a

silent apology to Mrs. Winkle.

"I'll say. You might as well believe in hobbits," he muttered before going back to his reading.

Fiona caught my eye and gave an encouraging little nod. She had been delivering pep talks for several days about how I should use my study time with Jack to build a relationship of trust and mutual respect that would allow him to open up and share his feelings about his brother's disappearance and perhaps help him reach some sort of closure, which is so vital to the grief process and absolutely necessary for future psychological growth . . . or something like that. My mind usually started to drift after about thirty seconds.

I flipped through a history of western New York State but found nothing on Lily Dale. That book went into my reject pile, and I picked up the next one with a sigh. Our table was stacked high with books. I had grabbed every book on local history from the library shelves. They all had titles like *The History of Western New York State from 1700 to the Present Day*. And if the titles sounded boring, the actual books were even worse.

The books on Jack's side all had titles like *Spiritualism Exposed: A History of Frauds and Cons Among Mediums, Psychics and Channelers*. For the last fifteen minutes he had been reading out tidbits of information to demonstrate that any rational, thinking, sane person could never believe in ghosts.

"Listen to this," he said. He had opened a book titled *The Skeptic's Guide to Psychics*. "'Most psychics start a reading by quickly running down a list of general facts, such as "I see an older woman, perhaps a grandmother or aunt," or "I sense that you've recently had a time of trouble." These statements are so general that there's a good chance that at least some aspect of them is true. Most people over the age of twenty, for example, have an older female relative who has died. The medium then watches for subtle body signals, such as eye movements, facial expressions, and unconscious nodding or shaking of the head. The medium then tailors the rest of his comments accordingly.' "

I looked at Jack through narrowed eyes, trying to interpret his "subtle body signals." Hmm . . . a gleeful grin as he read about a medium who used ventriloquism to impersonate spirit voices. An eager glance as he pushed *Spiritualism Exposed* across the table to me. A sarcastic roll of his eyes as he flipped through an old copy of *Fate* magazine (cover story: "Ghosts Made Me a Millionaire!"). If I had to take a wild guess, I'd say that maybe he was, oh, I don't know . . . a skeptic?

"Sounds like a lot of work," I commented.

"But worth it if you make a lot of money." He flipped the page. "Did you know that Spiritualism started in Hydesville, New York? Two teenage girls—"

"The Fox sisters," I said wearily.

He glanced up, surprised. "Yeah. You've heard of them?"

"Of course." I sounded testy, and Fiona shot me a warning glance, but I was getting impatient. The Fox sisters were as well known to mediums as George Washington is to the average American. In 1916 the Fox family's house had even been moved to Lily Dale as an exhibit (it had burned down in 1955). "Back in 1848, a spirit started coming through to them with a message," I continued, showing off a little. "He said he was a peddler who had been murdered and buried in the cellar. And then in 1904"—I gave Jack a significant look—"a skeleton was found in the cellar wall."

"But Margaret later said she and her sister had faked everything," he said triumphantly. "She showed people how she cracked her toes to make it sound like ghosts were rapping on tables!" He grinned at me in a friendly manner. "Think you could do that?"

"I have a lot of talents," I said coolly. I wasn't feeling friendly. "Cracking my toes isn't one of them."

Fiona cleared her throat loudly at this response, but Jack just shrugged. "Too bad. I'd pay good money to see that. In fact I bet a lot of people would!" He put on a booming TV announcer voice. "You too could have a lucrative career as a psychic!"

"I'd never try to fool people for money!" I closed my book with a bang. Fiona looked alarmed.

"I never thought you would," Jack said, puzzled.

"I hate con artists! I hate fakes!" I could feel the pulse pounding in my temple and my face flushing with anger. In one small, distant part of my brain I realized that I was overreacting, but I didn't care. "But what I *really* hate are narrow-minded, judgmental people who call other people fakes—"

I was interrupted by the librarian, who was now standing over me. She looked as if she had a headache. "Perhaps," she suggested with a forced smile, "we could keep it down to a dull roar over here?"

"Sorry," I murmured. I sank down in my chair and opened another book, carefully not looking at either Jack or Fiona. I had found this book, *Guiding Spirits: The Life of a Medium,* propping up one leg of a kitchen chair at home. It was written in the early 1900s by a Lily Dale resident who had channeled spirits for hundreds of people, including a few minor celebrities. I leafed through it, hoping that my eyes would magically stop at an interesting paragraph. After a few minutes I realized that this was a futile quest. I'm sure Anna May Dodds had a fascinating life, but she somehow made the telling of it duller than . . . well, than *The History of Western New York State from 1700 to the Present Day.*

I sighed deeply and turned a few more pages until I found a photo of the medium sitting in a spirit cabinet. Her hands and feet were tied so that she couldn't create mysterious noises by bouncing an apple on the floor, banging a tambourine under the table or snapping her fingers. Although, I thought bitterly, she could probably still crack her toes.

I heard a slight cough from the next table.

I turned the page and concentrated studiously on the text.

Another cough, this time louder.

I made a note to myself on a legal pad and kept reading.

Now there was a series of racking coughs that culminated with a book falling off the table and landing on the floor near my foot.

Resigned, I leaned down to pick it up. A piece of paper stuck out of the pages. I pulled the paper out and handed the book back to Fiona, who was unwrapping a cough drop with a look of utter innocence on her face.

I unfolded the note. "Be sweet!!! *Jack is reaching out to you!!!* Seize The Moment!!!" It was signed with an enormous initial *F* and a hasty sketch of two intertwined hearts.

I raised my eyebrows. Nine exclamation points. Clearly, attention must be paid.

Jack leaned over the table to whisper, "So, um, have you found anything more about why Spiritualism was so popular around here a hundred years ago?" He casually picked up the biggest, heaviest book—*Spirited Lives: Nineteenth-Century Mediums and Changing Views of the Afterlife*—and moved it to the side of the table closest to Fiona.

"Tons," I whispered back, a little puzzled by this question. All I had been doing for the last hour, after all, was reading about that very subject. I watched as he took two more books and stacked them on top of *Spirited Lives*. "I think we need to find more dates, though. We don't have much of a time line yet."

"No problem. I got a lot of stuff from this book," he said, picking up another massive volume and putting it on top of the others.

I could see Fiona eyeing the growing wall of books. The stack was now a foot high.

Jack lowered his head toward the table so that the books blocked him from sight and gave a conspiratorial wave to indicate that I should do the same.

"What?" I whispered as I leaned toward him.

"I think this library is far too crowded and noisy for serious research," he said seriously. "Do you want to come over later to work on the project? We can do some Internet research on my computer, and I think we'll have fewer, um"—he shifted his eyes in Fiona's direction—"distractions."

"That's a great idea," I said.

There was a small coughing fit from the next table.

I ignored it.

Chapter 19

"Favorite ice-cream flavor?" Jack asked.

"Vanilla," I said, opting for honest.

"That's pathetic." He smirked. "Mine's pistachio."

"And that's trying a little too hard to be interesting," I countered.

We were walking to Jack's house after school. Somehow the conversation had moved easily from the Great Ghost Debate to What's Your Favorite——? (fill in the blank). We had compared notes on favorite foods (mine: pot roast, Jack's: sausage pizza), favorite words (mine: *serendipity*, Jack's: *effervescent*), and, now, ice cream.

"Favorite movie of all time?" I asked.

"No contest. It's gotta be—" Jack stopped suddenly. His smile vanished and was replaced by a tight-lipped glare. "Shit!"

"What?" I followed his gaze and saw a chubby, balding man standing across the street, peering at us through black-framed glasses. "Who is that?"

Jack took my elbow and began moving me faster toward the driveway, all the time glaring at the stranger as if he were a career criminal with bad intentions.

The man didn't seem that threatening. He wore a rumpled gray suit. His tie was loosened, and the side of his shirt was coming untucked. His shoulders slumped as if it took all his energy just to stand there. He looked like a mournful baby elephant.

"Jack?" I said again. "Do you know him?"

Jack looked at me as if he had just remembered that I was standing there. "No," he said in a totally unconvincing manner. "Let's go inside." He was still holding on to my arm, and now he began steering me up the driveway.

"Jack!" the man called out. I turned my head and saw that he was crossing the street in our direction. "I'd like to talk to you." Even though he had raised his voice, he wasn't yelling. He sounded reasonable, even friendly.

"I think he wants to talk to you," I said, unnecessarily.

"I don't want to talk to him." Jack tightened his grip

and walked faster, pulling me along like a guard marching a prisoner to a cell. "Hurry up."

As anyone in my family could have told him, the best way to make me do something was to command me to do the opposite. Especially if the command was issued in an edgy voice and accompanied by an impatient little jerk on my arm.

I stopped walking and did my best to become a dead weight. He yanked on me again, but I didn't budge.

"Will you move?" he snapped, glancing over my shoulder.

"Not unless you stop pulling on my arm!" I snapped back. "And you could say 'please' once in a while, you know."

"Fine!" He dropped my arm and took a step back, his arms held out as if to demonstrate to a crowd of onlookers that he was no longer trying to force me to go anywhere. "Will you *please* move?"

By then, of course, it was too late. The man had reached us, huffing a bit (he really was too round for even a minor dash across a street). He pulled a handkerchief from his pocket, mopped his forehead, and smiled genially at Jack.

"Jack. Glad I caught you. You got a few minutes?"

"No." Jack turned to me but knew better than to

grab my arm again. "C'mon, let's go inside."

The man seemed unfazed by Jack's rudeness. "I just thought I'd stop by, see how things were going for you," he said calmly. "And for your family, of course. You're all doing well?"

"Yes." Jack spit out his one-word answers as if he couldn't stand the taste of them in his mouth.

"Good, good." The man sounded breezily unconvinced. His eyes seemed to sharpen a bit as he asked, "So, your dad's doing well then?"

Finally Jack swung around to face the man, his face blazing with anger. "We're all fine, okay?" he shouted. "We're great! And I'm not talking to you about my dad!"

The man held up his hands in a calming gesture. He moved closer to Jack and lowered his voice. "I just want you to know that I'm available if you want to talk. Anytime. Day or night."

Jack's hand clenched into a fist, and the man quickly stepped back, just as a car turned the corner. The driver swung into the driveway, fast, and braked hard enough to make the tires squeal.

He turned off the engine and stepped out. "What's going on here?" He was a thin man with graying hair, a stooping posture, and sad eyes. He looked at the strange man with barely concealed distaste. "Detective Calhoun. I thought I told you not to bother my family anymore."

"I just wanted to see how you folks were getting along," the man said again.

"Right," said the driver, who I had cleverly deduced was Jack's father. "You just happened to be driving by, twenty-five miles from home."

Detective Calhoun shrugged, a faint smile on his face. "I take cold cases very personally."

Mr. Dawson's jaw tightened, but he said, calmly enough, "We're doing as well as can be expected. Now, unless you have some news for us . . ."

He left the question hanging. After a long pause the detective shrugged and shook his head. "No. No news."

Mr. Dawson nodded curtly, as if that had been just what he expected. "Then it's time for us to have dinner. Good night."

He turned on his heel and marched to the door, with Jack following. I walked more slowly after them. As I reached the door, I turned to look over my shoulder.

The detective hadn't moved. He was standing at the end of the driveway, watching.

* * *

We stood in a cavernous kitchen that was filled with shiny state-of-the-art appliances and absolutely no evidence that food was ever cooked or consumed there. Mr. Dawson stared down at the gleaming white tile floor, lost in thought. I heard a drop of water drip from the faucet into the stainless steel sink. It seemed to echo in the room.

Finally Jack cleared his throat. "So, Dad—"

Mr. Dawson looked up, startled. "Oh, sorry." His voice was thin and gray and sad. "I was just thinking. . . ." The words trailed off as if he were too tired to remember what he was going to say.

"This is Sparrow. She's in my history class. We're doing a project together." Jack sounded as if he were reciting lines in a school play. Lines that did not inspire him at all.

His father sounded as if he had been cast in the same dispiriting play. "Very nice to meet you, Sparrow. How are you enjoying school so far?"

"It's great," I said woodenly. Oh, great. Now I was in the play, too. "I really like it."

"That's good. School is important." Mr. Dawson paused for a long, long moment. Was he waiting for his cue? Finally he nodded, as if remembering the next line, and went on. "What's your favorite class?"

"I like English. And history, of course." I stopped. I would have kept talking if I could have, just to fill the overpowering silence, but my mind was completely blank. The atmosphere in that kitchen made me want to find a dark corner, curl up into a little ball, and weep for days.

The three of us looked at one another, no one saying a word. Fortunately, Jack's mother walked into the kitchen a few seconds later, carrying an empty wine-glass. She smiled brightly at all of us.

"Sparrow, it's lovely to see you again!" She reached across Mr. Dawson to pick up a wine bottle and filled her glass. "Would you like something to drink?" She gave a brittle laugh. "Not the Cabernet, of course! You have years before you're ready for that! But we always keep lots of soda for the boys, so if you're thirsty. . . ."

I swear I felt Jack flinch when she said "the boys."

"No, thank you, I'm fine," I blurted. "But we should probably get started on our project. My mother wants me home before dinner."

A complete and utter lie, of course. There was a reading tonight in the parlor, so my family would assume that I was hiding in my room, as usual. But Jack seized on this excuse, his face practically incandescent with relief.

"No problem. We should be done in an hour." To his

parents, he added, "We'll be working on the computer in my room," and then moved toward the door.

"Door open," his father called after us. I gritted my teeth with embarrassment and carefully avoided looking at Jack.

His mother called after us, "Well, let me know if you get hungry. We have lots of snacks, too. In fact, the pantry is full of chips and cookies. Or you could microwave some popcorn—"

I had already edged out the door. I glanced back and saw Jack put his hand on his mother's arm.

"It's okay, Mom," he said softly.

She looked at him, and he nodded reassuringly. "We're fine."

She sighed, and I could see her shoulders relax and her smile become a real smile, not the painfully bright and false one that she had been using. "Yes, I know. I do."

He patted her arm again and came toward me. Over his shoulder I saw Mrs. Dawson's smile slip as she took another sip of wine.

The first thing I noticed about Jack's bedroom was all the maps. I felt a little shock of recognition as I saw them, papered onto the wall behind his desk, floor to ceiling. "Cool maps," I said, walking to get a closer look. Colorado. Wyoming. Utah. Montana.

"Thanks." He reached around me, his hand brushing my arm, to turn on his computer.

I jumped at his touch, and he jerked back; I tried to move out of his way and tripped over my feet; he put out a hand to catch me and knocked over the desk lamp.

"Sorry, sorry," I said, flustered.

"No problem." He leaned down to pick up the lamp just as I did the same thing.

"Ow!"

My hand went to my nose. Jack fell back into his chair.

"I think I'll get out of your way," I said weakly.

"Good idea," he muttered, rubbing his forehead. "Safety first."

I moved across the room and stared with intense interest at a bookcase, trying to regain my composure. After a few seconds my attention was caught by a collection of figurines on one of the shelves. They all were characters from *Star Wars*: Darth Vader, Princess Leia, a few random storm troopers. I picked up Yoda.

"Those aren't mine."

I turned to see Jack, looking embarrassed. His eyes met mine. "I mean, they're my brother's. Not that he's a geek or anything," he added quickly.

"No, they're kind of cool. Really." I carefully replaced Yoda and patted his head with one finger before sitting down next to Jack at the computer.

"Yeah." He frowned at the bookshelf, then looked around and spotted the Luke Skywalker figure on the windowsill. "I don't know why Mom keeps moving my stuff," he muttered as he picked it up and brought it over to put it with the others. "They're all vintage," he said, nudging Darth Vader and Obi-Wan Kenobi back into line. "The complete collection."

"Really. It's probably worth a lot of money."

"I'd never sell it." Jack's voice was abrupt.

"Oh, right. Sentimental value—"

His frown deepened. "I'm not sentimental!"

"No, of course not." I had a terrible feeling that I had just accused him of being unmanly. A quick change of subject seemed to be in order. "So, who was that guy?"

"What guy?" He managed an expression of honest bewilderment that was almost completely convincing.

I chose to play along. "The guy outside," I said patiently.

Complete and utter incomprehension. "What guy out—"

"The detective!" I snapped. "The detective who

wanted to talk to you, the one your father ran off, the one who kept making mysterious hints, that guy!"

Unexpectedly he grinned. It lit up his whole face and made him look, for one brief instant, like the person in the newspaper photo.

"What's so funny?"

"I was waiting for you to stamp your foot in frustration."

"You what?"

"I've never seen someone stamp her foot in real life, only in the movies," he explained, still grinning. "I thought if I kept playing dumb, you might do it. You looked like you were on the verge."

I grinned back at him. "You do an *excellent* job of playing dumb," I said, using the breathless tone of an ardent fan. "I mean, I *so* can't believe you didn't win the Oscar last year!"

"No, no." He waved his hand in airy dismissal, pretending to be embarrassed by the praise. "It's nothing, just an enormous gift that I happened to be born with. I can't take any credit, really."

I laughed just as Jack's dad knocked on the door frame and stuck his head in. "You guys getting a lot of work done?" he asked mildly.

Jack sobered up immediately. "Oh, yeah." He pushed

the mouse and his Lucha Libre screen saver was replaced with a Web site about Lily Dale. "Just doing some Internet research."

I could see his dad's eyes flick over the screen. His eyebrows raised in surprise, he asked sharply, "This is for a school project?"

"Yeah. History." Jack's answers were getting shorter. I remembered his dad's opinion of mediums—con artists, criminals, frauds—and hurriedly stepped in.

"We have to do a report about local history," I said. "We picked Lily Dale because it seemed, um, I don't know, interesting?" My voice trailed off in the face of his tight-lipped expression.

"Mmm." He was trying to seem neutral, I think, but that little murmur managed to sound disgusted all the same.

Jack swiveled his chair around to click the site closed. His back to his father, he said, "We have a lot to do."

"Sure thing." His dad hesitated, but Jack didn't turn around. "Okay, then. I'll leave you to it." His father rapped a couple of times on the door, as if tapping good-bye, and walked away.

Jack stared at his computer and clicked on one link after another, checking out Web sites on spirit photography, séances, slate writing, spirit trumpets. I watched the screens flash by and tried to think of the best way to reintroduce the topic of Detective Calhoun. Nothing clever or subtle or convincingly off-hand came to mind, so finally I just asked him. "Jack. That detective. You don't have to tell me if you don't want to, but—"

That "but" seemed to hang in the air for a long time as Jack kept his eyes fixed on the monitor and chewed his bottom lip, clearly trying to make up his mind. After a long moment he said, "Okay, I'll tell you, but you can't tell anyone else." He turned to give me a fierce look. "*Nobody*. Agreed?"

"Agreed."

He took a deep breath and let it out slowly. "Okay," he said. "See, I have this brother."

He stopped, as if replaying what he had just said. "He ran away last year. Or—well, he's gone. Disappeared." He was staring down at the floor as he said this, but I still tried to look as if this were news to me.

"Oh. That's terrible," I said. "What happened?" The words sound stilted and false to my ears, but Jack didn't seem to notice.

He shrugged and began pushing the toe of his sneaker back and forth on the rug. "I don't know.

Nobody does. I got up one morning . . . it was a Saturday. Luke—that's my brother—likes to sleep in on weekends. I made myself some cornflakes. I played a couple of video games. My parents came downstairs."

He frowned slightly. Maybe he had replayed this memory so many times—for the reporters, for the police, for himself—that he was just tired of telling the story again. "Then it was time to eat lunch, and Luke still hadn't come downstairs. So Mom went up to check his room. His bed was still made. It didn't look as if he had slept there. His backpack was gone."

I found that I was sitting on the edge of my chair, even though I knew, only too well, how this story ended.

"Anyway. He never came back."

I stood up abruptly. "So where do you think he is?"

As soon as I said it, I knew it was a stupid question, but I didn't care. Because Jack shot me a withering look, which was a hundred times better than looking as if he were about to cry.

"I have no idea," he said, adding, very slowly, as if speaking to someone who didn't understand the language, "that's the problem."

His scornful tone would have made me blush a week ago. But now I ignored it and walked over to the maps.

"That's what these are for," I said, tracing a road with my finger. "You're trying to find him."

He gave me a sidelong look. "Yeah. Luke and I always talked about working as white-water guides in the summer, and all the best rivers are out West. So I've been calling some of the outfitters we found on the Internet, asking if he maybe signed up with them."

Jackson Hole, Wyoming. Big Sky, Montana. Deadwood, South Dakota. It was easy to imagine Luke living somewhere in those wide-open spaces, steering a raft through white-water rapids, making a campfire in the crisp evening air, hiking up a snow-peaked mountain. The images were so real that it took a second for me to remember that Luke would never do those things. He would never make it out West.

"That could take forever."

He shrugged. "Not searching for Luke would take the same amount of time." I heard a faint echo of Luke's matter-of-fact logic. Jack stood beside me and pointed to a river. "That's the Shoshone. Supposed to have the best white water in the country."

Standing this close to him, I could feel the warmth of his body. It was the exact opposite of standing next to Luke, but I still shivered and moved away.

He kept his eyes on the map and said softly, "I don't

get why he didn't tell me he was going."

There was nothing I could say to that except a lie (I'm sure he meant to call) or the truth (actually, he didn't call because he's dead, and oh, by the way, here's how I happen to know that). Neither option was possible.

"So, that detective?" I prompted.

Jack threw himself back into his chair. "Yeah. Detective Calhoun," He mimicked the detective's voice. "'I just stopped by to see how you were doing.' I just stopped by to pump you for more information is more like it."

"He's still working on the case? It's been, what, a year since Luke left, right?"

"In two weeks." He smiled at me sardonically. "The anniversary is going to be pretty low-key. No balloons or confetti or anything."

I shifted my gaze over his shoulder to several snapshots pinned up in a row on the edge of the map. I got up to look more closely and took in a quick breath. Luke was smiling out at me. His hair was a little too long, just like it was now, and he was wearing an old army jacket.

I glanced down at Jack. He looked down at his jacket, then back at me. "I don't know why he left this," he said. "He used to wear it all the time. Drove my dad crazy."

"It's really cool," I said, trying to make my tone as colorless as possible. I didn't want even a hint of what I was thinking to show up in my voice.

Because I was thinking was this: Jack knew that if Luke had run away, he would have taken his jacket. He knew that Luke would have told Jack where he was going. He knew that Luke would have made plans for them to get together. He knew that Luke would have called or written or been in touch somehow.

Which meant that Jack had to suspect that Luke was dead.

Chapter 20

"So, you saw Jack today."

Luke had taken his usual spot in the window seat. I was sitting in the rocker, trying to concentrate on *Pride and Prejudice*. Mr. Darcy had finally shown up, and the book was indeed getting much better. I could hear distant yelling and banging and sudden crashes from another part of the house, which meant that Grandma Bee had finally convinced Lark and Linnet to help her practice jujitsu throws in the parlor.

I turned to look accusingly at his profile. "Were you watching us?"

He shook his head. "I heard him ask you to come over. I don't hang out around my family much anymore."

"Too sad?"

He shrugged. "Too frustrating. I try to get through to them, but nothing works. They don't hear me when I talk. If they feel a sudden cold spot in the room, they just close a window. That day in the museum?"

I sat up in surprise. "What?"

"I managed to make my face appear in the spirit painting," he said, rather proudly. Then his smile dimmed. "It just freaked Jack out."

"No kidding," I said, remembering.

Luke frowned. "I've tried showing up in their dreams, moving stuff around Jack's room—"

"Luke Skywalker! That was you!"

"Yeah." He rolled his eyes. "You'd think that would be easy enough to figure out. I mean, come on. *Luke* Skywalker?"

"*Excellent* clue."

"Thank you." He nodded in acknowledgment. "Except, you know, for the fact that *no one got it*. In fact nothing I've tried has worked. Which brings me to today's argument—"

I groaned and dramatically collapsed on the floor.

"—for why you should help me."

I looked at my watch. "Ten minutes," I said. "Go."

But he didn't launch into his case immediately. Instead he leaned his head back and stared at the deepening blue sky. "One thing you should know about Jack. He's very stubborn."

"Really." My tone was as dry as the desert, and he grinned.

"We used to wrestle all the time. I'd usually pin him in two minutes, tops, but that kid would never tap out." He shook his head, remembering. "I mean, I'm two years older, about fifty pounds heavier and"—he shot me a quick grin—"an incredibly gifted athlete."

"Not to mention modest."

He nodded modestly and went on. "He'd be on the floor, arm twisted behind his back, about to pass out, all scraped and bloody from friction burns—"

"Excuse me," I interrupted. "This was in fun?"

"Yeah, of course," he said, as if this were self-evident. "But no matter what I did, he would never give up." He turned to look directly into my eyes. "Ever."

I looked away first. "And your point is?"

"If he thinks that I'm still alive, roaming around the Wild West in search of adventure—"

"It's one of the stages of grief," I said, more authoritatively than I felt. "Number three, I think. Denial. He'll get over it."

"No, Sparrow." Luke's voice was sad. "He won't. Jack will keep searching for me until the end of his days."

I shifted uncomfortably, feeling some sympathy for Jack. Luke had me pinned in—I glanced at my watch—less than five minutes.

Luke settled into a gracious silence, allowing me (I thought bitterly) a generous amount of time to consider this new argument. He sat in the window seat and amused himself by blowing on the glass and watching ice crystals form into patterns as I frowned down at my book.

Finally he took pity on me and introduced a new subject. "Did you get that trail map? Maybe we can take a look at it now."

I pulled the map out of my backpack with relief and spread it out on my desk.

"See, here are the trails I usually took." His finger traced them for me. "That's where the park rangers searched, of course." He pointed to another spot. "Now. See here? I had wanted to try this trail for a long time."

It led up the other side of the mountain, far away from the other trails. "It looks steep," I said, eyeing the topographical lines.

"It is," he said calmly. "Very."

"So you decided to try it at night," I said sharply. "Alone. Without letting anyone know where you were going."

"Stupid," he said. "Although, in my defense, I'd like to point out that when I started the hike, it was still light outside. But once you've made one stupid decision, it gets easier to make even stupider ones. Which is why when I got to this spot"—his finger moved on relentlessly—"I decided to step to the edge of a cliff to get a better view. It was a beautiful night, and I could just about see Orion, but there was this tree blocking my view, so I . . . Anyway. The fact that the ground under my feet was loose shale didn't give me a moment's pause."

As soon as he said that, I saw it happen. The dark trail up the mountain. The clouds scudding across the moon. The step onto loose rock, casual, just trying to get a better look at a constellation . . . and then the sickening plunge.

"But why didn't you just break your legs or end up paralyzed or something?" I sounded argumentative and angry. I felt close to tears. "Why did you have to die?"

"Because I fell off a forty-foot cliff. You can't argue with reality, Sparrow."

And with that he was gone.

I didn't sleep well that night. The next morning I woke up late and got dressed in record time. As I dashed through the kitchen, Grandma Bee blocked my way and thrust a piece of toast in the general direction of my mouth.

"Hey!" I wiped a smear of butter from my chin.

"You're not getting out of this house without eating something!" she said. "I need you in fighting shape tonight!"

"Um, why?" I asked, knowing I would regret it.

"I'm learning to extend my ki force so I can do a no-touch throw," she said, a manic gleam in her eye. "I'll be able to slam you to the ground through the sheer power of my mind."

"Sounds like fun," I said insincerely as I took the toast from her hand and started toward the door.

She blocked my way again, staring pugnaciously into my face. "We can start right now!" she cried. "Try to shove me out of your way! Go ahead, push me as hard as you can!"

"Please, I've got to get to school—"

"Go ahead, try! You'll see, I'm solid as a rock!"

"I'm already running late—"

"You won't be able to move me an inch! My mind is a mighty weapon—"

A few moments later, as the door swung shut behind me, I heard her yell, "I wasn't ready! My thoughts weren't collected! My feet weren't planted! Come back, I'll let you try again."

Fiona caught me by the arm just as I was about to go into history class. "Hold on a sec," she whispered. "I need to talk to you."

"What about?" I cast a worried look through the classroom door at Sergeant Grimes, who had just picked up the attendance book from his immaculate desk and was surveying the room with his usual forbidding air. "The late bell is about to ring—"

"I know, I know, but *listen*!" Her eyes were sparkling with excitement. "I called Merri last night to ask her about our Spanish homework, you know Senorita Reilly always talks so fast when she gives the assignment that I can't understand a *word* she's saying, especially because it's always in *Spanish*—"

"I know, I know." I was bouncing impatiently on my toes.

"—so *anyway*, Merri and I started talking about other things, you know, like that boy she likes who plays on the JV basketball team and whether Jeannie Bartlett is *really* going to New York to be a model after graduation—"

"Uh-huh." I made a wrap-it-up motion with my

hand as I glanced nervously toward the door.

"—and then we got on the subject of the Halloween dance." She came to a complete stop and gave me a meaningful look.

I gave her a puzzled look in return.

"*The Halloween dance*," she said again, with significant emphasis.

"Yes, you said that already," I pointed out. We were really going to be late if Fiona insisted on saying everything *twice*—

"It's a Sadie Hawkins dance," she said, pronouncing each word very distinctly. "Girls ask boys."

"Oh, right." I looked at the floor, the ceiling, the door. "Well, that's a long way away—"

"Not that long. And Merri told me—"

The late bell rang, a jarring clang that echoed through the halls like an air-raid signal.

"Oh, no, I *told* you we were going to be late!" I started to open the door.

Fiona tugged on my arm, pulling me back into the hall and completely ignoring Sergeant Grimes's thunderous expression.

"*What?*"

"Merri told me that Clare told *her* that she heard Chad talking to Sam and that *he* thinks that Jack wouldn't mind too much if you asked *him*." She stopped to take a breath and beam triumphantly at me. "Isn't that totally *cool*?"

I hesitated, parsing that sentence in my mind. "So *him* is?"

"Jack, of course!" Fiona patted me reassuringly on the shoulder as she opened the door and swept into the classroom. "Don't worry, I'll talk you through the whole thing. This is going to be so so *so* much fun!"

I soon realized that it's very hard to get through life when you're too distracted to pay attention to what's going on around you. By the end of the day I'd been yelled at twice for not paying attention in class. I had flunked a pop quiz in biology. And during a vicious game of volleyball, my lack of focus had resulted in the ball's smashing into my face not once, not twice, but *three* times.

I was sitting alone at the bus stop, wondering if my nose was broken and thinking for the hundredth—okay, the thousandth—time about what Fiona had said, when I felt a touch of dry ice brush my left arm.

I sighed and turned my head to see a middle-aged man wearing a dark suit and narrow tie sitting inches away from me, smoking a cigar. His old-fashioned fedora was pushed jauntily onto the back of his head. His right elbow was hooked over the back of the bench, and his left ankle was propped on his right knee.

"Hey, kiddo," he said. "I heard you're finally open for business."

Oh, no. *Go away, leave me alone, I don't want to talk to—*

Oh, what the hell.

"What business are you talking about?" I asked tersely.

"The ghost talking business, of course." He nodded in approval. "That'll be a nice little moneymaker for you. I got a nose for these things."

He blew a smoke ring in my direction. "I was regional sales director of the year ten years in a row, you know. Had a whole wall full of plaques." He waved his hand in a wide arc to illustrate. "'Course then I died. After that I have to say the plaques didn't mean as much. But I still get to pass on business tips once in a while to folks down here on the earthly plane. Take you, for example—"

"Forget it. I'm not going into the ghost talking business."

He raised his eyebrows in surprise. "Sure about that?

'Cause a girl with your kind of talent could charge a bundle."

"I'm sure."

"Okey-dokey." He blew two more smoke rings. One floated delicately inside the other. He watched it for a moment with quiet pride, then winked at me.

"Don't you know smoking will kill you?" I snapped.

He laughed. "Black humor. I like that in a girl."

I started to say something nasty back when I heard a slight cough behind me. I turned to see Detective Calhoun eyeing me.

"Sorry to interrupt," he said, "er, whatever it is you were doing."

"Oh. Um. Just . . . practicing for a play."

"By the way, it wasn't smoking that got me in the end," the ghost said. As he faded away, he added, "Here's another tip, kiddo. Never eat sushi at a diner called Mom's."

"Ah," Detective Calhoun said. "A play! It's always a pleasure to meet a fellow thespian. You know, I did a little acting in high school, too. Harry the Horse in *Guys and Dolls*." He sighed happily at the memory. "Great part. Great play. If you ever get a chance to see it—"

"What do you want?" I interrupted.

He blinked, as if he had been awakened from a

particularly pleasant dream. "Right to the point, I see. Well. I don't know if you remember me? Detective Calhoun? We met outside the Dawsons' house yesterday?"

"Uh-huh." I waited, wary.

"I thought we might have a little chat."

I glanced at my watch. "My bus will be here any minute."

He didn't take the hint. "You seem to have become good friends with young Jack—"

Young Jack? Where were we, in a Dickens novel? I looked at him in disbelief, but he rolled right along.

"—so I'm sure he's told you about the recent tragedy that his family suffered."

A long pause here as he looked at me meaningfully. I made my face as blank as possible and looked unhelpfully back. If he wanted to pump me for information, he'd have to do better than that.

The silence stretched out for almost a minute, which is actually quite a long time to go without speaking. There was a sudden breeze, and a few leaves fell from the tree behind us. I squinted down the road, looking for the bus and concentrating on not speaking.

Finally he sighed heavily and said, "Yes. Well. I'm sure you'd like to help them any way you could."

I stared at him without blinking.

"If young Jack has said something to you, for example, that might shed some light on his brother's disappearance—"

"I've only known Jack for a few weeks," I said. "He didn't even tell me about his brother until last night."

He sighed even more heavily, as if that were exactly what he would expect me to say. "I see. And what did he tell you?"

"I'm not sure I should say," I said cautiously. "Wouldn't that be betraying a confidence?"

"Would it?" He somehow made me feel that just by asking the question, I had revealed something sinister about the Dawsons.

"Yes. Yes, I think it would." I tried to sound definite and assured.

"All right." He shrugged. "Of course you may be able to tell me something that would help Jack and his family," he added thoughtfully. "It's a funny thing, even people who are perfectly innocent don't always trust the police—"

"Why should they?" I demanded hotly. "When you show up at their school and their home and practically stalk them, how do you think they're going to act?"

"Jack said that I was stalking them?"

Damn! Did that sound like he was overreacting, covering something up, hiding something suspicious? I clamped my mouth shut and looked away.

"Nothing you say will get anyone into trouble, Miss Delaney. I promise."

I kept my eyes fixed on a distant line of trees, silhouetted against the sky. I wouldn't say another word, I promised myself. Not another word . . .

"Unless, well—" He paused in such a heavy-handed and obvious manner that I was glad I had missed his performance as Harry the Horse.

I pressed my lips together more tightly. He crossed his arms and joined me in staring at the horizon.

Fine. We can both sit here as silent as stones for the next week.

Seconds ticked by.

I noticed that my foot was tapping nervously, and forced myself to stop it.

Finally I couldn't help myself.

"Unless *what*?"

"Unless the Dawsons do have something to hide," he went on smoothly. "I'm sure they don't. It's just that if this case is never solved, well, there will always be that faint suspicion—"

"Of what? Luke was fighting with his father, so he ran away. Out West someplace. Wyoming, maybe. He's working out there as a white-water guide. . . ." My voice trailed off. I was so eager to defend Jack and his parents that I had almost forgotten that this story was a total fiction.

"That's what Jack told you?" A tone of mild surprise, underlaid by another, sharper note. Sudden, intense interest.

"Well . . . yeah."

"I see." He let that hang in the air for a few seconds while I wondered if I had just said something really stupid. When I didn't respond, he said, "Well, if you do hear or see anything else that might help the investigation, perhaps you'll give me a call?"

He searched several pockets before finding a card, which he handed over with an apologetic air. I stared down at it. It was gray and wrinkled, rather like his suit. There was a light brown stain over the words *Missing Persons Bureau*. It looked as if someone had spilled coffee on the card, then thriftily dried it off instead of throwing it away.

As he started to walk away, I called after him. "Detective Calhoun?"

He turned wearily.

"I just wanted to ask you—" I hesitated for a moment, then plunged on. "You search for missing people?"

"Every single day," he said.

I hesitated. "How often do you find them?"

"Not often enough. Why?"

"Well . . ." I took a deep breath. "Say someone left on a trip about ten years ago and said they would come back. And they sent a few postcards that kept saying they were on their way, but they never showed up. And then, after a while, even postcards stopped coming. I was just wondering. . . ." My voice dwindled off as I saw him shaking his head with regret.

"This person was an adult?"

I didn't even try to keep up the fiction that we weren't talking about a real person. I nodded.

"After that many years the odds are slim. You could try hiring a private detective, of course."

"I don't think that's an option." I didn't know anything about private detectives, except that they sounded expensive.

Detective Calhoun ran a hand over the top of his balding head. "Well, even they might not have much luck. It's a pretty big world. Still lots of room to get lost, if that's what you want to do."

"Yeah," I said stiffly. "Well, I just thought I'd ask."

He glanced over my shoulder. "I think your bus is coming. Have a good evening."

The bus wheezed to a stop, and I climbed on. I leaned back in my seat, closed my eyes, and imagined the world and all the places where someone could still get lost.

Chapter 21

When I walked into the kitchen, Grandma Bee was hunched over the table, peering shortsightedly through a magnifying glass. "Good, you're finally here," she greeted me without looking up.

"Finally?" I protested mildly. "I came straight home from school!" I opened the pantry and peered inside without much hope. "Why don't we ever have any cookies? Or crackers even."

"Forget cookies, forget crackers, I need your help," she snapped. "Take a look at this spider. Your mother thinks it's harmless, but you know how softhearted she is. I think it could be a black widow myself. Maybe something even worse."

I approached cautiously. "Is it dead?"

She took her gaze off the spider long enough to scowl

up at me. "Of course it's dead!" she snapped. She glanced down to see the spider scuttling behind the sugar bowl. "Oh, damn it!"

She grabbed a dish towel and swatted at the sugar bowl, which of course meant that it crashed to the floor and broke, scattering the unpaid bills that had been stuffed inside. Wren, ever alert to any kind of domestic crisis, came running at the sound of smashing china.

"Oh, no!" she said. "Not *another* broken dish!" She knelt to pick up the pieces.

"Wren, for goodness' sake, sweep that mess up and throw it away," Grandma Bee snapped.

"But I might be able to glue it back together."

"You're fussing over a silly piece of china when my scientific investigation has been completely destroyed!"

Wren looked at me fearfully. Grandma Bee's last scientific investigation had resulted in a massive kitchen explosion and gallons of an unidentifiable green slime that smelled like rotting seaweed.

"Maybe a poisonous black widow," I said in answer to her unspoken question. "Maybe a harmless house spider. Now we'll never know."

"Oh, is that all?" She tried to sound casual, but she

looked a bit nervous as she reached for the broom. She began sweeping with the intense concentration that other people reserve for high-stakes poker games.

"All?" Grandma Bee pushed herself to a standing position and began lurching around the kitchen, staring at the floor with a gimlet eye, lips pursed with serious scientific purpose. "What if that spider is a Sydney funnel-web? Its bite delivers the mostly deadly toxin in the animal kingdom!"

At that moment Mordred padded into the kitchen, tail held high to show his complete disdain for all of us. He weaved between Grandma Bee's legs, threatening to tip her over, and she swatted at him.

"Get away from me, you disgraceful creature!" Mordred hissed and retreated to the far corner as Grandma Bee continued talking to Wren. "I would think that you'd be more concerned about potentially poisonous creatures living cheek by jowl—aha!"

She spotted the spider near the stove at the same moment that Mordred did. Grandma Bee moved fast, but Mordred moved faster.

One lightning-quick feline leap, one paw slashing down, and that spider was ingested by Mordred before any of us could blink.

"Damn it!" Grandma Bee glared at Mordred.

Mordred glared right back. "You old reprobate. That's another investigation cut short."

Wren looked more closely at our cat. "He just ate a poisonous spider? Do you think he might die?" I knew she was trying not to sound too hopeful.

"Never." Grandma Bee was definite. "Not that spawn of Satan. I keep getting my hopes up, but he just keeps on living. It's unnatural, is what it is."

It's true that Mordred has an iron constitution; he's eaten dead wasps, rancid socks, and a quart of Grandma Bee's weed killer without showing the slightest ill effect.

Still, I reached out to stroke his back. He hissed and raked his claws down my hand.

"Ow!" I jumped back as tears came to my eyes.

"That's what you get for trying to be nice to the most evil creature on the planet," Grandma Bee said unsympathetically. "And I'm including pigeons."

I finally set the table (after dousing my hand with the strongest antiseptic in the medicine cabinet). Wren finally finished making dinner (after fishing a refrigerator magnet out of the saucepan and complaining vociferously about people who did not put refrigerator magnets *on the refrigerator*). Lark and Linnet finally finished tossing the salad (after having their usual heated argument with Grandma Bee, who hates green peppers and considers their presence in her meal a personal affront).

When we all sat down to eat, four people weren't on speaking terms, two people claimed to be on the verge of starvation, and one person (me) was worrying about cat scratch infections.

Grandma Bee's glasses were even more askew than usual, and she kept smacking her lips to keep her dentures in place, a sure sign that she was trying to repress great inner excitement. Finally, after we had settled in to eating our meal, she cleared her throat portentously.

"I heard something quite interesting at the post office today," she said, trying (and utterly failing) to sound casual and offhand. "Maude Canterville stopped by while I was there. The Assembly just had a request for an additional message service. It seems that a local TV reporter is working on a story, and she wants to feature Lily Dale—"

"Not again!" Raven groaned.

"Please don't tell me it's going to air on Halloween," Oriole said.

"That would be so typical," Wren said.

This was not the reception that Grandma Bee was

hoping for. "I should think that this family would show at least a little interest in getting positive media exposure for our profession," she said coldly.

"Well, dear, the town hasn't come off very well in the past," my mother said placatingly. "Reporters always make it look like the people who live in Lily Dale are such—" She peered vaguely into the gravy boat she was holding in her hand, as if she might find the word she was searching for there.

"Weirdos," I said succinctly. "Con artists. Cheats. Delusional, mentally deranged, New Age flakes—"

"To be fair," Dove said, "there *is* a quirky element."

"*Anyway*," Grandma Bee said quite loudly in order to refocus attention on her, "the story is about some boy who went missing."

I put down my fork and sat very still.

"*And* the family has insisted that the message service be filmed." She sat back in satisfaction at the stir this caused. Lily Dale never allows filming or recording during services; it's as unthinkable as having a camera crew invade a regular church service.

"I guess the family consulted some woman who said she was a medium a while ago, but no luck." Grandma Bee sniffed disdainfully. "Sounds like they went to someone who was about as psychic as a poodle. But they've agreed to try again because, of course, there will be many very talented psychics in attendance at a Lily Dale message service. Someone"—and by "someone," she clearly meant herself—"is bound to get a message of comfort and healing."

A small, hard, cold ball had formed in my stomach. I pushed my plate away as Grandma Bee went on.

"What if this boy isn't dead?" Dove asked. "You said missing."

Grandma dismissed that with a wave of her hand. "Then he might see the show and decide to call his mother! Or a person who knows where he is will see it and turn him in. Still a happy ending. *Plus* Maude said that one of the network producers in New York has been looking for a psychic to star in a new TV show. Someone with talent and, of course"—Grandma Bee picked up her napkin and delicately dabbed at her lips—"stage presence."

The long silence that followed this announcement was filled with the subtle vibration of nine minds thinking furiously.

"So one of us could be on TV?" Lark asked.

"And all we have to do is channel this lost boy?" Linnet added.

"Do we get paid for this?" That was Wren, of course, focusing on the practical.

Grandma Bee snapped her dentures in irritation. "*Money* is not the issue!"

"Yes, it is," Wren said stubbornly. "The electric bill is three months past due. Not to mention the heating bill, and the grocery bill, and the telephone bill, and the car's broken window, and two bald tires—"

"So," Lark repeated, clinging to her main point, "one of us could be on TV?"

Glances darted around the table.

"Now, darlings," my mother said hastily, "you are all *extremely* talented—"

"Except for Sparrow," my sisters chorused.

"Well, we'll see about that," my mother said comfortably. "At any rate, I don't want this to turn into some kind of competition. That would be most unseemly. And hurtful."

"And useless," Grandma Bee said, adding smugly, "After all, I think we all know who has the most experience, talent, and charisma in this family."

"Mordred?" Linnet asked innocently.

Grandma Bee shot her a poisonous look.

My mother stepped back into the fray. "You know, there's no reason this show would have to feature just one medium," she said. "The reporter might want to interview several people from Lily Dale. And I think we have quite an interesting story, don't you? Three generations of psychics, living in one household, carrying on a proud family tradition?"

"Hmmph." Grandma Bee looked disgruntled at the idea of being lumped in with everyone else.

"Headed, of course," my mother added craftily, "by a strong, wise, and powerful matriarch who has helped so many, many people during her lifetime."

There was a long pause as Grandma Bee thought this over.

"You mean me," she said at last.

"Of course!" My mother beamed at her.

Heads were nodding around the table.

"We could all be on TV," Raven mused.

"*If* this spirit actually comes through," Wren said rather dampingly. But even her eyes were sparkling.

Oriole didn't say anything, but she glanced dreamily in the mirror over the sideboard and tossed her hair in a most becoming manner.

"People are so uplifted by seeing loving reunions from Beyond and hearing messages of love!" Dove said. "It wouldn't be like normal news story at all! It would be positive and uplifting! A way to use television for good!"

Lark turned to look at her twin. "We'd better practice doing our makeup."

Linnet nodded, serious. "And our hair."

I was sitting still and silent. I don't think the phrase *frozen in horror* would be out of place here.

"Um," I said at last.

Everyone turned to look at me.

"I hate to be a wet blanket, but you *know* what this story is going to be like," I said. "You all said it five minutes ago. Clichéd, stereotypical, humiliating. Why would we want to be a part of this?"

"Fame?" Lark suggested.

"Fortune?" Wren insisted.

"A chance to do good in the world?" Oriole chimed in sweetly.

"*If* someone sitting at this table can actually channel this spirit," I pointed out. "*If.*"

Grandma Bee glared at me. "You think we can't?" she asked belligerently.

"Jealousy," Raven whispered under her breath. "Such a terrible thing."

"I am not jealous," I said huffily. "I am *sensible.*"

Raven snickered. The others stared down at their plates or took thoughtful sips of their iced tea.

"Sparrow's right. We shouldn't count our chickens," Dove said peaceably. "There's no guarantee that this story will even make it on the air."

Grandma Bee sulkily picked green peppers out of her salad and piled them in a little heap by her plate.

"Although"—Dove continued sweetly—"it does sound like such fun."

Again the excited babble broke out. Grandma Bee held up a spoon, trying to see her reflection. "Which side of my face is more photogenic?" she asked the room. "My right or my left?"

I may be stubborn, but I can also recognize defeat when I see it. I slumped back in my chair and closed my eyes in surrender.

Chapter 22

I was taking my history book out of my locker the next morning when a hand shot over my shoulder and slammed the door shut. I whirled around to see Jack Dawson facing me.

"What the hell did you think you were doing?" he yelled.

I stared at him, openmouthed. "What—"

"I told you he's been sneaking around, trying to get dirt on us."

"Who? What?" I was so taken aback I couldn't even form a complete, coherent sentence. "I have no idea what you're talking about!"

Jack glanced around and saw that half a dozen students had stopped to listen to this impromptu drama with every appearance of enjoyment. He leaned closer to me and said, in a much quieter voice, "Detective Calhoun. I saw you yesterday at the bus stop, talking to him!"

I blushed. Unfortunately, this is my default reaction. I blush when I'm embarrassed, angry, nervous, or uncomfortable. But Jack doesn't know that, so of course I just looked guilty.

"I can't believe you would talk to him about my brother," he said with utter contempt. Then he started to walk away.

"Wait!" I finally found my voice. "Jack, I didn't say anything to him."

He kept walking. I hurried after him. "I would never tell anyone something private, especially not that detective!" Jack didn't slow down. I took a deep breath and tried again, even though I was getting a little annoyed at talking to his back. "He asked me questions, but I just told him that you thought Luke had gone out West. That's it, I swear!"

He finally stopped and turned to face me. "Yeah, right."

"Please believe me." My voice was less than a whisper. "Please."

He looked at me, then down at the floor for a long moment. Then he nodded to himself and slumped back against the wall of lockers. "Okay," he said, not looking at me.

"I'm not sure why he even talked to me," I said, relieved.

"He wanted evidence."

"Evidence?" I was baffled. "What kind of evidence?"

"Any kind that will prove his theory. He thinks my father killed Luke."

We skipped homeroom. I had never skipped class in my life, but this didn't seem like a moment to worry about breaking the rules.

Jack, of course, was an old pro at rule breaking. I followed him through a door clearly marked "Emergency Exit," up three flights of stairs that looked as if they were meant for maintenance workers, and through a door labeled "Authorized Personnel Only." We ended up on the roof, where I'm about 100 percent positive we weren't supposed to be. There were ventilation pipes sticking up into the air and a panoramic view of the brand-new football stadium to the west. Jack slipped the lock off the door of a small cinder-block hut and ducked inside.

After a moment he stuck his head back out the door. "Well, come on," he said. "Someone might see you standing out there."

I followed him inside. There were mops, brooms,

and various metal tools that looked heavy and dangerous. A couple of folding chairs, a well-used pack of cards, and a wooden crate that could serve as a table indicated that it was a place of leisure, as well as work, for the school's janitorial staff.

I perched gingerly on the chair, which had seen better days. Jack was sitting with his elbows on his knees, staring at the floor.

"Nice spot," I said in an effort to break the silence. "Very homey."

"Yeah. I like to have a place where I can be alone."

His words echoed Luke's so closely that I shivered.

"Are you cold?" he asked.

"No, not at all." I crossed my arms. Then I thought that made me look too stern, so I uncrossed them and tried to look open and encouraging. "So why does Detective Calhoun think that your dad . . . that he's a suspect?"

He pressed his hands over his eyes. "It's so stupid. Luke and Dad weren't getting along that well last year. They were arguing a lot."

"About what?"

"Not anything big, just"—he waved one hand vaguely—"stuff."

"Like—?"

He shrugged impatiently. "Like . . . wearing his army jacket all the time. It's the jacket that Luke's dad wore in Vietnam, so you'd think Dad would understand why Luke wanted to wear it, but Dad still hated it." He smiled slightly and rolled his eyes. "Dad's kind of a hippie. Well, he would say *former* hippie, but you know. He still wears tie-dyed T-shirts."

"That doesn't seem like a big deal," I said. "Wearing an army jacket, I mean."

"Exactly. All their fights were about stupid stuff like that. Staying out past curfew, playing too many video games. And then Luke started getting all moody about something. He'd go off on his own all the time."

He rubbed his eyes again. "One time he got a little turned around on the mountain and it got dark and he had to make a temporary camp overnight. Once it was light, he was able to find the trail again, no problem, and he got home by lunchtime. He was totally fine, he's *always* totally fine, but my parents went ballistic."

"Still," I said, "murder."

"Yeah. I think Detective Calhoun has been watching too many episodes of *Unsolved Mysteries*," Jack said, the sardonic note back in his voice. "It can't be that Luke just had enough of the fighting and took off. No, it's got to be some big made-for-TV special."

"Did he actually accuse your father of murder?" I asked.

"Well, not *premeditated*." Jack lifted one eyebrow to underscore the slight distinction being made here. "His theory is that Dad and Luke got into a big fight and Dad hit Luke in the heat of anger and it was all an accident. Which, of course, is *way* better than planning it out ahead of time."

"But if there's no evidence—"

"There's no evidence *yet*," Jack corrected me. "That's why Calhoun keeps sniffing around. When we lived back in Collins, he came up to me at soccer practice and started asking me questions about Dad. You know, how we got along, if he ever hit me."

"You're kidding."

"I punched him in the face," Jack said proudly. "Broke his nose."

"Wow. Really?"

"Well, I made it bleed anyway." His grin faded. "You know what's worse than being accused of murder? Not being accused but having everyone think you did it anyway."

* * *

Later, in my bedroom, I paced the floor, lying in wait for the most sneaky, duplicitous, manipulative ghost in the afterworld.

I felt a gust of freezing air behind me and wheeled around to see him sitting in his usual spot, the window seat.

For once he wasn't smiling.

I yelled, "When were you planning on telling me?"

For once I didn't care if anyone heard me.

"Telling you what? And don't you think you should keep your voice down?" He looked at the door as if expecting a police raid. "If your sisters hear you—"

"The police think your father killed you!"

"Oh, that."

"Yes, that. Kind of a big secret to be hiding." I couldn't remember ever feeling so furious.

"I did tell you there was a terrible wrong to be righted," he pointed out.

I sat on the edge of my bed and put my head in my hands. "What am I going to do?"

"Tell my family what happened," he answered in a matter-of-fact tone. "Tell them where my body is. Go to the funeral, maybe say a few heartfelt words—"

I shot him a disbelieving look.

"Okay, maybe not. But the rest of it . . . it's all perfectly simple, really."

"I can't."

"Sparrow." He seemed to be feeling his way. "If someone could tell you where your father was—"

"Stop it!"

"I'm sorry." He held his hands up in surrender. "That wasn't fair."

I opened the window and crawled out onto the roof. I lay back, staring at the stars. Luke manifested a few careful feet away.

"If I pass on your message," I said slowly, "you'll be able to move on to . . . wherever."

"That is the plan," he said equably. "I realize of course what a sacrifice you'll be making."

I glanced at him sharply.

"You won't be able to hide anymore," he reminded me, as if I needed to be reminded. "You'll have to let the world know who you are."

"Hmmph."

"Although I can assure you, the world will like the real Sparrow Delaney," he added. "Very much, in fact."

I took a second to absorb that. Downstairs a series of crashes and raised voices indicated that most of my family was home and engaged in what passed for quality time.

"But if I pass on your message," I said again, even more slowly, "you will move on."

There was a long pause. His outline began to fade.

"Yes," he said finally.

Then he vanished, so my response was whispered to the air. "Then how can I help you?"

Chapter 23

"There is quite a sense of expectation tonight!" Prajeet peered at the dozens of people who were finding their seats in the auditorium and talking excitedly to one another. "Quite an anticipatory buzz, I must say! Don't you feel that?"

"Actually, I feel sick," I answered.

I was lurking behind the lattice screen. The temperature had dropped steadily during the day, so all the auditorium windows were closed. A rising wind whistled through the trees and rattled the shutters—unnecessary extra drama, in my opinion. I was already tense and jittery with nerves.

"In fact," I added thoughtfully, "I may throw up."

"Breathe, Sparrow," he said calmly. "Breathe."

"Yeah, right," I muttered, but I did. I breathed.

A few breaths later I felt calm enough to peer through the screen and scan the audience. I saw Miss Canterville, who would be leading this evening's service, standing ramrod straight next to the stage. I saw Fiona's mother next to her, double-checking her makeup in a pocket mirror as her cameraman fiddled intently with lenses and lights. I saw Fiona bouncing with anticipation in her seat. I saw every Lily Dale medium, as well as psychics from other nearby towns, sitting throughout the auditorium, bright-eyed and alert, ready to jump up if called by Spirit. I saw ghosts lining the walls, hovering on either side of the stage, and standing in the aisles. Their faces looked as expectant as everyone else's.

But I didn't see the one particular ghost I was looking for.

The front row where my family usually sat had been reserved with a bright pink ribbon, but the seats were still empty. Although my family had been supplanted from the first row, Grandma Bee had commandeered the second. She sat dead center, clutching a cracked leather purse on her lap. In honor of the occasion she had actually tried putting on some makeup: a slash of red across her lips, two spots of blazing pink blush high on her cheeks, and a thick powdery coating of turquoise eyeshadow, which seemed to be giving her problems. She squinted into the middle distance, blinking.

Raven was muttering darkly to herself, as if preparing to bully any spirit that showed up into talking to her. Dove looked serene and unworried, while Wren seemed to be mentally calculating how many bills were still unpaid. Oriole freshened her lip gloss, as Lark and Linnet giggled and poked each other, completely ignoring the sense of occasion. My mother glanced casually around the room, as if looking for someone. After surveying every corner, I could see her shoulders droop, and I knew that she had been looking for me.

I felt a twinge of guilt, but not enough to join them.

The smell of baking cookies, overlaid with the medicinal odor of liniment . . . I turned my head and smiled weakly at my spirit guides.

"It looks like there's room to squeeze in there if you want to," Floyd said in my ear.

"I think I'll sit this one out."

He nodded benignly. "Well, we're here if you need us, honey."

"We always are, you know," Prajeet added.

Professor Trimble nodded in agreement, then said to the others, "We should take our places."

They wafted over to sit in the reserved section. They took up only half the bench, and that was good, because just then Jack and his parents arrived and walked down the aisle to the front row. Every head swiveled to gape at them. Mr. Dawson looked wary and grim. Mrs. Dawson looked hopeful and worried. Jack's face was blank.

The Dawsons sat down, with Jack sitting closest to my guides. I saw him shiver and frown a little as he edged away from them. "And *that*," I whispered with satisfaction, "is your proof that ghosts exist."

"I think Jack will need a little more evidence than that," said a voice behind me. "You know how skeptical he is." Luke was leaning on the wall, one ankle crossed over the other. He seemed totally at ease, if not for the fact that he was, for the first time since I'd known him, biting his lip. He moved over to stand next to me and peer through the lattice screen at the growing audience.

"Looks like quite a crowd," he said. He sat down abruptly, frowning and tapping his foot. After five taps he jumped up and walked back over to the screen. "My dad doesn't look like he wants to be here."

I raised one eyebrow. "Feeling a little nervous, are we?"

"Never." He winked at me, but it was a worried wink.

"Uh-huh," I said.

The audience hushed as Miss Canterville moved to the front of the room.

"Good evening," she called out.

"Good evening!" everyone in the audience responded.

Luke straightened his shoulders and even ran one hand through his hair, as if anyone but me could see him. "I think that's my cue," he said softly. "See you out there."

"No, you won't," I whispered. I watched as he strolled to the front of the room as if he had all the time in the world. He edged past the cameraman, who shuddered a bit, looked nervously over his shoulder, and moved a few steps away.

Miss Canterville said, "Is anyone receiving any messages?"

It felt as if the whole world were holding its breath.

And nothing happened.

After thirty seconds of silence Miss Canterville's eyes started shifting around the room. After a minute Raven whispered something to my mother. Grandma

Bee turned around to see if perhaps something astonishing was happening in another part of the auditorium. Mr. Dawson shifted impatiently in his seat, and his wife put a hand on his arm, patting it gently. My gaze shifted to Luke, who was looking back at me expectantly.

"Come on in," Luke called to me. "The water's fine."

Scowling, I shook my head.

"I'm counting on you, Sparrow," he said. "Don't let me down."

My heart jumped a bit at that, but I shook my head again, even more emphatically. Just in case he hadn't gotten the message, I mouthed the words *Leave . . . me . . . alone.*

He held my look for a long moment, then nodded as if accepting a challenge.

He walked over to the front row, where his mother was now whispering urgently in her husband's ear. Jack was slumped down in his chair, his arms crossed, but I could see his leg jiggling nervously. Luke stood just far enough away so that Jack and his parents wouldn't feel his chill. He watched them for a minute with an expression of utter love and utter sadness.

Then he glanced over me and gave me a friendly, conspiratorial smile. I gritted my teeth and clenched my hands and repeated over and over in my head the mantra that I had been using for years: "Go away. I will not help you. Find somebody else."

Then he leaned over to touch his mother's face, gently, just like that.

"Oh, unfair," I whispered.

And without willing it, without meaning it, without wanting to do it *at all*, I found myself walking out into the open, out to the front of the room, and saying to the Dawsons, "May I come to you?"

Chapter 24

For the space of one breath, no one moved. I had the sudden, giddy thought that perhaps I hadn't really stepped out from behind the screen. Perhaps I had just imagined it so vividly that I *thought* I was standing alone in front of two hundred people, but I was in fact still safely hidden. . . .

Then the cameraman moved so that his lens was pointing right at me, and there was a wave of movement as everybody in the audience turned either to stare at me or to whisper to a neighbor, and the spell was broken. Even the ghosts edged in a little closer, as if they wanted to make sure they didn't miss a thing.

I looked into the camera's round black lens—it felt remarkably like looking at the end of a gun—and had the sudden, clear realization that I hadn't considered the possibility that I would end up on television. And I was wearing my oldest jeans, a faded Lucky Charms T-shirt, and last winter's jacket, which was now at least one size too small. Oh, well. Once again I wouldn't be named to the year's best-dressed list. I stifled a slight giggle at the thought and wondered if I was about to have hysterics.

"Larry!" Fiona's mother whispered to the cameraman. "Closer!"

The cameraman moved up the aisle, his camera lunging at me. I gulped.

I only *thought* I felt sick before. Now my hands were icy, my head seemed to be floating a foot above my body, my breath was coming in gasps, and I couldn't feel my feet. Noises seemed to come from a long way away. My eyes flickered around the room so that I saw quick little snapshots of people in the audience, as if a camera shutter were going off rapidly, *click click click.*

Click. My mother looking radiant and disbelieving and tearful.

Click. Wren looking confused and a little miffed by this decidedly disorderly turn of events.

Click. Dove and Oriole beaming encouragingly.

Click. Lark and Linnet jumping with glee at the sensation I had caused.

Click. Raven frowning darkly.

Click. Grandma Bee looking so smug that the words might as well have been written over her head in neon letters: *I told you so*.

"That's my girl," Luke said, smiling.

I relaxed a tiny bit, just enough to smile back.

Then I looked at the Dawsons and forgot to breathe.

Mrs. Dawson was clutching her hands together so tightly the knuckles had turned white. Mr. Dawson gave her a worried glance, with a look of dawning anger. Jack stared at me, the shock on his face shifting in an instant to betrayal. *Clickclickclick*.

Prajeet must have seen the panic in my eyes. "You're doing fine, Sparrow," he said.

"May I come to you?" I said again.

"Yes!" Mrs. Dawson said. Her husband made a move, as if to stop her, but she went on. "Please—"

"I see a young man—" My voice was barely a whisper. I cleared my throat and tried again. "I see a young man, about seventeen." The words were louder, but I still sounded unsure of myself. Even though I could see Luke, clear as day, I felt like an impostor, saying the words that I had heard other mediums pronounce with such authority over the years.

"Keep going, sweetheart," Floyd said. "You know what you're doing."

I went on, trying to sound more authoritative. "He has blond hair and hazel eyes. His name is Luke."

Mrs. Dawson gasped. Fiona's mother looked back and forth from the Dawsons to me, every line of her body at attention.

"You're saying that Luke is dead." Mr. Dawson's voice rang harshly through the auditorium.

"Well, yes—"

"*My boy is not dead.*" Mr. Dawson's voice got louder.

"I'm s-sorry, but he is—I mean, he has C-crossed Over," I said, and cursed myself for stuttering. "I can see him! He's standing right there, just behind you—"

There was an interested murmur as everyone in the audience looked where I was pointing. The cameraman automatically swung his lens in that direction as well, then pulled his eye away from the viewfinder, as if surprised to see nothing but decidedly human audience members.

"This is ridiculous!" Mr. Dawson stood up. "Sarah. Jack. Let's go."

Fiona's mother moved forward as if to stop them from leaving, but before she could say anything, Luke's mother touched her husband's arm.

"No, wait," she said. "She's Jack's friend. Let's at least hear what she has to say."

I met Jack's eyes, blazing with contempt. "Yeah," he said. "Let's hear what Sparrow has to say."

I cast a helpless look at my ghosts. I can't do this. I really, really, really can't—

"Sparrow!" Professor Trimble snapped. "Plant your feet. Stand up straight. *Own your ground.*"

Without thinking, I did as she said and immediately felt more centered.

"It's not about what I have to say," I said firmly. "Luke is all right, and he has a message for you. Do you want to hear it?"

Jack's father stared at me for a long moment. Finally he gave a slow nod.

"I need to hear your voice," I prompted.

He nodded again and said, "Yes. I want to hear it." His voice had a sarcastic edge, but it did the job.

"Thank you." I turned to Luke, who was wearing an expression of long-suffering patience. "Go on."

"So. Please tell them I'm fine," Luke said. "And happy."

I rolled my eyes. "That is *such* a cliché."

"Unoriginal," he said calmly, "but true. And . . .

reassuring, perhaps. So if you wouldn't mind—"

"He says he's fine and he's happy," I said to Mrs. Dawson. I avoided looking at Mr. Dawson. Or Jack.

"*Really*," Mr. Dawson said sarcastically. "I never saw that one coming."

Grandma Bee leaned forward and poked him in the shoulder, hard. "Show some respect!" she said fiercely. "That's my granddaughter you're talking to." She added a couple of menacing clacks of her dentures, and Mr. Dawson, clearly unnerved, shrank back into his seat.

"Shh," Mrs. Dawson murmured. "Just listen."

"This girl goes to school with Jack!" Mr. Dawson sounded incredulous. "She's only fifteen years old, for God's sake!"

Of all the condescending, patronizing, dismissive comments . . .

I lifted my chin an inch and said frostily, "For your information, I've been talking to ghosts since I was five."

I glanced at my family and shrugged. "Sorry."

They all seemed stunned, of course, but there were other emotions on their faces as well: Outrage (Raven), Gratification (Mother), Relief (Dove, Oriole), Irritation (Wren), Amazement (Lark and Linnet), and Complete and Utter Vindication (Grandma Bee, who caught my eye and gave me a roguish wink).

"Since she was five," Mr. Dawson said to no one in particular.

"Yes." Then, in order to keep things moving along, I added, "I'm getting another message," and looked inquiringly at Luke.

"Right. Well. Let's start with my dad." Luke paused for so long that I thought perhaps he had forgotten that everyone was waiting to hear from him. Then he nodded to himself and said, "My dad and I had a fight the night I died. About washing the car, which was really just so . . . *stupid.* But I was mad and I wanted to be alone and there was still some light in the sky, so . . ."

I waited.

"So I decided to try a new trail. I slipped on some loose shale and—and—" He stopped again. "Maybe I shouldn't go into all the details."

I sneaked a quick look at his parents. "Good idea."

"But please tell him that wasn't his fault that I died. Once I got on the mountain, I had forgotten all about our argument. I was just . . . thinking about other stuff and not paying attention and—anyway, tell him not to blame himself."

I carefully repeated all this, doing my best to use his exact words. Mr. Dawson didn't say anything, but the anger seemed to drain out of his face, leaving it waxy and still.

"Tell my mother that she doesn't need to worry about me anymore." Luke smiled down at her. "Tell her everything's copacetic. She'll know what you mean."

I repeated that. "Copacetic" was obviously a hit. When I said that, Mrs. Dawson made a little sound, half sigh, half sob. She glanced over at her husband, as if checking his response. Mr. Dawson pressed his lips together so hard they turned white. Jack was shaking his head, over and over. I don't think he was even aware that he was doing it.

"Now. Jack," Luke went on. "Please tell him to stop calling every white-water outfitter in the West and get on with his life," he said with some exasperation. He paused and then added more softly, "And tell him that I'll always watch out for him, okay? I really want him to know that."

As I passed on the message for Jack, I found myself smiling. It was such a nice, big brother type of message, and Jack would be so happy to hear it—

"You're lying." Jack's words felt like a slap. "Luke would never talk like that."

"Like what?" I asked with an edge in my voice.

"Like a damn greeting card!" Jack put on a fake spiritual voice. "'I will watch over you, my dear brother, from the Great Beyond!' This is *total bullshit*!"

"Please," Miss Canterville murmured a mild reproof. "This is a religious service."

His father shot him a warning look about the language, but it was halfhearted at best. If anything, he looked sorry that Jack hadn't said something more colorful.

"That's not what he said!" I said. "You're just trying to make me sound stupid!"

"I don't have to try! This is completely stupid because *Luke isn't dead*!"

"Ask him about the museum," Luke interjected. "Ask him about the painting."

I flung the question at Jack. "What about the spirit painting at the museum, then?"

Jack's eyes widened with shock, then narrowed again. "What about it?"

"Ask him whose face he saw," Luke said helpfully.

"Whose face did you see—"

"Nobody's!"

"It looked like Luke, didn't it?" I listened to Luke. "That photo of him from last year, the one where he's standing by the creek."

That stopped Jack, but only for a second. "I told you all about Luke last week," he said accusingly. "About how he disappeared and how we've been looking for him. Why didn't you say anything then, if you were already talking to him?"

"Because—" I stopped. The truth—that I wouldn't help Luke because I didn't want people to think I was a freak—did not seem calculated to please anyone in this audience. I started again. "Well, you see—"

"You didn't tell me either." A voice rang out from another part of the room. Fiona was standing, hands on hips, eyes blazing, red hair floating around her head as if electrified by her anger. "And I thought you were my friend!"

"I was," I stammered, totally unprepared for this secondary attack. "I mean, I am."

"Really? Because friends tell each other everything," she said sharply. "And you didn't breathe a word about any ghosts or spirit messages or—or anything! Even after I told you my mother was doing this story!"

"Yes, but—" I started to protest.

But Fiona had more to say. Unfortunately, she had *much* more to say.

Like, "You never said anything when we Googled Jack—"

A sharp glance from Jack.

"—or when we read all those articles about Luke's disappearance—"

An accusatory glare from Mr. Dawson.

"—or when you saw Luke's photo in the newspaper—"

A tearful look from Mrs. Dawson.

My face was red hot with embarrassment. "I only read about Luke on the Internet after he had already started appearing to me." It sounded lame, even to me.

A sigh of disappointment rustled through the audience. I saw Professor Trimble, Prajeet, and Floyd exchange looks of distress. Grandma Bee was glaring at Fiona so fiercely that I was a little surprised that she was still standing.

"Right. That's very convincing." Mr. Dawson stood up, then grabbed his wife's elbow. "This has gone on long enough. Come on. We're going home."

I felt tears brimming in my eyes and quickly blinked them back. This must be the way those poor accused women felt during the Salem witch trials, I thought. Like, they just couldn't believe how everyone was getting everything *so wrong*.

"Please," I said to Luke. "You've got to say something else, something they'll believe."

Jack and his parents started walking up the aisle.

"Come on, Luke. Please."

Surprisingly, Luke grinned. Then he said, "I want to say something to Jack."

"Wait," I called out. "Luke has a message for Jack."

They stopped. They turned. They waited.

I listened.

Then I said to Luke, "I am *not* going to say that."

"Believe me, this is the only thing that will convince him—"

"No. Absolutely not." Serving Spirit was supposed to be a higher spiritual calling. Messages were supposed to be inspirational and uplifting. And I wanted my debut as a psychic—since apparently I had to have one—to be remembered for something other than third-grade humor.

He looked positively gleeful. "Don't be so prissy, Sparrow."

I rolled my eyes, but I already knew that I would do what Luke wanted. "He says to tell you this: May the farts be with you."

Lark and Linnet (and several of the ghosts) snickered, but the audience of living, breathing people seemed taken aback by this message, which was definitely less than spiritual.

"I *think* he's trying to do an impression of Obi-Wan Kenobi," I said nastily, "but it's absolutely terrible."

Jack gave a snort of laughter.

I smiled back at him.

But as soon as I smiled, his face was wiped clean of emotion. Then that stony, disdainful glare returned.

"Luke isn't dead," he said flatly. "I don't know why you want to make us think that he is, but you're wrong."

Then he marched out after his parents.

But just for a second I had seen the look in his eyes. I knew that, just for a second, he had believed me.

Chapter 25

"I have long predicted this day, and it has now come to pass," Grandma Bee said grandly (and loudly, so that everyone standing within ten feet—not to mention the TV camera—would be sure to catch her words). Then she dropped the oratorical flourishes to add grumpily, "I don't know why none of you ever believe me."

"We did believe you. Of course we did," my mother said soothingly before turning to me. "Sparrow, I'm so proud of you! I always knew you could serve Spirit if you tried!"

My family had gathered around me at the foot of the stage, while my three spirit guides hovered behind them. The rest of the crowd was still milling around in the auditorium, casting curious glances my way. No one seemed to want to leave yet; even the ghosts were hanging around. An excited buzz of conversation rose and fell in the background as my family, and my ghosts, beamed at me.

"Great job, honey," Floyd said.

"You looked like a real professional out there," Oriole said. She tilted her head and squinted at me. "But maybe we should talk about wearing some makeup next time."

"And you should blink once in a while," Raven added. "You looked like a deer caught in headlights."

"Gee, thanks," I muttered.

She added grudgingly, "You did get some major hits, though."

"Indeed you did," Prajeet said. "A most impressive debut."

Lark and Linnet were bouncing up and down on their toes, too excited to let the other finish a thought.

Lark said, "Now we've absolutely *got* to get our TV back, so we can watch Sparrow on the news!"

"We should tape it too!" Linnet added, her eyes sparkling.

"Yes! Mother! We *have* to buy a VCR!"

"Oh, yes," I said. "We really *must* have a tape of my public humiliation."

"Humiliation?" Professor Trimble's eyes were gleaming. "It was a triumph!"

I rolled my eyes. "Oh, *please*! I think triumph is a bit of an overstatement, don't you?"

Everyone in my family stopped talking. They looked at each other, then back at me.

"Sparrow?" Wren piped up. "Who are you talking to?"

I sighed. "One of my spirit guides," I admitted.

This caused another stir of interest, resentment, surprise, and agitation among my family.

"You have spirit guides?" Raven snapped. "Since when?"

"And you said *one* of your spirit guides," Wren said before I could respond.

"Yeah, exactly how many do you have?" Linnet wanted to know.

"Three," I murmured with resignation as I watched the last of my secrets revealed to the world.

"*Three?*" Lark sounded outraged. "How come you get *three* ghosts to help you out?"

"I'm not sure 'help' is precisely the right word," I said with a sharp look at Professor Trimble, who was actually smirking. "More like nag and bully until I'm driven to the edge of insanity."

"Well, we're all born with certain gifts." Professor Trimble shrugged modestly. "Although I've always done my best to *develop* what I was given—"

My family kept babbling questions at me, but I suddenly felt that I couldn't stand being around people for another second.

"I need to be alone for a while," I said. I pushed past my sisters only to find my way blocked by Fiona's mother.

"So, Sparrow, you put on quite a show tonight!" She gave a brittle laugh that didn't sound very pleased. "But I wish you had told me about your . . . hidden talents earlier. I would have been better prepared. Still, that was an amazing performance."

"It wasn't a show," I said coldly. "I wasn't performing."

"No, of course not." She gave me a long, assessing look. "Now, may I ask you a few more questions, while the experience is fresh in your mind?"

"Maybe later." Maybe never, I thought as I sidestepped her, only to run smack-dab into Fiona.

"Sparrow Delaney, I am *so disgusted*!"

"I know, I know, I should have told you, I'm sorry, everything is completely my fault, now can I please *go?*" I said, trying in vain to move around her.

But Fiona planted herself firmly in my way and went on, her voice getting louder with each word. "In fact I am more than disgusted! I am distraught! I am angry! I am absolutely speechless!"

"Not noticeably," I said sarcastically.

And for once she *was* speechless. She stared at me for a few seconds, then said, in a remote voice, "Fine. I thought you were my friend, but I guess it's better that I know the truth right now. I'll see you around, Sparrow." With great dignity, she walked away.

I pushed myself through the rest of the crowd and ran off into the night.

It was dark now and getting colder. I could see my breath in the air as I ran down the street. Nearly every house had wind chimes on the porch, and they were clanging wildly in the rising wind. As I got closer to the lake, I could smell autumn leaves, damp earth, grass. I even imagined I could smell the moonlight; it was clear and sweet.

Finally I got to the lake, where I sat down on a log, panting. I stared out over the silvery water as my breathing slowed down. I hadn't been thinking as I ran, and I didn't intend to start thinking now. In fact, if I could have put off thinking about what had happened tonight for, oh, the rest of my life, I would have been quite happy—

"Nice job. Thanks, Sparrow."

"Are you kidding? That was a disaster." I didn't need to turn my head to know that Luke was now sitting beside me. I could feel an icy chill down my right side; even compared with the cold night, it was freezing. "Your dad is furious, your mom doesn't know what to believe, and Jack—"

I stopped.

"He can't go on thinking that I'm rafting in Wyoming somewhere," Luke said gently.

"Why not? What would be the harm in letting him"—my voice wobbled—"letting him think that? Just for a little longer?"

"The harm," he said, "is that it's not true."

"Oh, right. That." I put my head in my hands.

"I had hoped this would be easier, but—well, it wasn't." He sounded tired and disappointed, but when I turned to look at him, he managed a smile. "On to Plan B."

"Plan B?" I asked dangerously. "*What* Plan B?"

"Sparrow," he said, his voice stronger, "there's *always* a Plan B. We just have to figure out what it is." He seemed to have recovered his confidence remarkably quickly.

I opened my mouth to argue, but I was interrupted

by the sound of a branch breaking with a loud crack. I jumped up and saw Jack standing in the shadows of a tall maple tree.

He stepped toward me, into the moonlight, and I could see that he looked suspicious, wary . . . and scared.

"Who are you talking to?"

"Who do you think?" I said, exasperated. "How long have you been standing there?"

He waved the question away, still staring intensely at the log where Luke was sitting. "How did you know all that stuff you said back there?" he asked abruptly.

I was getting really, really, really tired of going over this. "Luke told me what to say."

He ran one hand through his dark hair as he glanced from the log to me and back to the log again. "Right."

"You don't believe me."

"No, I don't," he said slowly. "Except that . . . well, Luke does do terrible impressions." He bit his lip, looking troubled. "And he and Dad did have a big fight the night he left—"

"*None* of which you told me," I said. "And it wasn't in any of the newspaper articles either. So how do you explain that?"

"I don't know." He shook his head fiercely, as if

trying to wake up from a dream. "But the idea that you can talk to ghosts . . . I'm sorry. It's just so *freaky*."

"Right. Freaky." I clenched my fists as a surge of hurt and anger flooded through me.

Slowly and deliberately, clipping off each word, I recapped some of the things Luke had told me during our long conversations. "Luke's favorite snack was a toasted chocolate sandwich. He loved to read about the decline and fall of ancient civilizations. He was always doodling, and he got in trouble in sixth grade for drawing in his textbooks. When you were eight, he warned you not to touch his comics, so you used to stand in front of the bookshelf and breathe on them instead. In third grade you camped out in the backyard, and Luke pretended to be Bigfoot and you screamed loud enough to wake up the neighbors. He went to last year's homecoming dance with Beth Lowell and all he would tell me about *that* was that he had a, quote, really good time, end quote. His last hike was up Hunter's Mountain, on a trail he never tried before. He asked me to get a map. He showed me where he fell." I stopped, breathing hard.

His face was pale in the moonlight. Then a cloud drifted across the moon, and he was in shadow again. Tree branches swayed in the wind, and a sudden shower of leaves fell all around us.

Then the moon came out again, and Jack was staring at me. He looked sick.

"Are you all right?"

He swallowed a couple of times. "Yeah," he said.

"Now do you believe I'm telling the truth?"

He nodded. "Yeah, but—"

"But what?"

He cleared his throat. "You're saying that Luke is dead. But the first thing anyone thought was that he might have been hurt on a hike. And the park rangers never found him. They looked and looked."

"They weren't looking in the right place."

"But I can't believe . . . I *can't*—" He stopped, then started over. "I can't believe Luke is dead just because you say you've seen his ghost. I need real evidence. I mean, I'd have to actually see his body or something."

"No. Absolutely not. That is a completely insane idea." Jack and I were squared off, glaring at each other. I waved a hand at the sky. "Have you noticed all that black up there? That's called *night*, Jack."

"There's a full moon."

"It's cold."

"We're wearing coats."

"We'll get lost."

"You said"—Jack tilted his head to one side and

looked at me through narrowed eyes—"you *said* that Luke told you to buy a trail map."

"He did!"

He folded his arms, his chin jutting forward stubbornly. "If you're telling the truth, you'd be willing to check it out."

That "if" stung, and he knew it would. "All right," I said, trying to ignore the thought of finding Luke's body. "Tomorrow. I'll go with you tomorrow."

"Tonight." Jack gave me a challenging stare.

"*Why does it have to be tonight?*"

"Sparrow." I had been so focused on my face-off with Jack that I had almost forgotten that Luke was still sitting on the log, listening to our argument.

I looked over at him. "Go." He glanced away, as if listening to someone, then nodded reassuringly to me. "Yes. Go. It will be okay. I promise."

"Really?"

He smiled. "Trust me."

So I turned to Jack and said, "All right."

Chapter 26

Jack stood behind the garage, peering dubiously into our backyard. "Are those, um, graves?"

"Yes," I whispered. "Wait here."

I eased the back door open. I knew Raven was in her bedroom—I had seen her through the window as I walked across the lawn—and the bathroom pipes were gurgling, meaning that Oriole had settled into the bathroom.

I could hear Grandma Bee, my mother, Wren, and Dove in the parlor, rearranging chairs in preparation for the next reading and talking in low tones. I was halfway across the kitchen when the sound of Wren's worried voice asking a question floated toward me. I couldn't hear her words, but my mother must have been closer to the door because I clearly heard her say,

"Sparrow needs some time to absorb everything that has happened, that's all. . . ."

I felt a pang of guilt and hesitated mid-step. Then a sudden crash from the dining room (Lark and Linnet, practicing their juggling act) spurred me on. I climbed the stairs, carefully avoiding the creaky steps, and slipped into my room.

I grabbed the trail map and gloves, then rummaged through my closet. After a few minutes of excavation (oh, so that's where my old paint set went), I found a flashlight. As I was about to leave, I had one last thought and went to my desk to scrawl a quick note. Then I headed downstairs, my heart thumping.

I closed the back door softly and ran across the lawn to Jack.

"This way," I whispered as I led him in the side door of the garage. "Let's move it down the block before we start it." I got in the front seat of my family's car, a rusty 1978 station wagon with a cracked windshield and upholstery that smelled like a combination of cat, spilled soda, and incense, with a faint overlay of skunk. I moved the gearshift to neutral and waved at Jack. He started pushing as I steered.

Once we were on the street, I braked and let Jack get in the driver's seat. I saw him sniff the air and surreptitiously wipe his hand on his pants (the steering wheel was always a little sticky), but he didn't make any comment.

"Are you sure it's okay for you to drive?" I asked.

"I have my learner's permit," he said absently as he examined all the controls. The windshield wipers started moving with a horrific screech.

"Shit!" Jack jumped, then quickly turned them off with an embarrassed sideways glance at me.

"Don't you have to have an adult in the car, though?" I persisted. "Legally, I mean? If all you have is a learner's permit?"

"Sparrow," he said, "we're *stealing a car*."

"True," I said faintly.

He held out his hand to me. "Keys?"

"Lost," I said. "We hot-wire it."

"Every morning?"

"Yep." I reached under the dashboard, located the ignition wires, and handed them over.

Several seconds ticked by as he stared blankly at them. I waited, enjoying the moment, then took the wires and crossed the ends. The motor started up immediately.

"Thanks," Jack said. He cleared his throat and added, "That was actually somewhat impressive."

I grinned in the dark as he accelerated down the street.

For the first twenty minutes, I felt bold and reckless. As we drove down toward Zoar Valley, however, the sky got cloudier, and the wind blew harder, and the night got colder. My spirits sank. What in the world were we doing?

Just then Jack reached over to fiddle with the dashboard controls, and the car veered toward the other lane.

"Watch it!" I yelled.

"I am!" He jerked the steering wheel, and we were back in our own lane. "Don't worry!"

"We could have been killed!" I said, which was, of course, both obvious and completely unhelpful. "What were you trying to do anyway?"

"I was trying to get some heat going!"

"Forget it." I didn't bother to twiddle with the dials. "The heater's broken."

"Great." He glared out the windshield. "How old is this thing anyway?"

I felt called upon to defend the honor of the family car. "At least it's *running*."

"Barely."

I sat in silence and stared out the window at the

black mass of trees lining the road, thinking dark thoughts about boys who talked people into stealing cars and then complained about the condition of said cars. We drove on for half an hour without talking. Finally, Jack pulled over into a small parking lot.

He looked at my map, then pointed toward a group of trees that looked exactly like every other group of trees we had passed. "The trailhead's over there."

"Are you sure?"

"*Yes*, I'm sure!"

"Okay, just checking."

We walked over to a weathered sign with an arrow pointing straight ahead. I peered into the underbrush, trying to figure out where, exactly, the arrow was suggesting we go.

"There." Jack pointed again.

Now I could see a slight break in the underbrush that could have been a path of some sort. "Maybe this wasn't such a good idea." A few snowflakes drifted lazily through the air and landed on my sleeve. "It's starting to snow."

He glanced at the sky, then shrugged. "Just a few flakes." He turned on his flashlight. "Scared?"

"Of course not." I raised my chin defiantly and started toward the trail. Then I heard a rustle from the trees and stopped. "Are there bears out here?"

"Yep. And wolves and cougars, too. But they're scared of people, so they won't bother us." He paused, then added, "Probably."

"Oh, well, that's all right then," I said airily.

I had taken three more steps when he called after me, "Watch out for snakes."

A branch lying on the ground instantly became a rattlesnake. I jumped back, bumping into Jack, who swore under his breath and laughed at the same time.

"Why don't you lead the way?" I suggested sweetly.

So Jack walked to the trailhead, pushed some branches out of the way, and disappeared into the forest, vanishing as quickly and completely as any ghost.

After a heartbeat's hesitation, I followed.

We walked for fifteen minutes in silence. The woods were full of sounds: Mysterious rustlings in the bushes. Wind sighing in the trees. The far-off rushing of a stream. Thankfully, nothing that sounded like bears, at least so far.

Gradually the trail started to twist up the side of the mountain. I found myself thinking less about snakes and more about putting one foot in front of the other. The edges of the trail were starting to whiten with snow.

I squinted up at the sky. "I think the weather's getting worse."

"No, it's not." Jack kept walking, the beam from his flashlight moving back and forth across the trail.

"Jack!" I stopped. He kept going for a few paces, then turned around and stared at me in exasperation.

"*What?*"

I took the flashlight from him and pointed it at the ground. "That's snow. We've been walking for almost an hour, and it's getting colder by the minute. I think we should turn back."

Instead of answering, he held out his hand for the flashlight. I gave it to him, and he studied the map, muttering to himself. "Okay, we're right *here*, and the trail curves around *here*—"

"Did you hear what I just said?" I yelled.

"Yes, I heard!" Jack yelled back. "I'm ignoring you! Got it?"

I took a deep breath, held it, let it out. Count, Sparrow, I reminded myself. Three, five, seven. Okay. Now I felt calmer—

"Are you a *complete idiot?*" Well, so much for mindful breathing. "This is crazy! We both could die, just like Luke!"

There was a long, long silence as Jack stared at me.

Finally he said, "Look. We've been hiking for almost an hour. So if we turn around"—he made a U-turn signal with his finger; I never knew that a simple hand gesture could be so sarcastic—"we'll have to hike another hour to get back to the trailhead. We might as well keep going."

He gave me a hard look. "Of course, you can go back if you want to. By yourself."

Now it was my turn to be silent. Finally I said, "I think we'd better stick together."

"Whatever." He turned his attention back to the map, clearly indifferent to whether I chose to stay or go.

Where was Luke? I thought miserably. He'd said everything would be fine. He'd said to trust him. And now here we were, alone on a mountain in freezing weather, on a dark night, following a trail we didn't know, hoping to find . . .

No. I refused to think about that.

What did a body look like after lying outdoors for a year? Jack said there were bears and cougars and wolves around here. Even if he was making that up to scare me, there were other, smaller animals. Foxes. Raccoons. Buzzards. Not to mention all kinds of bugs.

Ivory bones lying at the bottom of a cliff, the skull

grinning up at the sky . . . I shuddered.

"Okay, it looks like the trail divides up ahead," Jack said. "You marked the left fork. So that's the way we should go?"

"Yes," I said shortly. If Luke had gone to the right, he might have been fine. He might have still been alive.

"You're sure?"

"Yes, of course I'm sure!" I pulled my collar up around my ears and jammed my hands into my pockets.

"Okay." He turned and started up the trail. He didn't look back to see if I was following.

"But, Jack," I said to his back, "what are we going to do when we find Luke?"

He didn't respond right away. Then I saw him shake his head as he kept walking. "If we find him," I heard him whisper. "*If*."

"It's snowing harder, Jack."

"No, it's not, Sparrow."

"Yes, it is."

"No . . . it . . . is . . . not."

Snow was starting to pile up on the edges of the trail and on the branches of the trees. The flakes were falling faster, swirling down from the black sky.

Clouds moved across the sky, covering, then revealing the moon. One moment it seemed that world was made of nothing but shadows; the next, nothing but inky darkness.

As we got closer to the cliff, Jack started walking faster. I gritted my teeth and kept up.

It was then, as I was willing myself to keep going, to match Jack's pace, that I tripped and went sprawling awkwardly on the path. My right knee landed, hard, on a rock, and my right ankle twisted under me.

Jack stopped and turned. I had a few seconds to note that he looked exasperated with me and to feel irritated in turn by how unfair that was.

Then I felt the pain, and I screamed.

"What? What?" Jack was kneeling beside me, his hair in his eyes. He tried to help me up.

I screamed again. "No, don't touch me!"

I was breathing in sharp little gasps, but not crying. It hurt too much for tears.

"Sparrow!" Jack's eyes looked scared. "What happened?"

"My ankle—" I took a deep breath, held it, let it go. Then another.

My voice was almost steady as I said, "I twisted my ankle."

"Is it broken?"

"I don't know. Maybe just sprained," I said, with little hope.

He reached out, as if he were going to try to touch it, and I yelled, "No, don't!" and he snatched his hand back.

"Okay, okay," Jack said. "Hold on. You'll be fine."

I had managed to get to my knees, but I couldn't imagine standing up yet. "I don't think I can walk. I don't think I can make it."

Then, as if my body wanted to underscore the point, I leaned over and threw up.

Jack stared at his shoes.

"Sorry," I murmured.

He caught my eye. "Feel better?"

I tried to match his dry tone. "Much."

"All right." Jack straightened up. "We need to find some shelter." His gaze swept the area, then returned to me. "Can you move over here?" He helped me sit on a nearby boulder, then patted my shoulder. "Don't worry." He walked away, his flashlight beam bobbing in front of him. Then the path curved, and he disappeared.

I sat very still. Every slight movement hurt. Just getting up off the ground had sent hot flashes of pain up my leg. I tried closing my eyes, but that made me feel even sicker, so I opened them again and focused on my breathing.

Breathe in for three counts.

Watch the snow swirl down.

Hold for five counts.

Wait for Jack to come back.

Breathe out for seven counts.

Look for Luke.

Breathe in.

Breathe out.

Chapter 27

After what seemed like fifteen hours, although it was probably only ten minutes, I looked up to see that the snow was falling faster. The wind was blowing harder. I was shivering violently. My ankle was throbbing with pain. Jack still hadn't returned. And I felt totally, completely, utterly alone.

To cheer myself up, I began to curse Luke under my breath. After all, it was his fault that I was sitting on a mountaintop in a blizzard with a broken leg, wasn't it?

I mentally replayed all the events that had led up to this moment. Yes. Yes, it was.

I had just reached a quite satisfactory level of obscenity when I heard a whisper in my ear.

"The pain and the shivering are actually a good sign, Sparrow. Means you're still alive."

I turned my head sharply to see Luke sitting on a nearby boulder.

"It's about time you got here."

"I thought I'd keep you company until Jack comes back. Which won't be long." He crossed his legs and looked around calmly. "It's interesting to be on this trail again. I didn't notice much the last time."

"Why not?" My teeth were chattering, and my face hurt from the cold. Any kind of conversation, even random and surreal conversation with a ghost, might keep my mind off all the different kinds of discomfort I was experiencing.

"Too caught up in my own thoughts. Worrying about this and that. You know what that's like." He gave me a brief smile. "Listen, Sparrow, I think I have a Plan B—" He stopped and glanced past my shoulder. "Ah, here comes Jack. I think I'll leave you two alone for a while."

"Wait!" I said. "We need your help."

"You're doing fine, Sparrow. This is the way things have to happen. Trust me."

He vanished just as Jack came back into view.

"I found a shelter," he said. "Are you okay? Can you walk if I help you?"

"I'll try." I stood up and leaned on his arm. We

started slowly up the trail, with me hopping on my good leg and Jack awkwardly supporting me and moving me forward at the same time.

The trail twisted back and forth as we walked uphill. Finally Jack said, "Here." To the left was a high outcropping of rock. He pulled back a branch and revealed a shallow opening. I bent down, squeezed inside, and found myself in a small cave.

Jack watched me, his eyes dark with concern. "Okay?"

"Yes, fine. Well," I amended, "better anyway." I looked around at the rock walls and added, "At least it's not snowing here."

"Hold on." He ducked back outside. I could hear leaves rustling and wood snapping, and then he was back, his arms filled with twigs and branches.

He knelt and began piling the brush into a heap. "I'll make a fire. We should be warm enough. We have warm clothing, we're out of the wind, and there's enough brush here to keep a fire going for hours."

I nodded, but I was thinking about Luke. Jack leaned over and put his hand on my forehead.

"Hey!" I jerked backward and felt a sudden flash of pain. I glared at Jack. "What are you doing?"

He pulled his hand away. "Checking to see if you have a fever," he said in an injured voice.

"I'm perfectly fine!"

"Well, excuse me for caring!"

"Just leave me alone! It's *your* fault we're in this mess!"

"My fault? I'm not the one who made up some insane story about talking to a dead person!"

"Well, at least you're finally admitting that Luke is dead!"

I stopped abruptly, wishing with all my heart that I could hit a rewind button and scoot about thirty seconds back in time. Jack was staring at me, looking angrier than I'd ever seen him.

He opened his mouth, then seemed to think better of whatever he was going to say. He closed it again, shook his head briefly, and began stacking the twigs in a methodical Boy Scout fashion. I watched for several long, cold, silent minutes as he made tiny adjustments with the same level of concentration needed to dismantle a nuclear bomb. Finally he pulled a matchbook from his pocket. He took a match and lit it by snapping it on his thumb. As it burst into flame, I said, "That was actually somewhat impressive." Then he dropped the lit match on the tinder. My tone wasn't exactly warm, but I thawed the icy edges just a bit, to show that we were still friends. If he wanted to be.

"Yeah, well." He didn't look at me, but his voice was edging toward room temperature as well. "That's just about my only party trick."

"At least it's better than flipping your eyelids inside out," I said without thinking.

The next second Jack was on the other side of the cave, as far from me as he could get, his back pressed hard against the rocky wall. I could see the whites around his eyes as he stared at me.

"How do you know about that?" he asked hoarsely.

"Luke told me," I said wearily. "Actually, he showed me. It was disgusting."

"Ri-ight," Jack said softly. He looked like someone trapped in a cave with—I winced at the thought—a strange and dangerous animal.

You see? I wished that Professor Trimble, Floyd, and Prajeet were here to witness my direst predictions coming true. *And it's actually worse than I thought. Jack isn't just laughing at me. He's afraid of me.*

Jack poked at the fire with a long stick. The flames jumped up, sending wavery shadows across the walls.

I eyed the pile of branches that he had put to one side to feed the fire as it died down. "Is that enough wood to last the night?"

"Probably."

Probably? I tried to suppress a vivid image of us freezing to death.

"And if it's not, there *is* a forest right outside."

I eased my sleeve back to look at my watch. Morning wouldn't come for hours and hours. In the meantime, the silence in our cave deepened until I imagined that I could hear snowflakes landing on the trail outside.

"I left a note," I said finally. "On my bed. So my family would know where I was. People are probably on their way right now—"

But he was shaking his head. "Not at night. Too dangerous. You don't want the rescuers getting hurt. That's just more people to worry about."

"Oh." I hadn't thought of that.

We both were watching the flames, but I could see that Jack had relaxed a little. He was sitting on the ground now, his legs crossed.

But he still had his back to the wall.

I jerked awake and looked at Jack.

"Jack?"

He was staring at the fire. "Yeah."

"Maybe we should talk or something."

He didn't look up. "Why?"

"Well, to keep from falling asleep," I said. "You know, from hypothermia? And it could scare away the bears."

Now he looked at me. "Bears? What bears?"

"You know. The ones that prowl around in the woods, looking for stranded hikers to eat."

He rolled his eyes. "Sparrow. Most bears are getting ready to hibernate right about now. And if a hungry bear did happen to find us, a little light conversation is not going to scare him off."

"Still."

He sighed, but he wasn't gazing at the fire anymore. "Okay, sure. What do you want to talk about?"

"Well . . . can you explain something to me?"

"Depends."

"What's up with all the *Star Wars* references?"

Jack blinked. Whatever question he was expecting, it wasn't that. "What?"

"Every time Luke tried to do an impression, it was always something from *Star Wars*." I mimicked Luke. "'Help me, Obi-Wan Kenobi, you're my only hope.' 'Feel the Force, Luke!' And that reminds me—" I glowered at Jack. "Why in the world did he want me to pass on that stupid message? 'The farts are with you'? What's up with that?"

Jack was laughing.

"No, really," I said, trying to maintain my outraged expression. "That's not the kind of dignified image that Lily Dale mediums are supposed to project. Not *at all.*"

"His dad loved *Star Wars*. His dad who died, you know. My uncle." Jack glanced over at me to make sure I understood. I nodded. "When he came back from Vietnam, he was all depressed and angry for a few years. Then *Star Wars* came out, and something about it . . . gave him hope, I guess. Anyway. He even named Luke after Luke Skywalker."

Jack shook his head. "That movie was Luke's blueprint for life, I swear to God. We must have watched it once a week. He could recite all the dialogue from heart. So, one time when we were nine or ten years old, we were watching it for the ten millionth time and, instead of saying, 'May the Force be with you,' he said, 'May the farts be with you.' We thought it was hysterical."

Apparently Jack still did. He fell all over himself, laughing. I just waited with, I was sure, an expression of patient forbearance on my face.

Finally my lack of reaction sobered him up. Well, a little. He shook his head. "You are such a *girl.*"

"Nice of you to finally notice," I said.

"Oh, I noticed," he muttered, staring at the ground.

His face looked slightly flushed, but he was looking into the fire again. It could have been just a reflection of the flames.

I hurried on. "Are you afraid of me?"

Once again Jack looked up, confused. "What are you talking about?"

"You seemed scared. Earlier." Now I was the one staring at the fire, refusing to meet his gaze. "So I just wondered. Does it, well, bother you that I talk to ghosts?"

"Not that you talk to ghosts in general, no," he said slowly. "But talking to my brother . . . I mean, if he can come back—"

He stopped. I could see a muscle jumping in his jaw. "I mean, we were tight."

"I know. Luke said you guys never even fought."

"He did?" Jack sounded uneasy.

"Yeah. Why?"

"Nothing." He still looked unsettled.

"How is that even possible?" I asked, thinking of the battles that my sisters and I waged for days, weeks, even months at a time. They were the stuff that epic poems were made of, if anyone still wrote epic poetry. "What were you, saints?"

"Hardly," he said dryly. For a second he sounded just like Luke. Then he shrugged. "Maybe it was because he came to live with us when I was three. I was old enough to remember the time before Luke and the time after. People always say that kids hate it when a new baby is born because they're not the center of attention anymore. Of course, not too many people get an *older* brother. Anyway, I don't remember being jealous at all. It was more like—" He paused, then smiled to himself. "It was like, there was the grown-up team, that's Mom and Dad. And there was me. But when Luke came, it was like, hey, finally I got someone on *my* side, you know?"

I nodded and eased myself into a different position, which was a mistake. I winced as my ankle began throbbing again. Jack didn't seem to notice. He was frowning at me, but it was a confused frown, not an angry one.

"So if Luke can come back," he said again, "why wouldn't he come back to me?"

I sighed. "Don't take it personally. Not many people can see ghosts. You have to have a special—"

I stopped in mid-sentence. After I had avoided that word for years, it was surprisingly hard to say.

"Special what?"

"Um, talent," I muttered, finally giving in.

Somewhere I knew, my spirits were smiling.

Then I heard a voice whisper, with great satisfaction, "That's my girl."

Luke was sitting cross-legged in front of the cave's entrance. "I wondered where you were," I said.

Jack followed my gaze and saw, of course, absolutely nothing.

"It's Luke," I said, answering his unasked question.

Jack sat very still. He was pale, and his eyes didn't move, as if he thought he could manage to see Luke again through a force of will.

"So, about that Plan B . . ."

I turned back to Luke, who was watching Jack with an expression of such intense compassion that I couldn't look away. I felt butterflies in my stomach and suddenly knew, without a second of doubt, that I was going to be asked to do something extremely difficult and unpleasant.

"Sparrow," Luke said, without looking at me.

"Yes?" My voice was shaky, just above a whisper.

"I know I've already asked so much of you—"

Oh, dear.

"—but if I could impose on you for just a bit longer." He turned to smile at me. I couldn't help myself. I smiled back, even though I knew I wasn't going to like what I was about to hear.

Chapter 28

"You're kidding." I was aghast.

"Not at all." Luke was calm.

"I can't do that!"

"You've never tried."

"What are you talking about?" Jack was still nervous, but that was quickly being overcome by irritation as he listened to one side of an increasingly heated argument.

I ignored him. "In fact I've never heard of any medium being able to do that," I said to Luke. "Ever. Even the ones who fudge the truth a little bit, even *they* never claim that spirits can take over their bodies."

"It is a rare talent," he admitted. "But we know you can do it, Sparrow." He raised one eyebrow. "After all, you are the seventh daughter of a seventh—"

"Oh, *please* stop right there."

He chuckled.

"Why can't I just pass on your messages the way I did before?"

He glanced at Jack, who was running his hands through his hair and looking rather wild-eyed.

"Quit fooling around, Sparrow!" Jack said. "This isn't funny."

"I'm not trying to be funny!" I snapped at Jack. I turned back to Luke. "That was good enough for you a few hours ago," I pointed out.

"Good enough for me, but not for Jack. I think we need to try something more convincing."

Oh, I liked that "we" part. *He* wasn't the one who was going to be invaded by another person's consciousness. *He* wasn't the one who was going to have someone else speak through his mouth. *He* wasn't the one who was going to relinquish control of his body.

I shivered. *We* indeed.

"But we're going to find your body!" I protested. "I'd say that's pretty damn convincing. And what if I try to do this and it makes me go crazy or something?" He smiled, and I said indignantly, "It could happen!"

"I think it already has," Jack muttered. Fortunately I was becoming quite good at ignoring him.

"I won't let any harm come to you," Luke said. "I promise."

I crossed my arms and stared at him. One of my great talents, I reminded myself, was a deep and abiding stubbornness.

I opened my mouth to say no, absolutely not, no way, not a chance. . . .

"Sparrow. I need to talk to my brother."

And I heard myself say, rather begrudgingly, "Yeah, all right, okay."

He smiled at me—a warm smile without a trace of mockery—and said quietly, "Thank you."

"What's going on?" Jack was getting freaked out now. "Sparrow?"

Then I explained to Jack what we were going to do.

Ten minutes later Jack and I were sitting next to each other, our arms almost touching. Luke crouched in front of me.

"Ready?" he asked calmly.

I licked my lips nervously and nodded.

He reached forward to touch my face. . . .

The freezing cold came first. I caught my breath as my lungs went into shock. On the plus side, I could no longer feel the pain in my ankle. On the minus side, I couldn't feel anything else either. I felt as though I had been turned into a frozen statue.

Then came the fog. My eyes blurred. Everything around me—the fire, the stack of wood, the flashlight lying on the ground, the drifts of leaves in the corner of the cave—was just indistinct shapes. I vaguely knew that I was someone and that I was somewhere, but nothing else. I could hear the fire crackling, but the sound was far away, and I could no longer feel the heat of the flames or the cold air that blew in from the entrance to the cave. Maybe, a remote part of my mind thought, this is what it feels like to be a ghost.

Then the fog lifted, and the cold went away, and I was looking at Jack, but it wasn't me gazing out at the world through this pair of eyes. It was Luke. I was Luke. The part of me that I think of as *me* felt like a small bee, buzzing around inside my head, watching and listening, an observer inside my own body. That tiny part that was still me could see Jack, but he seemed impossibly distant, as if I were looking at him through the wrong end of a telescope.

"Jack. It's Luke."

Jack jerked away, looking more scared than ever.

I didn't blame him. Luke's voice was coming out of

my mouth. I found it more than a little disturbing too, but it was too late to back out now.

"I did try to appear to you, you know. A couple of times I thought I was close, but in the end I just couldn't get through."

Jack stopped looking quite so scared and started looking more interested. "When?" he asked.

"That night you dreamed about me hiking through the woods? And I told you not to worry about me, that I was fine? That was *supposed* to be a clue." Luke shrugged. "A little cryptic, I'll admit. But I thought that when I kept moving that Luke Skywalker action figure around that you'd get the idea eventually. Especially since every time I was in your room, the temperature dropped by—well, by a lot. Didn't you ever notice that it was freezing?"

Jack looked stunned. "I thought I was just imagining things," he whispered.

Luke touched his shoulder. "It's all right. That's why I had to come up with another way to talk to you."

Jack moved away. Just a few inches, but it was enough. I could feel Luke's reaction—sorrow, understanding—and wondered what it was about. Jack looked even more apprehensive, a feat that I would have thought impossible. He seemed to be bracing himself, folding his arms tightly across his chest, clenching his jaw, and staring directly into Luke's eyes with a slight air of defiance.

"So, you're here," he said flatly. "Talk."

I swooped and buzzed a little more, out of sheer confusion. Only half an hour ago Jack had been upset that Luke hadn't appeared to him. Now he sounded annoyed for some reason—and after I had agreed to have a ghost take over my body!

I buzzed a little louder in indignation. Luke pressed his hand to his forehead, as if to calm me down. "It's okay," he murmured. "Just wait."

"What does that mean?" Jack was scowling.

"I was talking to Sparrow," Luke said. "She's pissed."

Jack grinned and relaxed a tiny bit.

"You know I was in a terrible mood that night. I would have fought with anybody who tried to stop me from leaving. You just happened to be in the way."

What was this? I buzzed around a little more. Luke ignored me. All his attention was focused on Jack.

"We never had a fight before that night," Jack muttered. "When you didn't come back, I thought—"

"None of this is your fault." Luke's voice got softer. "None of it."

Jack's jaw tightened. He shook his head and said

flatly, "I threw a punch at your head."

"I ducked," his brother said.

"I tried to smash you to the floor! With a double-leg takedown!"

"Yeah." Luke smirked. "Like you actually had a shot at making *that* work."

Jack grinned a little. Then his smile faded, and he looked away. "I said—" He hesitated. "I said I hated you."

"I didn't believe you," Luke said firmly. "Not for a second."

"Oh. Well. Good. Because, you know . . ." Jack's voice trailed off.

"Yeah, I know." I watched from far away as my hand reached forward to touch his shoulder. "So listen. I'll still be looking out for you, okay?"

Jack gave a quick nod.

"And when I offer a little brotherly advice, I expect you to take it, all right?" I could feel Luke being secretly amused about something.

Jack smiled faintly. Then he looked down to stare intently at a spider that was crawling toward his foot.

"Dude, you're not going to cry on me, are you?" Luke's voice was rough, teasing. "'Cause you know what happens when you cry. First, I get all choked up—"

Jack glanced up, his hair falling into his eyes. "—and then your voice starts quivering," he said in a mock-weary voice.

"—and before you know it, I'll be crying, too—" Luke continued.

"—just like a *girl.*" They finished together.

"I know," Jack said, smiling. "You are *such* a loser."

Luke put his arms around Jack and whispered in his ear, "I love you too."

Then I was myself again, back in my body, kneeling on the ground with Jack in my arms.

He had his arms around me too and was holding on as if he didn't want to let go.

So he didn't, and I didn't, and we stayed that way until morning.

Chapter 29

I opened my eyes in the hospital to see a ring of faces staring down at me. I blinked. They stood silent for so long—and Dove and Wren looked so tragic—that I finally snapped, "I'm not lying in my coffin, you know."

Everyone relaxed.

"It's about time you woke up," Raven grumbled. "We've been here for hours. I haven't even had any coffee yet."

Lark and Linnet gave me a long-suffering look at that, and I bit back a smile.

"We were so worried!" Dove said, tears (of course) in her eyes. Oriole nodded wordlessly and patted my leg. (Her lip gloss glistened perfectly and her eye shadow was flawless, but that didn't mean she wasn't sincere.)

"I told you she'd be fine," Grandma Bee said stoutly. "After all, she's inherited my wilderness survival skills."

I suddenly smelled the odd yet comforting combination of liniment, cinnamon, and incense. I looked past my toes to see Professor Trimble, Floyd, and Prajeet standing at the end of my bed.

"Indeed," the professor said complacently. "This entire situation has been resolved in a most satisfactory way."

"I always knew you would be a great medium," Prajeet said.

Floyd nodded. "You just had to get over that little doubt in your mind that you could do it."

Wren straightened my pillow and tucked a corner of the sheet in a little more tightly. "You could have died," she said softly, as if still stunned by the realization. "Do you know that?"

"But you didn't," Lark said quickly.

"And your rescue will look great on TV," Linnet said. "Very dramatic!"

"TV?" A horrible suspicion filled my mind. "What are you talking about?"

"Oh, didn't you notice the cameras waiting at the bottom of the mountain when the park rangers brought you out?" Linnet went on blithely. "You were all over the morning news!"

I groaned and closed my eyes.

"Your friend Fiona called—" Dove said.

"Five times!" Lark said. "She said she's '*so so so so so* sorry' she didn't believe you!"

Linnet giggled. "And can you ever ever in a *million trillion* years forgive her?"

Dove quelled them with a look. "She sounds like a very caring and supportive friend. Anyway, she said to give her a call. When you feel like it."

I felt a little cheerier at the thought of finally being able to tell Fiona—well, everything. Now that I didn't have any secrets to hide, I had a feeling that I was going to really like having a friend who was so so *so* interested in my life.

"I think we should leave Sparrow alone to rest, my darlings," Mother said. As everyone began to troop out of the room, she leaned over to kiss me on the forehead. "I'm so glad you're all right, Sparrow, but you did give us all quite a scare. And your poor father would have been devastated if anything had happened to you while he was away."

"I'm sorry," I muttered.

"Yes, well . . . the doctor said we could take you

home tonight. And then you and I"—she gave me a stern look over her glasses—"we are going to have a very serious discussion about this, understand?"

"Yes," I said meekly.

"All right." She started to go, then turned back at the door. "Last night, after we realized you were gone and we had to wait for all those hours until the rangers could look for you—" She paused for a moment, then went on. "Fortunately Mrs. Witherspoon popped in to tell me that you were being protected by the Other Side. But still, I must tell you, I was quite cross with you. *Quite cross indeed.*"

Then she came back to my bedside to kiss me again, before slipping out of the room.

The rangers found the skeleton the next day. A few days later the Dawsons held a memorial service in Collins, where Luke had grown up. I still hadn't gone back to school—the doctor said I needed a few days off to recover, and I fervently agreed—but my mother drove me to the church and sat with me as hymns were sung, eulogies were given, and prayers were said. I spent the entire hour staring at the large photo of Luke that had been placed on an easel near the pulpit, not hearing a word.

When it was all over, a crowd of friends and neighbors surrounded Jack and his parents. We slipped out the door and drove home in silence.

"Do you want some hot chocolate?" my mother asked tentatively as we pulled into the garage. "Or a cup of tea?"

"I think I'll just sit outside for a while."

She looked doubtful. "Are you sure? It's gotten rather chilly—"

"Just for a few minutes," I said. "Then I'll come inside and have some tea."

"I'll put the kettle on," she said, and drifted toward the house.

I limped my way through the bushes, even more overgrown now, until I reached the spot where Luke and I used to sit under the maple tree.

It's all over. I felt little pinpricks under my eyelids and squeezed them tightly to keep the tears from falling. *I helped Luke, and so he's gone away, and now . . .*

"I can't believe I'll never see you again," I said out loud.

Then I heard a familiar voice say, "I wouldn't say that, Sparrow."

I opened my eyes and saw Luke leaning against the Late Lamented's headstone, smiling at me.

A moment later: "Now don't cry."

"I'm not." I sniffed. "I never cry."

"I won't be far away."

"Really?"

"Well, not in cosmic terms anyway," he said, adding casually, "Edna told me I could still check in on you once in a while. Strictly on a need-to-know basis, of course, but still—"

Edna? For a second I was puzzled. Then the light dawned. "Do you mean *Professor Trimble*?"

"Yep. She's my guide on the Other Side. She met me when I first Crossed Over." He gave me a knowing look. "She's pretty, um, formidable, isn't she?"

"That's an understatement." I was surprised to find myself feeling a little jealous. "You call her Edna?"

"She asked me to." He gave me a sly look. "And then she suggested that I could help you, er, find your path."

"You mean she sent you to do her dirty work," I said baldly.

"Apparently you accused her of not understanding you? Because she's not young anymore?"

I blushed as I remembered that argument. Not my best moment, I must admit.

"Once she got over being really, really pissed—" He

tilted his head, as if listening to someone, and chuckled. "Excuse me. Once she got over being *livid with anger*, she realized that you may have had a point. That's when she asked me to step in and help you choose the direction you needed to take—"

"You were the guy at the crossroads!" I said. "The one Mrs. Winkle saw in her vision!"

"The one who was watching over you," he agreed. "Still is, as a matter of fact."

He started to shimmer.

"Wait," I cried. "Don't go! Not yet—"

"I have to, Sparrow." Even his voice was getting fainter. "Even though—"

"What?" I whispered. "What?"

But for the last time he was gone.

When I heard the leaves rustle behind me, I jumped up.

"Oh," I said.

Jack was standing there, looking crestfallen at my greeting.

"I'm sorry. I thought you might be—" I waved my hand in the air, and he caught my meaning.

"Oh, right."

"I mean, he came to say good-bye, so I don't know

why I thought . . . I guess I just . . ." My voice trailed off.

I hadn't seen Jack since the park rangers had helped us down off the mountain and put us in separate ambulances. Now we stood a careful distance apart. I studiously examined the moss on the side of the maple tree. Jack looked down and moved one foot back and forth in the fallen leaves.

After a few seconds of silence, I glanced over. Just then he raised his eyes and looked directly at me. I blushed, and one corner of his mouth lifted.

I blinked, but I didn't look away. "You're not wearing your army jacket."

He nodded and shrugged a little. "I don't think I need it as much," he said. "To feel that Luke is still around, you know? So, um, thanks." Then he gave me such a sweet smile that I smiled back.

"I saw you at the service," he said. "I wanted to come say hello and see how you were doing, but you left before I— Anyway, I thought I'd stop by." He gave me a rueful look. "Of course I had to get special dispensation from the pope."

"Grounded, huh?" He nodded. "Me too."

"Yeah. So. Anyway." There was another silence as it became clear that we had exhausted the topic of being grounded. Jack looked around the backyard, as if hoping that he'd spot a clue to what he should say next under a nearby bush. "When are you coming back to school?"

"Oh. Um, Monday, I think." Another silence. I glanced at him from the corner of my eye. He had his hands thrust in his pockets and was frowning at the ground.

"Hurry up, you laggards!" Grandma Bee's voice rang out from the back door. She was dressed in her karate uniform and had a bandanna tied around her forehead in a businesslike fashion. She marched over to the side lawn, trailed by Lark and Linnet, who were dragging their feet as if they were being led to an execution. "I don't know where I got such cowardly granddaughters! It must come from your father's side of the family."

Jack looked over at me and raised his eyebrows. "Who's that?"

"My grandmother. And two of my sisters." I paused, then added, "I have six of them, you know."

"Wow." He took a second to absorb this, then asked, "So, when we were driving up, I noticed . . . are those skulls on the front porch?"

"Oh. Yeah. Baboon skulls, actually," I said, and braced myself.

But Jack surprised me. "Cool."

I looked at him shyly, not sure whether he was making fun of me or not. "Really?"

"Absolutely." He grinned. "And I meant to tell you, hot-wiring your car was really awesome."

I grinned back. Now that several days had gone by, all the fear and worry of that night on the mountain were fading into memory. Pretty soon it would all seem like some kind of crazy dream—

"—this crazy dream," Jack was saying.

I came back to the present. "What?"

"I was saying I had a dream last night. About Luke." He half shrugged, not looking at me. "So . . . remember how Luke said that if he gave me some brotherly advice, I had to take it?"

"Yeah," I said slowly.

Jack took a step closer to me and looked directly into my eyes. "Well, all I'm saying is that this is what Luke told me to do in the dream, okay? So if you get mad"—he took a deep breath—"get mad at him, not me. Okay?"

I looked at him, puzzled. "Okay—"

And then he kissed me.

Some time later I heard Lark screaming, and Grandma Bee shouting, "She's fine! She's fine!" and a window banging open and Raven yelling, "Should I call nine-one-one?" and a door slamming as my mother hurried toward the latest disaster.

Jack glanced toward the house. "Um, it sounds like they might need you—"

"Yeah," I said. "They can wait."

Then I kissed him back.

Author's Note

Lily Dale, New York, really exists. It was founded as a Spiritualist community, in 1879. Every summer, roughly thirty thousand people visit the town to attend message services and to have readings with the mediums who live there.

But this is a novel, so I did tweak reality a bit. For example, most mediums do not see or talk to ghosts as clearly as Sparrow does. Although some do see spirits, others pick up spirit messages through smells, tastes, or physical sensations. Mediums usually meet one-on-one with each visitor who wants a reading, rather than hold group readings as the Delaneys often do. And although some mediums can sense pets who have Passed On, I haven't heard of anyone who could channel animals' messages as accurately as Miss Robertson!

If you'd like to know more about Lily Dale and its history, check out the town's website at www.lilydaleassembly.com or read *Lily Dale: The True Story of the Town that Talks to the Dead,* by Christine Wicker.